THE RULER

THE RULER

ROMAN REPUBLIC SERIES BOOK ONE

PENELOPE SKY

This is a work of fiction. Names, characters, organizations, places, events, and incidents are either products of the author's imagination or are used fictitiously. Otherwise, any resemblance to actual persons, living or dead, is purely coincidental.

Published by Montlake, Seattle

www.apub.com

EU product safety contact:
Amazon Media EU S. à r.l.
38, avenue John F. Kennedy, L-1855 Luxembourg
amazonpublishing-gpsr@amazon.com

ISBN-13: 9781662539237 (paperback)
ISBN-13: 9781662539220 (digital)

Cover design by Caroline Teagle Johnson
Cover image: © Michelle Lancaster PTY LTD

Printed in the United States of America

THE RULER

Chapter 1

Aurelia

After an hour flight from Rome to Catania, and then another hour drive from the airport, we arrived in Taormina, a quintessential Italian village with cobblestone pathways that led through little alleyways to reveal seafood restaurants that had been in the same families for generations, sandwich shops with freshly made focaccia bread, and little spots with Neapolitan pizza.

Paradise.

We'd planned this trip five months ago, and it was hard to believe it was finally here. With a packed schedule of visits to the wineries, the active volcano Etna, a trip to the Greek theatre, lots of cannoli and granita, it would be a trip to remember.

And we needed it now more than ever.

For the past couple months, Enzo had been noticeably withdrawn. It started off small, like not giving me the same focus he had in the past, missing whatever I was saying because his mind was somewhere else. It progressively got worse, and he didn't even bother to pretend to listen. Then there were other things . . .

He used to slip in behind me and join me in the shower. We never had sex in there, not when there wasn't room and the tiles were slippery and I'd fallen once before, but it always served as awesome foreplay before we made it to the bed and dampened the sheets. But he stopped doing that, and when I joined him instead, I could see his glimpse of disappointment. He tucked it away quickly, but not fast enough for me to miss it.

Conversations over dinner had grown stale and forced. He spent more time at work or out with his friends. He used to invite me to join him and his boys, but those invitations stopped.

Whenever I asked him about it, he said he was stressed at work, that he had a falling-out with one of his friends over a stupid argument, that his vertigo had come back with a vengeance . . . always something.

I'm not stupid, so I jumped to the conclusion every woman jumps to.

That there was someone else.

I wasn't proud of my actions, hated myself a bit for doing it, but I went through his phone and checked his messages. He'd never used a passcode, and I took that as a sign of committed transparency.

I never found anything.

I went to his work parties and knew all of his colleagues. He worked in finance, so most of them were men, and Enzo didn't strike me as the type of man to play for the other team. His boss was a woman, but she was about seven years older than him, with a husband and two kids.

So that was a dead end.

That led to one last possibility . . . and it was by far the worst.

That he'd just stopped loving me.

That I'd watched it happen, watched the love and desire slowly fade from his heart, watched the light fade from his eyes. They used to burn bright when they looked at me, with love and attention, and now there was just nothing there.

And the fact that he didn't acknowledge it when I asked, always had an excuse to explain his behavior, told me he didn't want to fix it. Didn't want to fight for this. Wanted to let our tree wither until it killed the roots and there was no going back.

He even tried to cancel the trip, said he had too many projects at work, but the hotel said our deposit was nonrefundable, so he conceded.

Maybe this trip would be a turning point for us. Maybe the sunshine and the warm beaches and the fancy dinners over candlelight would light a spark for a fire that had died in the depth of winter. Bring strength back to our broken bones and blood back to our hearts.

Part of me wondered why I continued to fight for a man who couldn't be bothered to fight for me. He'd been my boyfriend for two years, and we'd moved in together within the first three months of our relationship because it just felt so right. It was a whirlwind romance, uncontrollable laughter for jokes only the two of us could understand, a scorching chemistry that lit the sheets ablaze, a connection I'd never felt with another man.

I guess it just hurt too much to let that slip through my fingers.

The drive was spent in silence, the two of us in the back seat, Enzo constantly on his phone. He'd fire off a message and put it aside, but then it would vibrate with an instant reply, and he would be typing away again. That meant he was having a full-on conversation with someone.

He glanced at me when he felt my stare, and that was when he put his phone aside and ignored it when it vibrated a few more times. He focused his stare out the window and didn't explain the messages, even though he knew I was paying attention.

When we arrived at the little town of Taormina, the driver took us down narrow alleyways to get us to the small boutique hotel, Villa Fiorita. It was a short walk from the heart of town and had a pool on the roof. It wasn't a five-star experience, but it was an adults-only hotel, so that meant it would be quiet.

We checked into our room that faced another room across the hall. It had a double bed on top of a carpet that needed to be changed a decade ago. The bathroom didn't have a walk-in shower, but a shower in a tub that was slippery just to look at, and a single sink at the vanity that we'd have to fight over.

But at least we were here.

The second he put the luggage on the racks, he pulled out his phone and continued whatever conversation he'd been having.

I gave him space for a few minutes, sat in the single armchair, looked through old messages, and scrolled on social media. I checked my emails even though I knew there would be nothing to reply to because I'd cleared my schedule for this trip. I'd made sure all my clients got their photographs and had tied up all loose ends so I wouldn't have to deal with anything.

When I exhausted all forms of entertainment, I stared at him, leaning against the dresser with his fingers quickly typing away. Stared and stared while he typed and typed. My temper eventually got the best of me, and I snapped. "I made the lunch reservation for two, not three. Should I call and change it?"

His eyes finally left his phone and shifted to me.

"You know, for you, me, and your goddamn phone." I wanted to use this trip to reconnect the broken parts of our machine, but instead, my voice was more poisonous than the venom of a king cobra.

He didn't even bother to look embarrassed. He released a quiet sigh before he slid his phone into his pocket. "I told you I had a lot of projects at work—"

"Yeah, yeah, yeah." I tightened the strap of my purse and headed to the door. "Let's go before we miss our reservation." A reservation that had been hard to get. Like all the other reservations I'd made for this damn trip.

He did a better job of ignoring his phone for the next few days, but he still wore his smartwatch, and the screen lit up all the time. When I was able to catch a glimpse without making it obvious, I saw Luna's name on the screen—his boss.

So I guess he was telling the truth about work.

I kinda felt bad, but I also kinda didn't.

For lunch, we decided to try Rosticceria Da Cristina, a famous spot known for their arancini. Sicily was the birthplace of some genius culinary creations like granita, cannoli, and, of course, arancini. We had something similar in Rome, called supplì, not nearly as fried and with a different consistency. We grabbed one of each flavor, ragu with parmesan, peas, and mozzarella, and then pistachio, which contained pistachio pesto, cooked ham, mozzarella, and pistachio grains. There were a couple of other options, but each arancini ball was as big as my palm, so we picked one more, the eggplant option, and then sat at the outdoor patio seating since we'd chosen to do their takeaway option rather than dine in their restaurant.

My bar-top chair faced the restaurant, while Enzo's was pivoted the opposite way, the plate between us on the slender bar table that stretched all the way down for others to use too.

Enzo took the first bite, savoring the taste as he mulled over his opinion of it. "It's good." With dark hair and green eyes, he was a handsome Italian man with a nice smile. I noticed him the second we were in the same room together. And a lot of women noticed him when we went out together. It never used to bother me, but it bothered me a lot more now because our relationship seemed to have crashed on the rocks, no matter how hard I steered the ship back to sea.

I tried the pistachio and loved the combination of flavors, especially how crispy the outside was in comparison to the casserole-like concoction of rice and pesto and ham. "Ooh, this is worth the hype."

We tried the different flavors together, each rated them, and for a moment, it felt normal again. The two of us on an adventure, our only concern ranking the authentic cuisine in front of us, not worried about work or projects or anything else but this moment.

My hand went to his muscular thigh, an absent-minded and programmed gesture of affection, something he used to do to me but stopped months ago.

He didn't react to the touch, taking another bite of the arancini like he didn't notice my hand—or the act of possession didn't mean anything to him anymore.

Or maybe I was unfairly overanalyzing every little thing he did because I was riddled with insecurity.

I didn't recognize myself anymore. Desperate for his validation. Searching for any sign of desire on his part. Needing something he didn't seem to want to give. I was a beautiful woman who could find his replacement within a day, but I felt like the most undesirable woman at his side. Unwanted. Unworthy. Unremarkable.

With my hand on his thigh, I could feel his phone vibrate in his pocket over and over. His watch was going off too—Luna's name on the screen.

He quickly wiped his hands off with the napkin. "Sorry, I've got to take this."

I withdrew my hand. "It's okay, I understand." I tried to play nice after I'd snapped at him the other day. We never talked about the confrontation, and it kinda just went away in the silence. I hadn't directly accused him of infidelity, but I had indirectly. And then I'd gone through his phone, which I still felt guilty about. Guilty because when he said work had been overwhelming him, he'd been telling the truth.

I expected him to answer the phone right where he sat, but he left the barstool chair and walked down the alleyway past Rosticceria Da Cristina and then turned down another alleyway, like he didn't want me to see or hear him.

A wave of suspicion grew inside me, gnawed at my stomach, and then I felt a surge of rage that felt like a tidal wave. But I took a breath, swallowed it back, told myself I was being irrational and spiteful because things weren't where I wanted them to be.

I looked down at the plate of arancini and took another bite, even though I'd lost my appetite. I wiped the crumbs of the crust from my mouth and looked up the uphill passageway, waiting for Enzo to reappear.

But instead, I saw a man turn from the other street and begin his walk down the slope to the restaurant. In a black T-shirt that squeezed his thick arms that were covered in dark ink, and dark jeans that were low on his narrow hips, he headed to the side door underneath the sign, moving at a speed full of intention. With dark short hair and eyes the color of espresso and a distinct shadow on his jawline, he looked like an Italian model who hawked sunglasses for Tom Ford, somewhere on a yacht near the Amalfi coast, his skin coated in sunscreen that smelled like sex. I saw a flash on his wrist from a watch before he stepped through the open door and approached the counter.

The kitchen had ovens against the walls and a center table covered in different kinds of rectangular pizzas people could order by the slice and have reheated in a flash. And all the guys working there gave a loud roar of excitement—like they knew the guy who'd just walked in. They clapped and cheered, and the beautiful man walked right past the counter and joined them near the ovens. He smiled—and I'd swear to the pope that my entire body quivered.

The guys greeted one another with those embraces men did, when they clapped their hands together and then pulled each other in for a slap on the back. The beautiful man was the tallest and the most muscular, a fucking bull in a field of dairy cows. Words were exchanged, along with uproarious laughter.

I couldn't tell what the relation was or why I cared. Perhaps he used to work there. Maybe stopped by for a visit? But even if he did work there, it was a bit presumptuous to help himself to the kitchen like he had every right to be there.

He leaned against the counter, crossed his arms over his chest, and spoke with the guys with that same charming smile. We were at a distance from each other and divided by a window, but I could still see the sharpness in his eyes, like he was attentive, smart, and assertive.

I made a lot of assumptions solely based on his appearance, but the longer I stared, the more I found. Utterly hypnotized by a man I could only describe as the best-looking guy I'd ever seen in my life, I kept my eyes glued in place. Captivated like he was the subject of an award-winning photograph whose attractiveness was enhanced by the angle or the lighting or the pose, I couldn't look away.

But he must have felt my stare, even at this distance, because he suddenly shifted his gaze to me.

My breath was squeezed from my lungs just by his stare alone. Whenever an awkward moment like this happened, when I caught someone staring at me a little too hard or I let my gaze linger on someone longer than I should, my eyes shifted away like it never happened. But the command in his stare was so powerful that I lost the ability to control my own body. I was paralyzed, at the mercy of a stare so unbelievably confident but never on the threshold of arrogance. Someone might interpret it as hostile, but what I felt was intensity. The kind of intensity that, if it came from the sun, would burn you blind.

It lingered for seconds, but each one of those seconds felt like a minute, and the accumulation of the entire moment felt like a lifetime.

One of the guys said something to grab his attention, and his eyes left mine. He smiled at whatever was said and pushed off the counter before they headed into another room.

An indescribable wave of disappointment filled me when he left my sight. I mourned for the loss of someone I didn't know. Grieved the death of a life I'd never had. It was just a look, barely a moment, more a fraction of a second, but it was more than Enzo had given me in months. Undivided attention, feeling seen . . . being wanted.

I didn't even notice when Enzo returned to his chair. Didn't notice him come back because my eyes were still on the window where the beautiful man had disappeared. But Enzo didn't seem to notice that my attention was elsewhere because he was just as focused on the arancini as I'd been on the stranger.

Chapter 2

Aurelia

Enzo's phone didn't make a peep, but he was somehow worse.

Far more distant, far more irritable, barely looking at me even when I spoke directly to him. We were in the most beautiful place in the world, but it felt as if we were in a graveyard. Awkward and tense, like every fiber of his being didn't want to share the space with me.

Was it because I snapped at him a few days ago? Or did he just get fired for taking the time off when his boss told him they had too much work to do? Whatever it was, he seemed to resent me for something.

We sat together at dinner, a restaurant I made reservations at months in advance, but it was clear neither of us had an appetite. We sat on a balcony with a view of the water, but the ocean was invisible in the dark. A small candle was on our table, and it flickered every time the breeze picked up. It almost went out a couple times, but it somehow managed to hold on.

The way we were barely hanging on.

Enzo kept his gaze elsewhere, hand on his glass of wine, tension dripping off his body in waves.

I'd officially had enough of this. "I'm done."

His eyes flicked to me for the first time that evening. And he had the nerve to look confused by the statement.

"You're here, but you aren't *actually* here. Every time I confront you about your distance, you always have some kind of excuse. I'm done with excuses, Enzo." I noticed the waiter approach our table to take our order, but he must have caught wind of my words because he awkwardly turned around and addressed a different table instead. "So what the fuck is your problem?"

"Could you keep your voice down—"

"Could you be a man and tell me the truth?"

He slowly straightened in his chair, his hand leaving the stem of his wineglass as his arms folded underneath him. There was a pause, a heavy one under the weight of so many things he'd never said before. His eyes shifted away as he organized the words he was about to present. "It's time we end this."

"No shit, Enzo." There was a slight sting in my chest when he actually did it—when he actually dumped me. On an expensive trip where we should be drinking and fucking and getting sunburned from falling asleep on the loungers at the beach. "But I want to know why. Because you've been like this for months. Always making excuses about work or your friends or whatever bullshit comes to mind. I want the truth, Enzo."

He dropped his eyes again, trying to find a calculated answer.

"No thinking," I snapped. "Just tell me. Because we were really fucking happy, until one day we weren't. And I'm not the one who changed. I'm not the one who walked in the door one day as a different person. That was you."

"Keep your voice down—"

I lowered my voice, not because he asked me to, but because people were turning to stare and I did feel guilty for affecting their romantic holiday just because mine had gone to utter shit. "You care a lot more about strangers in a restaurant than the woman you supposedly love."

He searched for the waiter, and then he made a motion with his hand, asking for the check.

That somehow made me angrier, the way he wanted to get away from me like I was the problem. Like I was the irrational bitch who'd caused all of this. "Tell me what happened."

He sat there, slumped in his chair, looking at anything but me.

"Seriously?"

"What do you want me to say?" he asked, full of exasperation, like he was at the end of his rope of patience. Like being subjected to my company was that horrible. Like I was the most obnoxious cunt he'd ever met.

"You wait until we're on a trip to dump me? That doesn't make sense, Enzo."

"I told you I didn't want to come—"

"Why?"

"I told you I have a lot of shit going on at work."

"Another fucking excuse. Is there someone else? Just be a man and tell me. This is already a dumpster fire, so more fuel isn't going to make it burn any hotter."

He didn't react, didn't look at me.

"What the fuck is wrong with you—"

"It's done," he said, forcing himself to sound calm. "Let's just pay for dinner and go home."

"We've already paid for another ten days at the hotel. And the beach clubs—"

"I don't give a shit about that. I just want to leave."

"You mean leave me." It was the first time my voice was truly calm. The quiet acceptance hit me, having stared the truth in the face for months. It didn't matter what had compromised our relationship, if it was someone else or he really had just fallen out of love with me, if he really had just stopped being attracted to me. I meant nothing to this man. And every time I opened my mouth, every time I asked for the dignity of an explanation, I just irritated him more. Just pushed him further and further away.

I'd rather he tell me he fucked someone else and beg for my forgiveness. I'd rather he tell me he lied to me and promise to earn back my trust. But this indifference, this annoyance, this undeniable urge to leave and never think of me again . . . was fucking cruel.

Especially when I didn't know why. And I would never know why.

We didn't look at each other as we waited for the waiter to bring us the check.

It was one of the lowest moments of my life, my chest so tight with indescribable pain. The agony didn't come from the end of the relationship. It came from the way he looked at me—or *didn't* look at me, because I still remembered how it used to be. Remembered overhearing him talk to his friends and tell them he could see himself marrying me someday. The way he used to talk about us having three kids together. The way he asked me to move in by giving me one of his keys on my birthday. He put me on a pedestal.

And then he yanked it out from underneath me.

Back at the hotel, he packed his things in a hurry. Threw everything inside without discrimination. Threw his razor right on top of his blazer and then piled his shoes on top. His toothbrush was shoved into the side of the bag. An open tube of toothpaste was haphazardly shoved into one of the sleeves, and it would probably ruin a batch of his clothes during the flight.

But he didn't give a shit.

"You're going to stay here?" he asked as he zipped up the bag.

I wasn't going to sit on a plane with him. Wasn't going to return to the apartment we shared. I didn't have a plan for my next move, and I'd already sunk some serious cash into this vacation. I wasn't going to waste that, along with the last two years of my life. "Yes."

"I'll pack up your things." He put his suitcase on the floor and popped the handle so he could roll it out. "Let me know when you're ready to come get it, and I'll make sure I'm out."

"So you just assume you keep the apartment?" I asked spitefully.

He stopped by the door and stared at me. "You moved in with me, so yes."

What a gentleman. "All right, then."

He lingered in the doorway, as if he felt he should say something for the first time. Some goodbye words, provide some kind of closure.

I sat on the edge of the bed in my dress and heels. "Just go, Enzo." I was utterly defeated, somewhat relieved I didn't have a battle to fight anymore. Didn't have to wonder what would happen with us because I'd watched the ending credits of the film.

He hesitated for another moment before he opened the door and stepped into the hallway. The heavy door shut behind him the instant he was gone.

The curtains to the window were pulled open, and I couldn't see much in the darkness, just the light from the streetlamps against the leaves of the trees across the street. One of the lamps on the nightstand was on and cast shadows in the corners of the room. I felt the gravity of my loneliness in that moment, but realized I'd been lonely for a long time, long before Enzo had packed his bags and walked out.

I sat there for at least an hour before the tears flooded my eyes. The waves of agony hit me like ocean waves during a full moon. Why had I put up with this for so long? What had I done that made me so undesirable? What could I have possibly done to be so worthless in someone's eyes?

How could he tell me he loved me . . . and then make me feel so unwanted?

Walk out of my life without even an apology, let alone an explanation.

I wasn't worth either, apparently.

I didn't leave my hotel room the next day. Stayed in bed. Didn't look at my phone—not that I expected him to call or text. Didn't reach out to any of my friends to tell them what had happened. Even though I knew the end was drawing close, I still wasn't ready to describe how cruel it had been.

I didn't have an appetite, so I didn't order room service or go for some granita and brioche. I watched streaming programs on my device in the dark because I kept the curtains closed over the window. It wasn't until the next day that I took a shower and headed into town, but the idea of sitting alone in a restaurant made the situation feel too real, so I sat on the steps by the fountain and people-watched for hours. Everyone seemed to be having a great time on their holiday, while I lived through one of the darkest moments of my life.

By the third day, I was ready to get out.

I packed my camera and took pictures of the town. Went to the beach and climbed rocks and headed to Isola Bella to snap photographs. I was a professional photographer, and getting lost in art was the only coping mechanism I had.

When the sun set, I showered and got ready for my evening, choosing to visit the famous hotel farther up the road. It was the setting for a TV show about a murder mystery, and ever since the show debuted, it'd become a popular attraction for everyone who visited Taormina. I'd wanted to stay there in the first place, but it was *way* out of my price range. A single night there was a week's stay at the other hotel. I was certain it was worth it, but I just didn't have the money.

But anyone could visit the bar, so I put on a black dress and heels and braved the cobblestone walkways and the steep stairs, my ass a little plumper after the journey.

The second I entered the hotel, I heard the quiet music of the piano from the musician in the courtyard. The area was full of swivel armchairs and couches, all occupied by hotel guests or other people like me who couldn't afford to stay there. Full of trees in pots and potted flowers, the space was an oasis in the center of the hotel. There was also no vacancy, so I headed to the indoor bar, the lights low and most of the tables empty. The ceilings were coffered, with golden seashells, and the modern chandeliers that hung down only offered a slight increase in illumination. The mirrored shelves behind the bar were twenty feet high, stacked with every kind of liquor someone could possibly order. The bar also had a piano, but no musician to play it. Instead, music played from speakers overhead as the waiters circulated. Some couples were seated at the tables, but it was mostly men at the bar, who sat alone.

I found a table with two chairs and took a seat. A booklet menu and a low-burning candle were in the center of the table, so I flipped through the pages to see the tapas they had as well as their cocktails. They listed a spicy margarita with mezcal, my preference over tequila, so I ordered that when the waiter serviced me right away.

I took a sip, my phone on the table next to the glass. I should scroll through my social media or find an article to read instead of awkwardly sitting there, but at this moment in my life, I didn't care how out of place I looked.

The drink was thirty-five euros, and you got what you paid for, because it was *strong*. So strong that I would have a hard time meeting their two-drink minimum for those who weren't hotel guests.

Movement caught my eye, and my stare flicked to the left, to the second sitting area I presumed to be in the direction of where the hotel rooms were situated. In a button-up collared shirt with the sleeves pushed to his elbows, he entered the bar with a presence that commanded the attention of everyone seated. Even the guys seated at the bar glanced at him in the mirror.

Directly across the room from me was an open table with two seats, and he occupied one of the chairs as he pulled out his phone.

With dark-brown hair that looked black in this low light and eyes the color of midnight, he was the same prime cut of meat I'd seen outside Rosticceria Da Cristina a few days ago. Wearing dark jeans, he sat with his knees wide apart, elbows on the armrests as he quickly typed on his phone. A slight smirk sat on his lips, like whoever he was messaging with had said something that amused him. Maybe it was a woman he was flirting with. Maybe it was the same guys from the restaurant. My fingers around my glass, all I did was stare at a man more beautiful than all the sculptures of Apollo, god of music. All the sculptures of the emperors in Rome. A man too perfect to be a living being instead of an inanimate work of art.

If he was staying at the hotel, that meant he didn't live here. He must be visiting from somewhere else. All of his features were distinctly Italian, so I assumed he was from the mainland like I was. He was model material, so maybe Milan. So utterly entranced by the beauty before me, I could only stare.

It was the first break I'd received. To be consumed by something that didn't bring me misery.

A group of four girls entered the bar and passed me, and it was clear they noticed the same beautiful man, judging by the way all their heads turned in his direction while they slowed their pace.

He stayed on his phone, so he didn't notice his fan club.

They moved to a table farther down, the only one available that could accommodate all of them.

He finished typing his message just as the waiter walked over. He didn't look at the menu, already knowing what he wanted, and gave the order. He put his phone on the table and relaxed his muscular body into the chair.

The waiter walked off.

At first, the man looked at the wall across from him, eyes lifted upward as if he was admiring one of the large paintings that hung there. They lingered awhile before his eyes swept the bar, making a quick scan of everyone as his stare came toward me.

I had a quick opportunity to look away and hide my stare, but his appearance had me in a choke hold I couldn't fight. Frozen in place, I felt his eyes hit me like a searchlight, blanketing me in a glow that put me on center stage.

His stare didn't pass by me to the bar or another painting. His eyes stayed rooted in place, his stare slowly hardening into the same one he'd given me through the window at the restaurant. An intensity so severe, he almost looked angry.

I had no proof of my assumption, but I *knew* he remembered me.

Remembered me as well as I remembered him.

The stare went on far too long for strangers, but neither of us looked away first. Music continued to play overhead and drown out the conversations that took place at different tables and the bar, but it felt quiet in my head. His phone lit up with a message, the glow of the screen hitting one of his cheeks, but he didn't even glance at it.

Even when the waiter came over with his drink and placed it on a coaster, the man didn't break eye contact with me. I could see him mouth a thank-you to the waiter. One of his elbows was on the armrest, so he slid his closed knuckles underneath his chin, his fingers lightly touching the shadow on his jawline, the coarse hair that would probably feel sharp against the insides of my thighs.

Oh wow, did I really go there?

I just got out of a two-year relationship a few days ago, and I was eye fucking this guy across the bar. I was miserable not even five minutes ago, and now I felt a distinct tightness in every muscle of my body. Felt fire-breathing dragons fly around my stomach instead of butterflies from the garden.

I was the first one to look away, because the tension had become too much. I felt a flush on my neck that I knew tinted my skin all the way up to my cheeks. It'd been so long since I'd been available, and I couldn't remember how to be single. How to play it cool when my knees would buckle if I tried to stand up. I was devoid of confidence and not really sure why he stared at me like that, so I needed a moment of freedom from the suffocating power of his stare to think.

I could walk over there, but then what?

What the fuck would I say to a man who looked like that?

I'd had my share of handsome men, but this man . . . was something else. He had to be at least six foot four. Had to have at least a hundred pounds of muscles stacked on his arms, core, and legs. I bet he could crush a watermelon with his bare hands.

Light-years out of my league.

There was a pause in the music when the song finished. That was when I heard the group of girls from their table.

"Girl, go for it, or I'll go for it. Someone at this table is getting that dick tonight."

"He's probably married or has a girl," another one said.

My eyes were down on my drink as I listened to them, but I swore I could still feel his stare. I knew there was only one man in the bar they could possibly be talking about, and it was the same man I wanted for myself.

I couldn't remember what the women had looked like when they'd passed. I just knew they were well dressed and in heels. Probably attractive if they were confident enough to talk that way.

"Men like that don't have wives or girlfriends. They play the field until they hit forty, and then they marry a twenty-five-year-old," one of the girls said. "So I'm going for it unless someone objects?"

The heart palpitations in my chest were instantaneous. The man was a stranger, but I was suddenly under duress at the thought of losing him—when he wasn't even mine. My eyes flicked back up to his table.

He was still staring at me.

The next song came on, but I heard the distinct scratch of a chair against the hardwood floor as one of the girls stood up.

That meant I needed to haul ass if I wanted to beat her. If I wanted to stake a claim on this painfully gorgeous man.

Just when I was about to go for it, I was knocked over by a wave that no one else could see. Knocked on my ass by the painful reminder of the way I'd been neglected, forgotten, and then dumped. And the man across the bar was a million times better than Enzo ever was, so he'd probably be just as disappointed. Even if it was just a night in his hotel room, I was sure I wouldn't meet his standards, and it would end in sheer awkwardness.

I looked back at my drink and let her have him.

My eyes searched for the waiter who'd brought me my drink, and I made a quick gesture to signal for the check. To get out of there because I didn't want to watch him go to his room with someone else. Watch him buy her a drink, share a laugh, connect. I'd pay the fee for the second cocktail and just not drink it in order to get out of here faster.

I would go back to my hotel and find something to watch until I fell asleep.

It took a couple minutes for the waiter to walk over with my bill in a small leather folder. I kept myself occupied by using my phone, searching for emails that I knew wouldn't be there, looking at social media to see what my friends were doing. I hadn't posted any pictures of my trip, despite all the photos I'd taken the other day.

I placed my card in the folder and waited for the waiter to take it, desperate to get out of there, to walk home down one of the beautiful side streets and let myself breathe in the crisp air and the smell of dinner from the restaurants that I passed.

To try to forget the man who seared my skin with just his stare.

The waiter returned, and instead of taking the credit card I'd left in the folder, he pulled out the other chair and took a seat.

Then I realized it wasn't the waiter . . . but him.

My chin lifted, and I stared into the same eyes I'd studied across the bar and through a window from a patio. I'd never been this close to him, and the magnetic pull of his commanding air was even more potent at this proximity.

The fire-breathing dragons in my stomach started to burn everything inside me. The flush that had crept down my neck reverted with increased ferocity. I didn't know what had happened with the woman who'd visited his table because I hadn't watched and the music had drowned out their conversation, but I could only assume one thing.

That he chose me.

Chapter 3

Aurelia

With the same intensity in his stare that he showed across the room, he blanketed me in his ironclad focus. With quiet confidence, a command that rivaled the Roman emperors, he had an aura so distinct that I felt like I was in the presence of a president or a royal family member, someone of great importance.

Like prey that had been caught in the sights of the hunter, all I could do was remain still and wait for his next move.

After another stretch of silence, he spoke. “Constantine.” It was a single word, but the depth of his baritone was like a song. Deeply masculine, slightly grating, a bit intimidating. If he raised his voice a few octaves, every wall of the hotel would tremble.

I swallowed, knowing I couldn’t just sit there and continue my stare. I had to break the spell he cast on me and participate. “Aurelia.”

He gave a slight nod. “Beautiful name. It suits you.”

“It does?” I asked.

“It means gilded, golden. So yes, I’d say it does.”

This drop-dead gorgeous man had just chosen me over an easy lay . . . and called me golden. I’d never needed encouragement more than I did now, medicine for the disease that had nearly killed me. He had no idea what he'd done for me, pulled me out of the mud I'd allowed myself to wallow in, and he would never know.

For the first time, not in days, but weeks and probably months, I smiled. Felt the invisible pressure of twenty tons leave my shoulders and render me free. My smile felt lighter than a cloud, so natural and so genuine, and the flush in my neck filled my cheeks with a warmth I hadn't felt in my eternal winter.

His gaze shifted slightly, dropped down to my mouth before it returned to my eyes, like something about my smile caught his attention.

"Constantine suits you too. Named after a Roman emperor."

He smirked slightly. "You know your history."

"I'm Roman, so kinda comes with the territory." I straightened my spine, perked up my tits, grabbed the glass, and took a drink from the straw. The heat of the mezcal burned my stomach instantly.

He'd left his drink behind at the other table, but the waiter wordlessly presented a new one and placed it on a coaster. He also took the bill I'd placed on the table but left my credit card behind before he walked off.

As confused as I was, I didn't ask any questions.

"Are you staying at this hotel?"

"God no," I said with a quick laugh. "I'd have to start an OnlyFans to afford this place."

The smile on his mouth was instant and reached his eyes. He was so damn good looking when he wore that smolder, but when he smiled like that . . . chef's kiss. It was brief, but it was genuine before it faded back to a slight smirk. "You'd be in the presidential suite in no time."

"Would you be one of my subscribers?" I hadn't had confidence or courage like this in at least a year, but it came back to me like second nature, the old me finally reaching the surface and taking her first breath of air.

He smirked. "I prefer the live show."

The tightness in my stomach was so strong, I felt an invisible hand grip and squeeze. "You're in luck, because I think my next performance is really soon."

The smirk was still there, a distinct playfulness in his eyes. "How soon?"

I grabbed my glass and took a drink. "In the next hour or so." I didn't recognize myself at all, flirting with this man who could have anyone he wanted, basically inviting him to bed when all I knew was his name. But he'd made his interest clear when he came to my table, and I wanted my interest to be just as clear. A night with him would give me the biggest ego boost I could ever receive. Would put a swagger back in my step. Would give me the strength to grab my things from the apartment and flip Enzo off on the way out. Would remind me that I wasn't the problem—he was.

"Not gonna miss that." He reached for his glass and took a drink. It was amber colored, with ice, so I wasn't sure if it was whiskey and Coke or scotch on the rocks or maybe gin. But whatever it was, it was stiff.

"Are you staying here?"

He gave a slight nod.

"Presidential suite?" I teased.

The smirk that lingered on his lips finally faded away. "You'll find out soon enough." He was deadly serious, the intensity back in his gaze, and he pulled off something that no other man possibly could—effortlessly.

Thank god I shaved today. "What brings you to Taormina?" I changed the subject because if we kept talking about all the fucking we were going to do, I wouldn't be able to finish my drink.

"Family."

"So you're from Taormina?"

"Born and raised."

"And why would you leave such a beautiful place?" A place where you could walk everywhere, have the best granita and brioche in the world, to see beaches that rivaled the Amalfi coast.

"Work."

"What do you do?" Now I knew he had money, if he could afford a place like this. That meant he had an interesting career, maybe a business owner or a physician or a lawyer. But his vibe didn't fit any of those occupations.

There was a long pause before he answered, a pause that probably shouldn't be there for such a simple question. His eyes trailed away before they came back to me. "Private security."

Security. That fit him perfectly. I could tell by his tone that further questions weren't welcome. I wondered what that could mean, if perhaps he was part of the security detail that protected the president or even the pope. That would explain his wealth, his hard presence, his muscularity.

"What about you?" he asked. "You know, just until the OnlyFans career takes off." He smirked again.

When he smiled like that . . . oh fuck, my ovaries. That smile made me borderline unhinged, almost made me lean in and kiss him in the middle of the damn bar. How could he go from serious to playful with such ease?

When his smirk dropped and that intensity set into his handsome face again, I remembered he'd asked me a question.

"I'm a photographer."

"What kind of photographer?"

"I do a bit of everything. Photography and videography for new businesses or hotels. I also shoot weddings and corporate retreats. My passion is fine art photography, but it's hard to make a living that way."

"What is fine art photography?" he asked, the hardness in his eyes showing a sincere interest.

"It's basically a creative form of photography where you're trying to capture a vision rather than the subject. The best way I can describe it is, it's like trying to make a painting with a camera. Trying to make art with reality. A painter has the ability to do whatever they want, change the sky from blue to rain clouds, to change the features of the subject from happy to sad, free rein to show whatever emotion they're trying to evoke. But as a photographer, I'm at the mercy of reality. So it's very hard to do."

His eyes remained on mine, and he seemed absorbed in my answer. He didn't interrupt me to ask follow-up questions. Just listened. "And how does that kind of photographer make money?"

"They sell their photographs in galleries and at art shows. The best of the best sell them like paintings, making tens of thousands of euros per picture. Others go for mass production, so restaurants and other places can all buy copies and put them up on their walls. But then you see the same picture all over the place."

"And you'd prefer the first one."

"Yes." It was my passion, something I'd wanted since the first time I held a camera. I didn't have the talent or the eye to paint or sculpt, but I could work magic with a camera. The question was—did everyone else agree?

"Keep trying."

"I do," I said. "This is the only thing I want to do with my life, so I'll either make it . . . or I'll keep trying to make it until I die."

He crossed his arms over his massive chest and gave a slight smile. "I like that attitude."

"I'm not dedicated or ambitious. It's just the kind of passion that doesn't die."

"And very few people are that passionate about anything." He grabbed his glass and took another drink, practically ingesting diesel, based on the fumes I could smell.

Enzo had been somewhat interested in my photography in the beginning, but that curiosity had been short-lived. Whenever I showed him my photographs, he said they were nice, but he never really looked at them. Not the way I wanted the audience to look at my art. He worked in finance, so I knew he didn't have an eye for artwork, so I just excused it. But Constantine seemed genuinely interested, especially since he'd already secured me in his bed for the night.

I went out on a limb and asked a question that maybe I shouldn't. "What are you passionate about?"

He shook the ice that peeked from the top of his glass, then crossed his arms again. He considered the question with a stoic expression, but even then, he looked handsome. Deep in thought, eyebrows slightly furrowed, he really soaked it in. "Food. Family. And my country." When he was done answering, he looked at me again.

Family was an obvious answer, but the other two were surprises. "Could you elaborate on that?"

"Food and family are so close together they're practically the same."

"You just don't seem like someone who . . . you know . . . enjoys food." My eyes trailed over his hard body, a body that could only be created with intense discipline. Heavy weights every single day. A very specific diet. When my eyes found his again, it was obvious he'd watched me look him over.

"My family owns Rosticceria Da Cristina. Been in the family since before I was born. I worked there all throughout school. My aunt had a passion for that restaurant, and she didn't stop until she made it happen. She used all the recipes given to her grandmother from *her* grandmother. She still cooked dinner at night after a long day, hosted family dinners every Sunday, even when her hands hurt. To us, food and family are the same."

Now I understood why he was there that day. He must have just gotten into town and swung by to see friends and family at the restaurant. "Then that means you know how to make that arancini."

He smiled. "Along with everything else."

A beautiful man who could cook . . . damn. "That's pretty sexy."

The smile remained on his lips, like the compliment meant something to him. For a man who was so visibly hard and intense on the outside, he was actually charming and easy to talk to. Not arrogant like I thought he might be.

"Do you cook?"

"Not really, honestly."

"Then how do you feed yourself?"

"I go out a lot. Don't judge me."

"I didn't judge you for the OnlyFans, so I certainly won't judge you for that." He was also quick, witty, and funny. "How long are you in Taormina?"

"Another week. Do you visit a lot?"

"Whenever I can. Except in August."

"Why not August?"

"If you've ever been here in August, you would know why," he said with a chuckle. "Overrun with tourists. Can't even walk through the square with the clock tower without bumping into someone."

"This is my first time visiting."

"And how do you like it?"

"I love it." I hadn't been able to enjoy it much because Enzo was being an ass or I was too depressed after he'd left. But in this moment, I started to appreciate it.

"Are you here with anyone?"

The question made my chest tighten. It felt like an intrusion into a vault I didn't want to open. I didn't want to spill my soul to this man I barely knew. Didn't want to humiliate myself in front of a man I would never see again after tonight. Knowing another man had thrown me away wasn't exactly a turn-on. And knowing I'd stayed and fought for a man who didn't give a damn about me was the greatest embarrassment of my life.

So, I lied. "I came here with my friend Alex, but she had to leave . . . for work." I wasn't a liar, was pretty shitty at it, to be honest, but I wasn't about to drop a suitcase of baggage on the table and ruin the night. "I couldn't get a refund, so I decided to stay." I grabbed my glass and took another drink, letting the booze wash down the lie that continued to lurk in my throat.

His sharp eyes were still on me, but they gave no reaction to what I'd shared. The stare continued long after I finished talking, but he asked no additional questions.

The group of girls left their table and walked by.

I hadn't gotten a good look at them before, but this time, I watched them pass, and I didn't miss the sharp knives in their eyes. Potent hostility directed at me or Constantine, I wasn't sure which. Their heels continued to tap on the tile floor before they moved up the stairs and left.

I swirled my glass to dissipate the tension, but it lingered. "I'm not sure who they hate, you or me."

"Me."

My eyes flicked to his. "What did you say to her?"

"The truth—wasn't interested."

"Because . . . ?" Now that I'd gotten a better look, every single one of those girls was beautiful. All in short dresses and heels, long hair with earrings flashing in their lobes, ready to attract the attention of any man they wanted.

"Because I want you." His stare hardened on my face as he continued to meet my gaze. Maybe this was all an act he put on to get women in his bed. A tactic to close the deal.

And maybe I was the biggest fool on the planet for falling for it.

But when I looked at this man, I didn't see a performance or a charade. I saw the sincerity behind his dark eyes, saw a man who didn't play games. A man this beautiful didn't need lines or skits. He could have anyone he wanted, whenever he wanted.

So I chose to believe this was real—that he was real.

I'd been out of the game for years, so I didn't have any of my own moves to seal the deal. So, without thinking, I just went for it. I moved my hand to his muscular thigh under the table and gave a gentle squeeze. "Then take me."

Chapter 4

Aurelia

We took the elevator to the top floor and stepped into a long hallway with guest rooms on either side. Some faced the ocean, while others faced the gardens. When he walked beside me, I realized he had to be nearly six and a half feet tall, feeling dwarfed by his height even in my sky-high heels.

He kept his focus ahead as his hand snaked down and grabbed mine. His fingers were twice the size of mine, a single palm almost as big as my head. It was such an innocent touch, but it was enough to set off fireworks inside my chest.

A minute later, he reached the door and quickly pulled out his key to swipe it across the pad. The lock clicked and he opened the door, revealing a large suite with an entryway, two bathrooms, a separate bedroom, and a terrace that could easily entertain a dozen people.

I might have been more impressed by the room if I weren't so impressed by the man who'd brought me there. The lights were already dimmed, and turndown service had been completed, so the place was clean and tidy. He didn't fill the silence with conversation or offer me a drink. He turned toward me, slid his hand into my hair, and kissed me.

Kissed me good.

With masculine restraint and a purposeful embrace, cradling my head and angling his neck down so our lips could touch. He snaked his hand down my body to my ass, and he squeezed one cheek firmly in his grip before he suddenly lifted me into his arms.

I'd been picked up by a man before, but never with this level of ease, like I was a goddamn feather. And he held me with a single arm, sliding his other hand into my hair again, holding me like I weighed nothing.

Such a fucking turn-on.

And his kiss didn't suffer from the distraction of my weight. His mouth moved with mine, his tongue swiped at the perfect moments, and he cranked up my desire to a threshold I'd never reached before.

My dress popped up over my hips as I was held against him, exposing my black G-string, the material covering almost nothing. My hand dug freely into his short hair, and I felt the engine of my body rev to life. The sexiest man I'd ever seen wanted me as much as I wanted him. I'd stepped into a fantasy written just for me.

He carried me to the bed and gently laid me down underneath him. He broke the kiss right away, and while I wanted our embrace to continue, I was so white hot that I was about to combust if he didn't get inside me in the next couple of seconds. I'd been turned on since the moment I'd seen him in the bar, wilting under the heat of his stare. And with every smile and smirk, my thighs clenched a little harder, my uterus contracted, and I went slick with desire.

I quickly worked to unbutton his shirt, to expose more of the hard definition hidden from view. I saw his abs before I saw his hard chest, slabs of concrete that were hot from being exposed to the sun. Beautiful skin covered in the fresco of ink he had designed across his body. I didn't usually prefer a man with tattoos, but when done right, it was art.

And his were a masterpiece.

"Hurry," I said breathlessly, not recognizing my own voice because I'd never begged a man to fuck me.

He pulled his shirt free as a smirk moved over his lips.

It should piss me off, but it turned me on even more.

He unbuttoned his black jeans, kicked off his boots, and then yanked off the boxers underneath, a naked god at the foot of the bed.

Oh lord have mercy.

He had the lines over his hips where the muscles of his abs were separated from his hips. He was the first man I'd seen with an eight-pack, with nothing but muscle under tight skin, with veins popped from the flesh because of how tight everything was. I wasn't sure what I liked the most—his chest or his arms or his stomach. I hadn't seen his ass yet, but I was certain I'd add it to the list.

He finally came back to the bed, his knees making the mattress shift as he moved over me. He slid his hand across my stomach to my side, where the hidden zipper of my dress was located. He somehow knew it was there, like he'd spotted it in advance so he'd know how to take off my dress. He yanked it down, the dress came loose, and he started to pull it off me.

I didn't wear a bra underneath, so my tits were exposed first before the rest of me.

He threw the dress off the bed before he hooked his thumb into the literal string of material over my hip from my thong. Instead of ripping it off, he touched my hips, stared down at my body like he wanted to take a moment to gaze upon it. Then he slid his hand to the top of my ass, grabbed the barely there material, and lifted my hips as he pulled it free.

Once the material was gone, I tried to pull him toward me, to anchor his hips between my soft thighs, but he moved in the other direction, scooping his arms underneath my ass and thighs so he could kiss my aching flesh.

It was an offer I normally wouldn't refuse, especially from someone like him, but I didn't need another ounce of foreplay. Just looking at him was fucking foreplay enough. "No." I tugged him back to me. "I want you. *Now.*" I'd never been bossy like this, in any circumstance, but I wasn't myself at all right now.

He settled between my thighs as I asked, his narrow hips a perfect fit, and he tilted my hips back so he could fold me into the position that he wanted me in. He hooked one of his forearms behind my knees to keep me open, his massive body on top of mine, chiseled and hard, all for me to enjoy. "Pull out, or are you on the pill?"

He was going to fuck me without a condom, and because I wasn't myself at all, I didn't care. Delirious with my attraction to this gorgeous man, I wanted skin to skin, the consequences be damned. "Come inside me."

He inhaled a breath so sharp I felt the hard edge. There was no smirk like there'd been in the past, just that same intense stare he'd given me from the restaurant, from across the bar. He licked his palm and then swiped his wet hand over the head of his dick before he guided himself inside me and gave a gentle push between my lips.

He must have felt the pool right away, because he released the sexiest moan before he gave a hard thrust, pushing his fat length inside me where it belonged.

I gave a gasp because my body wasn't ready for it, but I loved the jerk of pain, felt the way my body struggled to stretch to accommodate him. But once it did . . . fuck. My nails clawed at the flesh of his arms, and I released the loudest moan of my life. "Oh . . . yes." I should restrain my enthusiasm and play it cool, but Jesus Christ, look at this man. Of all the women in Taormina, all the women in that bar tonight, he chose me, and that ego boost was the catalyst to the greatest orgasm in my life. I felt it start the second we stepped into his bedroom. The moment he kissed me, my body filled with an electric charge that grew in anticipation of the shock.

He thrust into me from above, holding his hard body up with his muscular arms and legs, his fat dick nailing me into the mattress over and over, a piston from a machine with the horsepower of a V12 engine.

I didn't moan like a normal woman, all sexy with parted lips and bedroom eyes. I completely came apart right from the start, like my pussy was filled with cobwebs because no one had touched me in years. The last time Enzo and I'd had good sex . . . I couldn't even remember. But it'd been so long since he'd fucked me like this that I certainly couldn't recall it. So I came in just a few seconds of Constantine's thrusts, squeezing his dick with my clenching body, my nails digging into the muscle underneath his tough skin. I didn't even see his reaction when I launched into the sky, not when my vision blurred with tears, not when my head rolled back and I said so many things between my moans like, "Fuck yes . . . yes . . . god yes." This wasn't the superficial high from a vibrator or my fingers. It was that deep combustion that could only be produced by a big dick and a hard pelvic bone right against my clit. "Sweet mother of God . . ."

His thrusts remained at full speed as I had the longest climax of my life, the intensity peaked all the way from beginning to end, one so strong I couldn't control the thrusts of my hips. I was just a body at his mercy, my soul already committed to heaven.

The wave passed and I breathed hard like I was the one doing all the work, and he continued to plow me with a dick sculpted by Michelangelo himself. Missionary and arguably vanilla, but damn, it was great.

He'd already done his job, delivered a promise that most men broke, and *way* ahead of schedule, so I kissed him to slow the thrusts created by that hard ass and roll him to his back. He was propped up by the pile of pillows at the headboard, and his skin was slightly slick from the sweat his hardworking body had produced.

I grabbed his dick that felt like a hot steel pipe and sank down over his length, sealing our bodies together much quicker than the first time because I was even slicker than I'd been at the start of this.

He gave a quiet moan as he gripped my hips in his big hands, his thumbs across my stomach.

My hands planted on his chest, and I rode that dick like a fucking American rodeo queen. The whole thing, tip to base to his sack. "You're so fucking hot," I said breathlessly, looking into those same hard eyes that had burned me with their stare from across the room. Every part of him that I touched was hard with muscle, not a layer of cushion anywhere. He possessed heavy shoulders and a bulletproof chest. The black ink over his tanned skin was beautiful, but I hadn't had the time to look at the art he thought was worthy of being preserved on his body. "Best fucking dick."

With nothing to lose, I felt free. I wouldn't see this guy again, and I could go back to my life with the confidence to face the next phase. Whenever I had to deal with Enzo's next wave of indifference, I would have this memory as armor, a reminder that there were plenty of fish in the sea.

Or plenty of dick.

His hands worked to help me up and down so I wouldn't fatigue too quickly. His strength was incredible, because sometimes I could feel him lift me, like I was a fucking barbell. All his muscles were flexed, the veins popping across his canvas of flesh, his jawline hard as he focused on me, those espresso-colored eyes borderline maniacal in their intensity.

I'd just gotten out of a long-term relationship, but I was bouncing on this man's dick and desperate for him to come inside me. I didn't know who I was. I didn't know whether I liked her . . . or thought she was kind of a slut.

His breathing changed, the tension tightened in his arms and his neck, the cords more prominent as he approached the finish. His hands dug into my flesh as he gripped me and increased the pace, telling me how badly he wanted to come.

I rocked my hips, gripped his shoulder like I was about to climb his mountain, and smashed that dick over and over. "Come inside me." I didn't know who the fuck I was. I'd never been a verbal lover. I'd never been such an emotional or chaotic mess. But I had nothing to fear, not when I would have a clean slate tomorrow, a new page.

I'd almost lost this opportunity because I was too much of a pussy to get out of my chair and fight for him. I'd chosen to waste my time fighting for someone who didn't give a damn about me. But I'd learned from that error, and now that I had this man to myself, I was going to fuck him like it was my last night on earth.

He came with a groan, gripping my hips and sealing me on his dick, dumping all his seed inside me, eyes almost angry from the surge of pleasure that hit him.

I'd never been more turned on.

He finished, his hands loosening their grip on my body, and the lethal edge to his gaze softened slightly. He slid his hands up my body, and he closed my tits within his grasp.

I waited for his dick to soften, waited for the come to start to sink toward my entrance, but neither of those things happened.

We both breathed a little hard as we looked at each other, the eyes of strangers piercing the other's depths. It was just a second or two, but it was a connection I would never forget, a memory that would give me chills every time I thought of it.

He started to sit up and take me with him, moving me to my back with my head at the foot of the bed. He pulled out of me, and his dick was still at full mast and coated with a shiny sheen.

Then he turned me over and grabbed me by the hips, putting my ass in the air and planting my face against the duvet. He gripped the back of my hair like it was a leash, and he shoved himself inside me again.

"Oh Jesus."

He pounded into me harder than he had before, clutching both of my wrists together against the small of my back, restraining me and pinning me to the mattress like there was somewhere else I'd rather be than taking his tank of a dick.

My body shifted with every thrust, my moans swallowed by the duvet underneath me, and my body quivered over and over as that thick pipe rammed into me with the force of a bulldozer. "Fuck me," I said into the mattress beneath me. "Yes . . . fuck me."

Chapter 5

Aurelia

I woke up to the sound of the click of the door. It was so quiet I probably wouldn't have normally noticed it, but I wasn't supposed to be there in the first place. I meant to let myself out once the fun was over, but I'd collapsed in his big bed and passed the fuck out.

I quickly sat up and looked toward the floor-to-ceiling window that led to the patio. The ceilings were twenty feet high, and the enormous drape of the curtains blocked out most of the sunlight. Some of it peeked through in the center.

"Shit." I shouldn't have slept over. Now we had to do the awkward goodbye thing. I had to do the walk of shame, leaving the hotel in the morning in a skintight black dress and heels. Everyone in the lobby would know I was stuffed like a cream-filled donut. If there was anything left inside me, I'd probably find it with my fingers and smear it over my clit back in my room and try to relive the best sex I'd ever had.

I got out of bed and began the scavenger hunt for my dress, panties, and heels.

He emerged from the entryway, in nothing but workout shorts and running shoes. He must have stripped off his shirt somewhere along the way.

I was just about to pick up my heel from the floor when I nearly toppled over at the sight of him. All his muscles were plump from his workout, the cords tight like strings on a guitar. He had a slight sheen of sweat, the same kind he'd worn when we'd fucked last night . . . over and over.

God, I'd forgotten how hot he was. "Um . . . morning."

He pulled his earbuds out of his ears and pocketed them. "Morning." His hard stare suddenly lightened when he smiled, a beautiful, breathtaking smile that made me want to jump right back into bed. "How'd you sleep?"

"Uh . . ." I finally picked up the heel, then searched for the other, which had been flung across the room next to the couch. I was buck naked, moving around his expensive suite, trying to find all my things that had been destroyed in the tornado that crashed through here last night. I finally found my little black thong near one corner of the table. "Yeah." Quickly, I pulled it on to give myself some kind of dignity.

With that same handsome smile, he watched me move to the dining table and find the rumpled black dress on the floor. "Yeah?"

"Uh-huh." I tugged it on, embarrassed that I'd overstayed my welcome. My eyes glanced to the alarm clock on his black nightstand and saw that it was almost eleven. "Oh shit." I'd really slept it up.

"Have somewhere to be?"

I moved back to the couch and started to get my heels on. "I just need to find my phone and my purse, and I'll be on my way." The last pieces of this fucked-up scavenger hunt.

"Hungry?" He remained in front of the large flat-screen TV on the wall over the ornate dresser. He pulled out his phone to check something before he set it on the surface next to the little decorative knickknacks.

"Sorry?" I asked.

"Stay for breakfast."

"Oh . . . um . . ." I didn't expect that offer. Didn't expect him to be polite or actually try not to be an asshole. This man could run me over with a car and I'd be the one apologizing for getting in his way. "It's okay."

"I'm not asking you." The smile was gone, and the intense man that I'd watched across the bar had returned. "Gonna shower. Order me an egg-white omelet and some coffee." He headed down the hallway to the bathroom and disappeared.

After he showered, he returned to the main room in nothing but gray sweatpants that hung low on his hips.

Only a man like him could make sweatpants look better than an Armani suit.

His hair was still slightly damp, like he'd done a quick towel dry. I'd opened the curtains, so the morning light struck his beautiful tanned skin and dark ink. He was even tighter first thing in the morning, his core strong and firm, distinct grooves between all the different planes of his stomach.

Room service had just set up the meal on the outdoor patio under the shade of the umbrella. It was a large terrace, with several different seating areas, including a few dining tables and a private plunge pool. The view of the Ionian Sea was breathtaking.

I was still on the couch, awkward and out of place in this sphere of luxury.

He looked me over before he opened the back door to the patio, the sunshine potent without a cloud in the sky. "Come on."

"Look, we don't need to do the whole charade," I said as I got to my feet, wobbling slightly because I wasn't prepared for the height of the heels. "I should have left last night, but I was knocked out cold—"

"If I wanted you to leave, I would tell you." He didn't raise his voice, but he somehow infused his words with unquestionable strength, the kind I was way too scared to challenge. Something about the look in his eyes and the way he held himself told me he was being sincere.

"Come on." He nodded toward the patio and stepped outside, barefoot, and pulled out my chair before he sat in his own.

I hesitated before I followed him, being hit with the sea air the second I left the suite and moved to the chair. When I tried to scoot my chair closer to the table, the legs got caught in the grooves between the stones, and it sounded like nails on a chalkboard.

He reached over, grabbed the bottom of the chair, and effortlessly pulled me to the table like the chair and I weighed nothing and the friction of the stone was practically smooth ice. He grabbed the steel pot of coffee and filled my cup before he filled his.

I was frozen to the spot, unable to believe I was sitting beside this gorgeous man in the light of day with this glorious view of the sea. He was even more handsome in daylight. His jawline was clean because he must have shaved after he took a shower. Maybe I should have let him go down on me last night so I could have experienced the coarseness of his beard between my soft thighs.

My eyes immediately shifted away when the heat surged through me.

Not over breakfast, girl.

I took a drink of the coffee and removed the lid from my dish to reveal the mulberry granita and brioche I'd ordered. I also had a side of scrambled eggs. There was a pastry basket on the table, but I hadn't ordered that.

I was a bit self-conscious of my appearance, especially in the brightness of the midday sun, because when I'd gone into his other bathroom, I'd seen my reflection in the mirror. I looked like I'd been hit by a car and dragged down the street. My eye makeup was a total disaster. I couldn't believe he'd seen me like that and invited me to join him for breakfast. My hair was a complete mess too, and I tried to manage it with my fingertips.

"Fan of the granita?" he asked.

Granita was similar to sorbet, but it had an icy texture rather than a creamy one. It wasn't very sweet, and spread over a warm piece of brioche, it just worked. I'd only had it once since I'd arrived here, which was a shame because I'd intended to eat it as much as I could on this trip. "Yeah, it's good."

"Tried Bam Bar?"

It was a famous spot in Taormina that was known for its granita. The restaurant was decorated in warm colors of yellow and orange with round tables made out of volcanic stone from Etna. I'd seen a lot of pictures online. "Not yet."

He took a bite of his omelet and chewed it. Then he sat back in his chair and watched me for a moment.

He watched me so hard that I had to ignore my food and meet his gaze.

"Don't do that."

Both of my eyebrows shot up my face. "Sorry?"

"You aren't being yourself."

The man barely knew me, but he called me out during our first meal together. "Well, I'm wearing a cocktail dress to breakfast, and I look like hell." I released a tense chuckle. "Just wasn't expecting this."

"Then take off the dress." A smile moved onto his face. "Won't bother me."

I felt the slight smirk come over my lips before I rolled my eyes.

"And you don't look like hell."

"Well, I look less like hell because I cleaned up the explosion of makeup on my face." I'd washed my face with the hand wash on the sink because that was better than letting myself look like a clown.

"You look thoroughly fucked." The smile was still on his face, a smile that I would love to see through the lens of my camera. "I like it."

My eyes flicked back to the granita, and I dug my spoon into the fruit and the dollop of cream on top before I smeared it on a piece of the brioche. I popped it into my mouth and chewed, aware of his stare on my face.

He turned his attention back to his omelet and took another bite.

For the first time, we fell into comfortable silence, the two of us just existing in each other's space. I felt my body relax and allowed myself to enjoy the sea view. There was a yacht anchored in front of us and a couple of fishing boats passing through.

"You don't stay with family when you visit?" I asked.

"Need my own space." He smirked slightly.

Because of all the women he picked up in town. I wasn't even jealous, just grateful I got to be one of them. I felt like I was in a special club.

"I have a house here, but it's being renovated. It's a big project, will probably take a year."

"This hotel is beautiful, so it could be worse."

"Could definitely be worse." He grabbed his coffee mug and took a drink. "You said you're here for a week?"

"Yeah." I continued to smear the granita on the brioche before popping it into my mouth. It didn't sound like a great breakfast on paper, but it was filling and somehow not too sweet, so it paired perfectly with my coffee. I wasn't sure if I even needed the eggs.

"Busy today but free tomorrow."

"Free for what?" I asked as I ripped off another piece of the brioche. It was a round bun with a circular nob on top, like a nipple. I always went for the nipple first.

He was quiet.

When he didn't answer my question, I shifted my eyes to him.

"For you."

I chewed the bite but nearly choked on it when I understood what he meant. That he wanted to see me again. "Um, why?" I blurted like an idiot, not understanding why this man would want to invest more time in me when he'd already gotten laid. He seemed like the kind of guy that didn't do back-to-backs. I'd expected him to be irritated when I didn't leave his room as soon as the deed was done.

His eyebrows rose slightly as his stare hardened. "Because I want you."

~

I made it back to my hotel room and showered.

The second I was dry and in a change of clothes, I knew I was a different person than I'd been yesterday. A walking zombie of grief and self-deprecation had transformed into . . . a fucking butterfly.

A slutty butterfly . . .

I sat in the only chair in the room, a small one that was distinctly unsteady, and once the high of the past twelve hours passed, a slab of guilt crashed into my shoulders.

My two-year relationship had just ended a few days ago, and I'd already jumped into bed with someone else.

And had the time of my life.

It seemed a bit small of me to do something like that, especially when I'd fucked him without protection . . . and asked him to come inside me. The guilt intensified, and a part of me felt as if I'd betrayed Enzo.

Or at least spat on the relationship we'd had.

The high I felt from Constantine immediately disappeared. I sat in silence, the old curtains open over the window to let the sunshine in. I should head outside and enjoy my time here, but now I was consumed by the darkness once more.

I was either hurt that Enzo had stopped loving me or ashamed of what I'd done.

There seemed to be no winning. It wasn't like me to hook up with a stranger in a bar, especially bareback. Not once had I ever done anything like that in my life. They said people did strange things in their grief.

Was this one of those crazy things?

I heard a few motorbikes pass in the street below the room. Heard a car or two, sometimes conversations from the people who passed by. But then I also heard a quiet vibration, one that didn't come from my phone on the table beside me.

I heard it again. And again.

It was coming from my room.

Then I heard a loud ringing noise—and it was definitely coming from inside my room.

I got to my feet and followed the sound, ending up on my knees on the floor. I approached the bed and lifted the bed skirt to see a bright light on the floor.

It was Enzo's watch.

He must have enabled the Find My Device feature to locate it. He'd probably been in such a rush when he left that he'd knocked it over and it had been kicked underneath the bed. It was still attached to the charging pad that was plugged into the wall. It had just fallen off the nightstand and landed somewhat behind it.

I took it off the pad and hit the button to make the obnoxious ringing stop.

He must have assumed he'd packed it in his suitcase but couldn't find it, instead of actually checking its location. He would probably do that next and realize it was here with me.

That was when an idea struck me.

When I'd checked his phone, his messages had been clean. So was his search history. But his watch stored messages on its own. If he didn't manually delete them from the device, they would still be there.

His watch had a passcode, unlike his phone, and I knew it after watching him enter it enough times, so I was in.

The top message was from Luna—his boss. Nothing suspicious there. I scrolled through the other message boxes to see if there were any names I didn't recognize. It was just his parents and his friends.

A new message popped up from Luna. Where are you?

An odd message from a superior . . .

Lost my watch. I'll leave in 5 mins.

K. She sent a bunch of heart emojis.

Okay, that was definitely weird. I scrolled back through their messages and realized there were so many. Far too many for a boss and her subordinate. When I'd checked his phone in the past, there had only been one or two messages from her, not a hoard of conversations like this.

I scrolled back to a few days ago, the day Enzo had left me at the hotel.

She blew up his phone with a ton of messages in a row.

Enzo, when are you leaving?

Don't ignore me.

Call me.

Why won't you fucking call me?

There were a ton of messages like that, trying to get his attention when he was with me. Without actual confirmation of what I expected, I still already knew what I would find. Knew it in my heart, soul, and bones.

Enzo finally wrote back. I can't leave right now.

Why the fuck not? You should have done this a long time ago.

It's complicated.

Well, Joe found out about us, so our lives just got more complicated.

Joe? Us?

She continued. I just left my husband and my two kids, and you can't ditch your girlfriend???

Oh Jesus.

What happened?

He packed his shit and left. Said he wants a divorce. Not how I wanted things to end, but at least it's done.

Are you okay?

I will be when you come home. I'm glad this is over. I'm glad the lie is done. I'm glad we can finally live our lives together.

I couldn't believe this. Right underneath my nose this entire time. The last time I'd seen her was at their company Christmas party. She hugged me . . . fucking smiled at me—all the while fucking my boyfriend.

I'll handle it and get on the next flight.

Handle it . . . handle me. I was something to be handled. And when I sat there at dinner and asked if there was someone else, he continued to lie. Now I understood why. It was probably because he wanted to protect Luna from getting fired. If I exposed their relationship, she would absolutely lose her job. Enzo too, but her position was more important because she made a lot more money than he did.

I could scroll farther back and read the details of their affair, but what was the point? I took a deep breath and suppressed the tears that wanted to fall. With sheer will, I defeated the urge. I made sure my ducts remained dry.

Because I wouldn't cry over this.

Over my dead fucking body.

"Well, at least I don't feel guilty anymore." I tossed the watch aside, then stared at my phone. I considered calling Enzo and airing my grievances, but he wouldn't care. He didn't care that he'd hurt me. If he'd cared about me at all, none of this would have happened in the first place.

But I'd never been one to take the high road. Never been one to remain cool and collected. I always liked to get in the last word if I could snatch it. So I typed a message to him, short and simple, something to make his heart drop into his stomach.

Wish you and Luna the best.

PS: You forgot to delete the messages on your watch.

PPS: 🖕🖕🖕

Chapter 6

Constantine

I texted her and told her to meet me at the fountain in Piazza Duomo. It was a circular fountain with four small horses as guardians. Only one of the horses worked as a fountain of fresh water. The rest had lost their ability through the ages. It was directly across from Duomo di Taormina, an ancient church that was still in use today.

I sat on the steps of the fountain in jeans, a short-sleeved shirt, and with sunglasses on the bridge of my nose. It was late May, a quiet time before the tourists flooded the area for summer, and the weather was already warm.

I noticed her when she entered the square, wearing a long sundress with platform sandals and a sun hat—perfectly dressed for a holiday. She had dark hair the color of cocoa, natural full lips that I was always a sucker for, and green eyes that were bright rather than hazel. I'd noticed them the first time I saw her outside my family's restaurant.

I rose to my feet and smiled as she walked toward me, a tall woman who was still petite in comparison to my height. I'd never been picky when it came to women, but I did appreciate a woman with legs for days, who was tall and elegant, someone I could kiss without having to break my neck.

She smiled back as she drew close, her hand moving to the shoulder where the strap of her bag hung. "Hey." She came to a stop before me, aviator sunglasses covering her eyes from my sight. She was awkward again, like she didn't know how to act around me, even though she'd already fucked my brains out.

I stepped closer to her, watching her reaction change behind the glasses, and slid my arm around the small of her back before I eased her into me and kissed her. A PG embrace suitable for the families nearby.

And I felt it—that same scorching heat.

Her hand automatically went to my forearm, and her posture changed. It softened, leaning into me like she was pulled by my presence. She sank into my lips a little bit, like she wanted to stay there.

I pulled away. "Come on. I'll give you a tour."

"Of Taormina?" she asked in surprise.

"Only the good spots."

She hesitated again, growing distant like she didn't belong there. "That's awfully nice of you."

"It's small, so don't sweat it."

"Still, you don't have to do that."

"Oh, I'm not doing this for free."

"You aren't?" she asked.

I grinned, watching the understanding enter her gaze once she comprehended my meaning. "You'll pay up later." I nodded toward the main street, Corso Umberto, only accessible by pedestrians. "Come on." The road passed all the souvenir shops and gelaterias and led farther into town and all the pathways that branched off it. "Our first stop—Bam Bar."

"The granita place?" she asked excitedly.

"The very one."

"Good. I'm starving."

We walked together down the main street, and I pointed out all the spots I recommended—and the others that were considered tourist traps. Cannoli made without love because they assumed passersby wouldn't know the difference. Souvenirs made in China instead of handcrafted items from the locals.

We strolled down a couple of streets, made our way slightly uphill toward the Greek theatre, and then emerged at the entrance to Bam Bar, a line of people already outside waiting for a table.

"Oh my god, it's so cute," she said. "I love the tables."

With a sun in the center and **BAM BAR** written in yellow, the tables were custom made by a local dealer. All the restaurants and cafés had the same furniture, just with different designs and colors.

Instead of heading to the line, I walked up to a waiter who had just bussed a vacated table. "Emilio."

He turned at the sound of my voice, and his tanned face immediately erupted in a smile. "Con, you're back in town." He returned the tray to the table he'd just cleaned and embraced me with a hand grab and a pat on the back. "How long you here for?"

"A week. Just visiting the fam. How's your dad?"

"He's good. On holiday in Egypt right now."

"Holiday?" I asked. "I don't remember him ever taking a vacation."

"Well, he had a heart scare a couple months ago and had to put a stent in. Has a new appreciation for life."

"I had no idea," I said. "Glad he's doing well."

"If you've got time, hit me up." He fist-bumped me. "We'll hit the beach."

I fist-bumped him back. "Sounds like a plan, man."

He nodded to the table. "Take this one." He winked and walked away.

I moved to the other side of the table and took a seat.

Aurelia joined me, hanging her bag over the top of the chair. We were covered by the awning, so we would be out of the sun and comfortable in the shade. She examined the table and touched the stone underneath her fingertips before she grabbed the menu. "Whoa, they have a lot of flavors."

"They don't offer those every day." I turned in my chair and peered inside the restaurant, seeing the sign they posted with what they offered for the day. I pulled out my phone and snapped a photo before I set it next to her to see. "This is what they've got."

"Oh." She held my phone and read the selections. "The lemon and the yogurt sound good."

I shook my head. "Those don't go well together. I recommend the coffee and the almond. But if you're looking for fruit flavors, strawberry and lemon pair well." I'd eaten a lot of granita growing up, and the locals always mocked the tourists when they made poor selections. I was just saving her judgment from Emilio and the others.

"Since you're the expert . . ." She closed the menu and set it aside. "I'll take your advice."

I smiled before I lifted my sunglasses onto my head, exposing my face now that we were in the shade. "Good choice, sweetheart."

She copied me, slipping her sunglasses into her bag. She had a small indentation where the spacers on the glasses had dug into her skin, but the rest of her face was perfection. She looked as she had in the bar, her beauty enhanced with subtle makeup rather than masked by it. She had full lashes, typical for an Italian woman, along with a sharp jawline and an elegant neck that I liked. Thick, long hair was around her shoulders underneath the hat, slightly wavy with gentle curls.

And her eyes . . . they just did something to me.

Emilio came back to the table and stopped my mind from drifting to the other night. The little tablet was in hand so he could type in the order for the kitchen.

"Two almonds and coffee," I said. "Cream on both with the brioche. And a bottle of water."

"You got it, Con." He left the table and helped the other customers.

She watched people pass on the street in front of us, sitting with her legs crossed, a golden necklace around her throat. "Did you go to school with Emilio?"

"Yeah. I've known him since I was a kid. Pretty much everyone I went to school with works in town."

"So you're the anomaly."

I'd taken a very different direction in life. A lot of people saw Taormina as a beautiful, peaceful town, and for the most part, it was. But Sicily had a long history that most people didn't know about. "I suppose."

She turned to look at me. "I can tell you love it here."

I'd walked these streets hundreds of times. Swam in the Ionian Sea, jumped from cliffs with the boys, explored caves that nearly got us killed. Had family dinners by candlelight next to the stone buildings. I had a lot of good memories here. "It'll always be home." Always hold a place in my heart of joy . . . and despair. "Where's home for you?"

"Rome."

"Same."

"Only an hour flight. Not sure why I didn't make this trip sooner." She turned to watch the people walk down the stone pathway again. There was a sandwich shop farther down, a local spot that tourists never visited because it was somewhat tucked out of sight. "I explored a bit the other day and took a lot of photos. A photographer's playground."

"Too bad your friend didn't get to enjoy it."

Her eyes came back to me, accompanied by a distinct flash of confusion.

I knew she'd lied before, but I gave her some grace and let it slide.

When she understood what I meant, she tried to brush it off. "Yeah, her loss." Her eyes immediately went back to the street to watch the couples pass, holding hands. Potted flowers were outside every door, flowers overflowing from the balconies of the buildings above.

I was a remarkable judge of character, could spot the most skilled liar with a devil's tongue within a few seconds, so when she'd hesitated and became visibly uncomfortable when she mentioned her *friend* who'd had to leave their holiday early . . . I knew.

I didn't respect liars, and anyone who chose to obscure the truth was someone I could do without, but she was so painfully bad at it that I knew it was one of the first lies she'd ever told. It wasn't her character. Wasn't who she was.

Now, I wanted to know *why* she lied.

When I'd felt her stare outside Rosticceria Da Cristina, I'd met her look. I'd expected a quick lock of the eyes and then an immediate dismissal. She was beautiful, obviously, but that wasn't why my stare lingered.

It lingered because of the grief.

I could spot it on anyone anywhere, even in the middle of uproarious laughter over a dinner party. I could feel the cold from the ice shards in their heart. Hers was just so raw and deep that it made me forget everything around me for a second.

When I'd spotted her in the bar, I'd noticed the exact same thing. An unbelievably beautiful woman anchored to a tombstone of grief. She wore a little black dress with pink and blue seashell ornaments on the straps, a delicate addition of color to her dark silhouette. She sat with a strong posture, but she lacked the confidence a woman of her caliber should possess. It was a dichotomy that I couldn't understand. She could hold my gaze when others would blink or look away, but when another woman approached to make a pass, she accepted defeat. Looked away and asked for the check so she could forget our stare had ever happened.

I didn't know what had happened to her—but I knew *something* had.

At the end of the road to the right was the Greek theatre, so I took her there to see what the Greeks had built when they conquered the island, before the Carthaginians conquered them, and then the Romans conquered them.

That's all history was—a series of conquests.

It was small, nothing compared to the Colosseum in Rome, but she seemed to enjoy it. Pulled out a high-end camera from her bag and snapped a couple photos, not of people or specific subjects, but angled shots, flowers, sometimes a broken piece of stone.

When we finished there, I took her to La Focaccia, a sandwich shop that was as popular with the locals as the tourists. With premium Italian meats like mortadella and capicola, along with pistachio pesto and burrata, it was always a stop on my list when I was in town.

"Those are big-ass sandwiches." She watched a customer walk away with the square piece of bread covered in waxed paper. For someone of her size, the sandwich would take up two of her hands.

"Want to split one?"

"I mean . . . if you don't mind."

"Sure. What do you want?"

"Uh . . ." She stared at the menu through the crowd of people. "You're the expert here."

I smirked then moved through the cluster of customers waiting for their sandwiches, hearing the high-energy American music over their speakers.

"Constantine!" Umberto stopped making his sandwich to raise his gloved hands in the air.

Raphael and Angelo both released shouts of excited surprise. "About time you show that ugly face around here," Raphael said.

Umberto ripped off his gloves, then came over to fist-bump me across the counter. "This your first stop?"

"You know you guys are the best," I said over the music.

All three of them made another shout to the music, the two in the back still working and dancing at the same time. La Focaccia was always a fun time, the guys in a good mood and entertaining the tourists.

"The usual?" Umberto asked.

"Yep."

He quickly glanced behind me to where Aurelia stood behind my shoulder. "And your friend?" He waggled his eyebrows.

I smirked. "We're going to share."

"Ooh . . ." He turned back to the boys. "They're gonna share a sandwich. Isn't that cute?"

I pulled out my wallet to grab my credit card.

"No, no, no." He waved the card away. "You know better than that, Constantine."

"Come on, you never let me pay."

"Your family never charges us when we stop by Rosticceria Da Cristina."

"But I don't work there or own it."

He continued to wave the card away like it was bewitched with a curse. "Con, your money is no good here. Stop it."

I sighed before I returned the card to my wallet. A couple minutes later, I took the sandwich, and Aurelia and I walked away from the crowd. There was an empty park bench farther down the curve of the road, so I took a seat and held out the sandwich so she could have the first bite.

"What have we got here?" she asked, taking the sandwich with both hands.

"Pistachio mortadella, stracciatella, pistachio pesto . . ."

She eyed the sandwich and tried to figure out her plan of attack before she went for the corner and took a small bite, missing pretty much all the good stuff.

"You can do better than that."

She took another bite, getting the meat and the cheese, and covered her mouth as she chewed. She nodded as she experienced the flavors.

I held the sandwich with a single hand and took a massive bite out of it.

When she finally finished her bite, she lowered her hand. "Damn, that's good."

We shared the sandwich back and forth, each taking a bite until there was nothing left but crumbs on the waxed paper.

"So you really know everyone around here." She sat with her legs crossed, the slit in her long dress exposing her beautiful tanned skin, the definition in her thighs and calves apparent.

"Yep." For better or worse.

"That's cute." She studied the street again, looking like a subject that belonged in front of the lens of her camera. "Anything else on our list?"

"You haven't experienced Taormina until you've had a cannoli."

"I actually had one when we first got here."

We as in her and Alex? Or *we* as in her and someone else? "But have you been to La Pignolata?"

"No, never heard of it."

"Then you haven't had a cannoli. Come on." I left the bench and tossed the waxed paper and napkins in the garbage.

"Wow, this is one hell of a tour. I'll have to leave you a nice tip." When we returned to the street, she gently came into my side, giving me a playful bump as she smiled.

I didn't bump her back, not when the slightest touch from my size could make her trip and fall. Instead, I moved my hand to her ass and squeezed it before I gave it a playful smack. "That's what I'm talking about."

~

I sat across from her outside the small café, watching her eat a massive cannoli with cream spilling out on either side of the opening. And of course, all I could think about was sticking my dick in her mouth.

Her dress was low cut in the front and showed the slight swell of her tits, and when she took a bite, a piece of the shell broke off with the cream and landed right on the exposed skin of her left tit.

She naturally stuck out her chest to look down at it before she brushed her hair behind her shoulder. With the cannoli in one hand, she used her other to wipe up the cream and suck it off her fingers. Then she ate the piece of shell that had broken off.

I was so fucking hard that I couldn't stand. Not when people would see my fat dick and I'd get a serious head rush from the loss of blood.

She must have felt the heat of my stare, because her eyes met mine as she sucked more cream off her finger. A sudden surge of confidence filled her, and she held my gaze as she took another bite of her cannoli, getting cream all over her mouth and swiping it away with her tongue.

Lord have mercy . . .

I'd watched women eat cannoli before, but it had never turned into a sex show like this.

She really should consider doing OnlyFans.

She returned the second half of the cannoli back to the paper basket it had come in. "You weren't kidding."

I was so uncomfortable I just wanted to adjust my jeans, but there was no way I could do it without making it obvious that my dick wanted to break my zipper. Aurelia already knew, based on the way she eye fucked me, but other people were around, including Hector, my old classmate, who stood in the window. And he didn't need to know how much this woman turned me on.

She cleaned her fingers with the napkin before she went inside and dumped her trash in the bin. But then she went to the counter and ordered another, clearly asking for it to go, based on the container they gave to her.

My pants were about to break.

She came back to the table and sauntered toward me, her hand moving to my shoulder and grazing over the muscles of my arm and chest. Her perfume hit me, as well as the scent of sunscreen. Her ass was right next to my shoulder. "Can I eat this in your room?" She slid her fingers up my neck, and her thumb brushed my bottom lip as she teased me.

I fucking loved to be teased. "Let's go, sweetheart."

~

The blackout curtains were closed when we entered my suite, but some streaks of sunlight poked through. Clothes were dropped, shoes kicked away, and I looked at her in her little pink thong and nearly growled.

Her lithe core showed the muscles of her abs, her tits were full and perky, big for her slender frame, and her legs . . . her legs drove me fucking mad. I slid my hand into the playground of her hair, and I fisted it as I kissed her, my other arm tugging her into me as I bent my neck to feel her lips. The second I had her, a heat flushed through me and lit every nerve on fire. I was aware of my own heartbeat, aware of the way it pounded in my chest like it might break my ribs. Sex was arousing, but generally soothing and calming. However, with her, it gave me the same rush of adrenaline as when I put someone in the grave.

I was about to throw her on the bed, but she beat me to it.

She guided me back, then shoved me.

Fuck me.

I was propped up slightly on the pillows at the headboard, my dick hard against my stomach, and I watched her take the cannoli from the package and saunter toward the bed.

Oh sweet mother of God.

She positioned herself between my thighs, lying on her stomach, and slowly dragged her finger through the cream on one side of the opening, then popped it into her mouth to taste it.

My dick twitched harder than a baseball bat about to hit a home run.

Then she cracked the shell, crumbs sprinkling into my lap, the ricotta filling coming free. Using her fingers as a spoon, she scooped it, then spread it up my length, getting the creamy mixture against my skin too. It was cold to the touch but ignited me like a match to gasoline.

She slowly worked to coat my entire dick with the dessert, her eyes seductive and confident, the version of her that only emerged under the right conditions. When she had enough drinks to take the edge off, when she stopped thinking about who she was and just lived in the moment. When she didn't have the chance to second-guess herself. When she didn't have to question whether she belonged . . . or she should give her spot to someone else.

She set the shell aside, then stuck out her tongue and grabbed the base of my dick—like my cock was a lollipop. She dragged her tongue up, caught the cream in her mouth, and when she made it to the top, she licked the dollop she left there and swallowed it like it was the best thing she'd ever tasted.

I propped my arm underneath the back of my head and dug my fingers into her hair to keep the strands from her face, watching her eat the white cream off my dick, taking her time like she was doing this for herself as well as for me.

She flattened her tongue and sheathed me with her mouth, the cream down my base catching on the sides of her lips as she moved down as far as she could go, maybe going a little too far, because she came back up and took a deep breath as if she needed to recover from the strain.

When she went down again, she was prepared for the hit to the back of her throat, and she was able to come back up and then lick another drop of cream from the top of my head, fulfilling a fantasy I didn't even know I had until now.

My fingers deepened into the curtain of dark hair, my hands cupping her face. "Attagirl."

When all the cream had been licked away, it turned into a straight blow job, but I didn't make it past the first minute before I released into that warm mouth.

And she drank every drop like it was just as sweet.

Chapter 7

Aurelia

Constantine stepped out of the shower, drops of water clinging to his naked skin like drops of dew on a summer morning. A living sculpture that had a beating heart, he moved to the dresser and grabbed a fresh pair of boxers. He ran his fingers through his damp hair absentmindedly.

Naked on his bed, I lay there and admired him.

"Do you like seafood?" he asked suddenly. He pulled on the black boxers before he tapped the screen of his phone to see what messages had popped up since he'd last checked it. There seemed to be nothing of importance, because he turned to look at me.

"Of course."

"I know a good spot." He grabbed a watch from the counter and slipped it onto his wrist before he clasped it closed. The face of the timepiece was turned toward me for an instant, and I recognized it as a Patek Philippe.

The most expensive watch brand in the world.

The only reason I knew that was because of some of the weddings I shot. Sometimes rich clients hired me, billionaires, and I'd seen glimpses of that world. They wore watches just like that. "For . . . ?"

"Dinner." He moved toward the bed, then took a seat at the edge. He reached for my ankle, his fingers lightly touching the skin and feeling the gold anklet that sat there. His eyes were on me like he didn't think twice about his actions. So subtle and quiet, but somehow sensual and intimate.

"The tour continues?"

His eyes held mine for an instant before a smile slowly lifted his lips. "Keep paying me well, and I'll show you the world." His fingers went still on my ankle before he rose to his feet and moved back toward his closet.

I watched him go until he disappeared, and my heart gave an inexplicable lurch. Even the simplest touches left invisible marks on my skin. I barely knew anything about the man except his name and his homeland, but I felt close to him. "Is it a nice place?"

"Yes."

"Then I'll swing by my hotel and change." I left the bed and pulled on everything I'd been wearing, before I grabbed my purse. "Want me to meet you there?"

He came back out of the closet, a black button-up shirt open across his tattooed chest. He worked the buttons without needing to watch his fingers work. "You think you could find it?"

"Heard of Google Maps?"

He smirked. "Then I'll meet you there in an hour, sweetheart."

When I arrived at Osteria RossoDiVino, Constantine was already seated at a table underneath an outdoor space heater. The patio was full of other couples enjoying a bottle of wine and their dinner.

It was a longer walk from my hotel than it was from his, but Taormina was small and safe, and walking alone down the cobblestone streets and the narrow alleys felt more like an adventure than a risk.

He sat with his arms crossed, a candle burning low on the table with a bottle of wine already placed there. He spoke with the waiter, and judging by their body language, they knew each other. The waiter said something funny, because Constantine flashed his signature mouthwatering, panty-dropping smile.

God, he was so hot.

Seriously, the hottest piece of man I'd ever laid eyes on.

And for tonight and hopefully the rest of the week . . . he was mine.

He seemed to know I was there, because he turned in my direction. His smile fell, and a hardened, intense expression replaced it—and that was the look I preferred. His eyes roamed down my body even though he'd taken me against the headboard before he'd showered and gotten ready for dinner.

When I reached the table, he rose to his feet, something I didn't expect him to do. He bent his neck and gave me a gentle kiss, even though I still must have tasted like him mixed with the cannoli. Eyes still focused on mine, he pulled out the chair for me and waited for me to sit.

It took me a second to shake off the magnetism in his eyes. To break the hold he had on me with just his stare. He could be such a gentleman but in a masculine way rather than a domesticated one.

He returned to the chair across from me, the candlelight highlighting the angles of his face. The sleeves of his collared shirt were pushed to his elbows to expose the chiseled muscles of his forearms, the black ink over beautiful tanned skin.

He grabbed the bottle and wordlessly poured me a glass.

I'd spent the whole day with him, but he looked so absolutely dreamy, it felt like the first time I'd met him. When I was so nervous I thought I'd throw up. When I felt completely unsure of myself, unworthy of his stare and his attention. I grabbed the menu just so I could break the connection between our eyes.

"Why do you do that?"

My eyes flicked back up to his, my heart in my throat like I'd been caught red handed robbing a bank.

He brought his glass to his lips and took a drink.

"Do what?"

"Pull away."

"I was just looking at the menu."

A smile moved over his lips, but it wasn't the kind he'd worn before. It was knowing, sinister, his eyes suddenly turning a little sharp. "All right, sweetheart." He took another drink of wine but continued to stare at me.

I felt a little weak at the comment, even more uncertain of myself now. I felt like I'd stepped into a poker match with a shit hand.

The waiter approached our table and placed a wooden table beside it. He returned to the kitchen and came back with a large tray piled with fresh fish before he set it beside us. "Our fresh catch of the day, sea bass. We can prepare it Sicilian way, baked with potatoes, tomatoes, vegetables, and oil. Is this something you're interested in?" He glanced to me, then back to Constantine.

Constantine looked across the table. "Would you like fish tonight, or did you prefer something else?"

I set the menu down. "You're the tour guide . . ."

I expected him to smile, but he didn't. He turned back to the waiter. "We'll split this one." He selected one of the fish that was presented on the tray. "Sicilian style."

The waiter nodded before he carried the fish back into the kitchen.

Constantine took another drink of his wine before he returned his glass to the table. "One of the things I like about this place. You get the freshest catch prepared authentically by people who take pride in their cooking."

"I'm sure it'll be delicious." I grabbed the glass he'd poured for me and took a drink. I let the previous tension fade away at the change of subject. I felt grateful for it, because the way he'd looked at me . . . I'd never forget it.

I felt like I'd just met a different version of him. "So, where do you live in Rome?" I didn't want to invade his privacy too much, but now that we'd spent the last couple days together, I felt like I could ask him.

He answered right away. "The Parioli area."

"That's a nice neighborhood." Which convinced me even more that he was wealthy. Really wealthy. Like significantly richer than a millionaire. I didn't have a ton of evidence for it except for the watch and the room he rented at the hotel, but his presence implied it.

"What about you?"

"The Prati area." I was just across the river from the Pantheon and the Trevi Fountain. I could also see the dome of Saint Peter's Basilica through my living room window. Well, my *old* living room, because I'd be moving out the second this fuck-cation was over.

"Also a nice area. You must do well with your photography."

"Not really," I said with a laugh. "I can only afford it because—" I swallowed, realizing the corner I'd just backed myself into. "Because I have a roommate." Because Enzo made good money working at his hedge fund company. I reached for my wineglass and took a drink, needing the bile of memory to be washed away.

Constantine said nothing. He just stared at me across the table like I might say more.

I cleared my throat. "How long have you lived there?"

He didn't answer the question right away. He continued his stare like his mind was elsewhere, so far away that it took time for him to come back to me. "Five years. You?"

"All my life." All the historic sites of that ancient city were second nature to me. Millions of tourists came to the Eternal City every year to see what I got to enjoy every single day. I couldn't count the number of times I'd done a shoot at the Colosseum or the Trevi Fountain. Ancient Roman history was just . . . history to me.

"What's your family like?"

"Well, I don't really have a family. Just a few friends."

He didn't press further with his words, but his eyes dug into me.

"My dad took off when I was young. Being a parent wasn't for him. And then my mom died."

The sharpness in his eyes dulled. "I'm sorry."

"Yeah, it sucks." I tried not to think about it too hard. Otherwise, I'd cry. She was what I'd needed these last few months. If I could have spoken to her, I was sure she would have helped me leave Enzo. Would have talked some sense into me. Slapped me if I needed it. "She got sick, and I took care of her until she died. I'm grateful for a job that allowed me the flexibility to do that. If I were stuck at a corporate job, that wouldn't have been possible."

He inhaled a slow breath, but I never saw him release it. "I'm sorry." He repeated his words like he forgot he'd already said them, or he meant them even more now than he had before.

"She didn't deserve it, but that's how it goes. I felt so much relief when she passed away on a truckload of morphine, because for the first time in months, her little body wasn't tense. She was just relaxed . . . and she slipped away."

He didn't apologize again, but he listened like every single syllable of my words mattered to him.

The sadness was dispelled by the arrival of dinner. The fish had been divided onto two plates, and it smelled heavenly. I didn't want to think about watching my mother die when I was in paradise with a man who was too good to be true. If she were here, I would have called her and told her all about it—and she would have told me to jump his bones.

We ate quietly for a while in the candlelight, just enjoying each other's company the way we had that morning at Bam Bar. There were times when I felt so comfortable with him, but the second I realized my comfort, I took a mental step back.

Because this was just a fling. I couldn't get too attached. I wasn't building a future with him—only memories.

"Headed to the beach tomorrow with friends. Like to join?"

I never assumed we had another day together. Any moment could be our last. He didn't owe me anything, and I owed him nothing in return. But it made my heart sing every time he asked. "I don't want to intrude—"

"I wouldn't have asked if you were an intrusion."

My heart tightened in my chest. It'd been such a long time since I'd been wanted that I wasn't even sure how to accept the inclusion. Enzo used to bring me around his friends . . . until he stopped. And now I knew why.

He was afraid they would tell me about Luna.

And that meant they knew everything. Assholes.

Constantine studied my face across the table like he knew my mind had slipped away.

I felt guilty. Horribly guilty for the lies I'd told him. Pretending I was here with a friend when I was getting over the worst breakup in my life. When I was cheated on, dumped, and then abandoned all on the same day.

I suddenly lost my appetite even though it was the best fish I'd ever had. I set my fork down on the edge of the plate. "Um, there's something I think you should know." Potent shame filled me like a cloud of smoke and coated my insides with soot. "I told you I came here with a friend and she had to head back for work." I kept my eyes on my plate because I could see his movements in the corner of my vision. See the way he gently set down his fork and rested both elbows on the table, his hands together. "Truth is . . . I was here with my boyfriend. Ex-boyfriend now."

Constantine was silent.

"He headed home. Said he'd pack up my things and I could collect them when I get back." I had no idea where I would live. I should probably work on finding an apartment now, but I didn't want to think about it. "I'm sorry I lied." I took a breath and finally had the courage to look him in the eye.

His expression was the same as it'd been before. He gave me nothing.

"I—I just didn't think I was going to see you after we met in the bar. I assumed it would be a onetime thing, so I made something up so I wouldn't have to talk about it. But now . . . I don't know. I feel like you should know." He might judge me. Think less of me. Assume he was a rebound and not want to see me anymore. Whatever his reaction might be, it wouldn't be good. It wasn't exactly sexy to be with a woman who just got dumped.

After a long stretch of silence, he spoke. "I already knew."

"You—you did?"

"I always know when someone's lying."

It almost felt like a threat. It made me swallow hard and made me feel really fucking stupid.

"I don't tolerate liars and cheats. But you're right. Neither of us knew we'd be sitting here right now. I was a stranger to you at the time. I can tell you're carrying some stuff right now, and the last thing you wanted to do was drop your baggage on someone you don't know." He gave a slight nod. "So, don't worry about it."

I felt pardoned and executed at the same time. I wasn't sure how to follow that. "So . . . the beach invitation still stands?"

"Why wouldn't it?" He grabbed his fork again, sliced it into the tender fillet, and took a bite. He'd already eaten half of his plate, because he always seemed to inhale his food when he ate. When we'd split that sandwich, one of his bites was the equivalent to five of mine.

"I don't know. Doesn't make me look very good."

"How so?"

"Well, I just got out of a relationship a couple days before I met you . . . and I jumped into bed with you pretty quickly." Instantly—and bareback.

"I'm not the judgmental type."

"You just said you don't tolerate liars and cheats."

"I don't," he said simply. "But you don't fall into those categories." He finished his fish, his elbows moving to the table with his hands together. "The relationship ended, and you're free to do what you wish—or whom you wish." A subtle, handsome smile moved on to his lips. "Unless there's a chance you'll get back together—"

"No." Every bone in my body wanted to scream. If Enzo came back to me because he realized his affair was just a mistake and begged for another chance, it would give me no pleasure, not when I never wanted

to see him again in any capacity—not even for that succulent revenge. "He's dead to me."

He gave a slight nod like he understood, when there was no way he'd understand at all. A man who looked like that had never been replaced by someone else. Had never been betrayed by a woman. Any woman who had the pleasure of his company held on until her knuckles snapped. "A liar and a cheat."

An astute guess. "That wasn't even the worst part."

He didn't ask for further detail, but his magnetic stare from across the table had the strength to pull it out of me.

I hadn't told anyone what had happened. I wasn't sure if Enzo had told his friends yet. So it was all crammed deep inside my chest, and the bars that kept it in place were growing weaker by the day. My friends would be supportive, but they would have that look in their eyes—I told you so. Constantine was a stranger in a bar who had quickly turned into my lover and my friend and . . . the perfect medicine for my misery. "I was the photographer for one of his work retreats. It moved really quickly, we moved in together in just a few months, and it just felt right. He told his friends he wanted to marry me. I found the family I'd been missing. But about six months ago, I noticed it."

He continued to listen.

"Noticed him fall out of love with me. A slow, painful death, just like my mother's. And there wasn't a damn thing I could do to fix it. I tried to talk to him, tried to plan special things for us, but the harder I tried, the more indifferent he became. I felt myself wither away as the defeat continued to suck me dry. I'm ashamed to admit this, but I started to snoop through his phone and try to figure out if there was someone else."

"Don't be ashamed. That's on him, not you."

"I violated his privacy."

"A man in a committed relationship doesn't need privacy." He spoke in his normal voice, all the tables on the patio filled with other guests, but his tone was so sharp it nearly cut me. "A man should make his woman feel secure. If he didn't, that's on him. You should never have to wonder, and if you do, then the relationship is done. Instead of being a man and telling you the truth, he forced you to do things you didn't want to do. He made you someone you didn't want to be, a woman who goes through his phone when he's in the shower, analyzes every word he says, searching for the truth between the lies, desperate for attention and validation. And the more he refuses to give it to you, the harder you work for it. He held the power over you—and he fucking knew it."

I stared, utterly mesmerized by this man.

"If he doesn't respect you, then you don't respect his privacy." His arms lowered on the table as he sank back into his chair, his dark eyes wreathed in viciousness. "That's how it works."

Did these heated words come from experience? I wanted to ask, but it didn't feel right in the moment. "I didn't find anything, because he was deleting his messages. We booked this trip a long time ago, and I thought it might be the right opportunity for us to find each other again. But he was more distant than he ever was until he just left abruptly."

He listened to every word, the candlelight reflecting perfectly in his eyes.

"But he left his watch behind, and those messages weren't deleted." I swallowed before I continued. "It ended up being his boss, a woman who's about seven years older than him, who's married with two kids."

His reaction was subtle but distinct, a shift in his eyebrows like even he was surprised.

"Her husband found out, and she wanted him to end things with me so they could finally be together . . . and he did."

"And not once did he tell you this himself." It was phrased as a question but more of a statement, like he was the judge about to decide the punishment.

"Correct."

He crossed his arms over his chest. "Now I understand."

"Understand what?"

He held my gaze for a while before he gave a slight shake of his head.

"Understand what?" I pressed.

His eyes shifted away as he considered my question, drafting his meticulous response. The pause was more than a few seconds, almost a minute, and his eyes continued to reflect the candlelight and the flames from the outdoor space heaters. "Why you didn't fight for me." His hand absentmindedly massaged the bicep of the opposite arm. "Why you let that other woman have me."

Chapter 8

Aurelia

We walked back to his hotel, taking the small alleyway to the main road and then the Piazza Duomo. Beautifully lit with the sound of the water from the fountain, it was a serene paradise.

I couldn't imagine experiencing it without the man next to me. They said people came into your life for a moment or a season . . . and sometimes forever. I knew he was just a moment, but it was a moment I would never forget. A lifeline while I was adrift at sea. Air that filled my collapsed lungs.

Halfway across the piazza, his hand snaked to mine and enclosed it.

Like a girl in middle school who had just touched a boy for the first time, my heart sprouted wings and flew to the sky. I moved closer into his side as we walked, my head rubbing against his shoulder. I could smell the scent of his clean shirt, the cologne underneath, the smell I'd noticed on his sheets.

He helped me down all the different sets of stairs in my heels before we crossed the road to the entrance to his hotel, a stone wall with a small open section in the center so no one could sneak in to the hotel without being checked by security.

I stopped feet away, and Constantine stopped with me, his hand leaving mine as he faced me. He was a behemoth compared to me, even in my five-inch heels. I was tall for a woman, so the dating pool of men was always smaller for me. I couldn't date a guy less than six feet tall, but most men liked petite girls, not someone who was just a few inches shorter. So that made Constantine perfect because he actually made me feel small. Not just in his height but the pounds of muscle on his colossal frame.

He patiently waited for me to speak.

"I'm gonna go to my hotel . . . I think I need to be alone tonight."

There was no sign of disappointment. Just acceptance.

"I'm just not really in the mood, you know." Something I didn't think was possible, because Jesus Christ, look at the man. I only had so many nights of this trip left, and I shouldn't squander them being alone in my cheap hotel room.

"I'd still like you to stay."

My eyes took in his, seeing truth burn bright like the North Star. He could let me walk back to my hotel and then stop by a bar on his way back and pick up someone else for the night. If I didn't give him exactly what he wanted, he could replace me with the snap of a finger. But he still wanted me. "You do?"

A handsome smile slowly spread over his face, the signature panty-dropper, the smile that made his eyes reflect a sea of candles that were nowhere nearby. It made me feel like the only woman who mattered to him—at least in that moment. He started to step away and gave a slight nod toward the hotel. "Come on, sweetheart."

We walked around the lobby and through the bar where we'd met. At one of the tables were the four women I'd spotted the other night. I remembered them, and they definitely remembered me.

I wasn't sure if Constantine spotted them or it was just a coincidence, but he grabbed my hand the way he had when we'd walked through the piazza.

The jolt in my heart was just as painful as it was pleasurable. Enzo didn't choose me—but Constantine did.

When we made it back to his room, housekeeping had already performed the turndown service. The lights were dimmed low. The living room had a full seating area with a large TV and a dining area. His bedroom alone was bigger than my whole room at my hotel.

He went into his closet and started to undress.

I sat on the couch by his bed and got my heels off, and I watched him enter the bathroom. The sound of the faucet was clear a moment later.

I stepped into the bathroom behind him, seeing him brush his teeth with an electric toothbrush in the large mirror that took up the entire wall. He was in just his boxers, his muscular back rippled with muscle, his ass tight. Still in my little black dress, I leaned against the doorway. “Mind if I wear one of your shirts to bed?”

He didn’t nod or stop brushing his teeth to answer. Just wore that smile of his that I couldn’t describe, the kind that was in his eyes rather than on his mouth.

I smiled back, then opened his drawer to find a clean T-shirt. It was black, and when I checked the tag, I saw it was an extra-large. It would definitely fit me like a dress, the most comfortable dress I’d ever worn.

I changed into it before I went back into the bathroom. He continued to brush his teeth, his eyes shifting to me before they returned to his own reflection.

I felt self-conscious taking off my makeup before bed, but if I didn’t, I would look like hell in the morning, my mascara and foundation all over the pillow. There were two sinks, so I used his face wash to clean my face and one of the washcloths to get all the makeup off.

When he finished brushing his teeth, he looked at my reflection in the mirror.

I felt on display, my eyes no longer pretty without the dark mascara and eyeliner, my lips no longer red and glossy because it’d all been washed away. All my imperfections were on display, the discoloration of my complexion, the old acne scars.

But a slight smile moved over his lips, and he slipped his hand underneath my shirt and gripped one of my ass cheeks before he gave it a playful smack. Then he walked out of the bathroom and left my sight.

I wasn't sure if he'd done it on purpose, but he made me feel more beautiful than I ever had.

I finished up in the bathroom, then joined him in bed, gentle lights underneath the bed frame to make it easy to find in the dark. He was on his phone, with one hand behind his head. Mine was left in my purse because there wasn't a single person in the world I wanted to talk to.

I lay there and got comfortable, his bed a million times more comfortable than mine at my hotel.

He set his phone on the nightstand, then came toward me, his big body enveloping mine, pulling me close, my back to his chest, cuddling with me like we'd just finished fucking. His shirt was so big that it slipped off my shoulder without effort, and when the skin was exposed, he dipped his head and kissed it.

Only four more days before I had to get back to reality, and I didn't want to think about that.

Constantine woke me up in the most tantalizing way, his mouth sealed over my folds, sucking hard before his tongue swirled my clit and jerked me awake with a gasp. He cradled my legs with his arms and devoured me like I'd asked him to do this.

"Oh my god." My voice came out like a croak, my throat dry and raspy from being dead asleep seconds ago. I was in a beautiful room at a famous hotel with the sexiest man in the world between my legs. It was hard to believe that my whole life had come crashing down just days ago.

He moved up my body underneath the sheets until he was over me, his arms still pinned behind my knees, tilting my hips even farther to get the angle right. He guided himself inside me and sank quickly, my body soaked for him, and he moaned when he made his entrance.

I gripped his massive arms, and then my body started to jerk as he pounded into me hard enough to make the headboard tap against the wall since it wasn't mounted to it. Dwarfed by his size and completely dominated, I just took the fat dick he gave me. "Oh god . . . yes."

His hand left one of my knees, then moved to my neck. He squeezed it, not hard, but enough to make me aware of his grasp. Aware of how big his hand was compared to my throat. That he could hurt me if he wanted to, but never would.

"Constantine . . ." I'd never said a man's name in bed with more enthusiasm. Never felt fuller with any other dick. All I had to do was lie there and watch this incredibly sexy man nail me like it was his honor to do so.

He squeezed me a little harder, his thumb swiping over my bottom lip, his hand so large it could cover my entire face. "Tell me you want my come, sweetheart."

"I want it." I obeyed immediately, digging my nails into him, letting him completely take me over. I had no power over my own body or my own life, and that didn't bother me in the least, not with him. "Fuck, I want it." I'd never been so turned on by a man's seed. Enzo had been cheating on me, so I guess I could easily give Constantine something. And I didn't know Constantine's past, so he could easily give me something, but neither one of us seemed to give a damn about that. We wanted each other so much, to the exclusion of everything else. And that realization made me burn so white hot that I exploded around his dick without warning.

His hand left my neck and slid into my hair, and he thrust a little harder, a little deeper, making me wince because it was too much dick, but he continued like he knew I could handle it.

We gripped each other and moaned together as we both hit our highs, our bodies ramming each other because everything still wasn't enough. He released inside me with a moan so deep and sexy, and I shed tears because it was just so damn good.

Was sex always like this for him? Because it wasn't like this for me—ever.

We finished and he kissed me, kissed me with crushing force, his hand deep in my hair. Then he abruptly pulled away, pulled his semihard dick out of me, and walked into the bathroom like what we'd just shared hadn't been explosive.

The shower came on, and I lay there, his come oozing out of me onto the sheets underneath. When I rolled onto my side toward the patio, I saw the sunlight coming through the closed curtains, knowing morning was already waiting for us. But exhausted from lying there and getting fucked like a whore, I closed my eyes and drifted off again.

I left my hotel and made my way to the sidewalk, where the black van waited for me. Constantine stood there in black swim trunks and a black T-shirt, talking on the phone with his sunglasses on the bridge of his nose. The driver had the back door open, and I helped myself inside so he could finish his conversation. I couldn't make out anything he said because he faced the other way. I didn't know if it was personal or work.

He finished up his conversation and took the seat beside me on the opposite side, leaving the middle open. But he absentmindedly reached over and placed his hand on my exposed thigh in my jean shorts as he looked out the window.

Every time he touched me, I felt higher than a cloud.

After a twenty-minute drive down the coast and the winding roads that hugged the cliff faces, we arrived at another hotel, Belmond Villa Sant'Andrea, to use their private beach club. We were dropped off at the top, and we walked down the pathway and then the stairs to the exclusive beach at the bottom.

The beach club was divided into two sections. On the left was a sea of loungers that couples used, and on the right was a section of private cabanas. That was where we headed, and when we approached one of the large cabanas that could easily accommodate twelve people, a group of guys was already inside.

Cheers exploded at the sight of him. "Con!" They all stood up and exchanged hand grabs, fist bumps, and hugs. They asked how much longer he was going to be in town, asked about one another's families, caught up in a couple of seconds.

Then the guys all turned their attention to me, flicking their eyes back toward Constantine as they waited for an explanation.

I felt a bit out of place, spoiling a guy hangout.

His arm hooked around my waist, and he gave me a gentle tug into him. "Aurelia. Aurelia, these are the boys. Aldo, Francesco, and Gianni."

I was a bit intimidated by these guys. They weren't in Constantine's league at all, but they were still good looking and muscular, and they looked at me a bit like they didn't know what to make of me. "I can tell by your faces that Constantine didn't tell you I was coming, so I'm sorry about that. But I promise, guy talk doesn't bother me one bit. Pussies and tits . . . I'm here for it."

Aldo smirked when he heard what I said. Francesco released a chuckle. And Gianni exchanged a look with Constantine before he nudged him in the shoulder when he passed to grab the menu. "I'll drink to that. Let's get the rounds going."

There was a rock fifty feet from the shore, stairs carved into the side, and the guys all swam out there, climbed to the top, and proceeded to dive, flip, and belly flop off the highest point like a group of kids.

I sat in the lounger with a drink and a full pizza all to myself, so I was just fine.

Whenever Constantine climbed to the top of the rock, he looked like Poseidon, god of the sea, his beautiful skin reflective from the drops of water that clung to his body. He ran his fingers through his short hair as he stood tall and proud, a sculpture that had come to life to enjoy a single lifetime.

I could stare at him forever.

I reached into my bag and pulled out my camera. Popped off the lens cover and then snapped a couple shots of just him, standing there like he owned the rock. One of his friends said something funny, and he laughed—and I got the shot.

When it was his turn to jump, he moved to the edge, then ran the last couple of feet, flipping in the air until he crashed into the water.

I got a couple shots of that too.

Once Constantine was out of the way, the next guy lined up and jumped. Constantine swam to the stairs and climbed up until he stood at the bottom of the stairs. He turned to me, saw me staring at him, and waved me to join them.

Yeah fucking right. I shook my head and gave a thumbs-down sign.

"Come on," he yelled, waving me over again.

"Not gonna happen," I shouted back.

A wave came and splashed the rock, but he remained steady where someone else would have slipped. "Get over here, or I'll come get you." He raised his voice. "What's it going to be, sweetheart?"

I felt like a commander was giving me orders across the battlefield, and I knew there would be consequences for my insubordination. So I closed my pizza box and set my drink aside before slipping on my water shoes and heading into the water. It was still a bit cold because summer hadn't kicked in quite yet, but after a couple steps, I got used to it.

Constantine continued to stand at the base of the rock as he waited.

I put my hair up in a quick bun, then started to swim, the waves coming to shore blocked by the rock. There were lots of small boats in the cove, people admiring the beach and the beauty of the hotels up on the cliffs.

I finally reached him, the swell of the waves making it difficult to grab hold of anything. "I don't know . . . it looks really slippery."

He slid back into the water with me, then pulled me close, his hand moving to my ass. "When the next wave comes in, climb up."

"I'm not really a rock-jumping kind of girl—"

"Yet." He smiled, and then the wave came in. He pushed me up like I weighed nothing, and I made it to the stairs without effort. "Attagirl." He climbed up despite the slickness of the rocks, like he'd done this a hundred times.

I grabbed on to the ridges of the stairs and climbed, and I felt his hand at my ass to support me until I made it to the top.

The guys all cheered when I got there.

"There she is." Aldo clapped me on the shoulder.

"Gonna dive or gonna flip?" Francesco asked.

"Uh . . . maybe just admire from a distance?" I said.

Constantine emerged from behind me, his hand giving my ass a playful smack. "All right, let's do it."

"How about you just do it . . . and I watch?"

"Come on, sweetheart. You've got this."

"I've never done this before." It didn't look that high from shore, but now that I was actually on top of the rock, I realized how far the fall was to the surface of the water. About thirty feet.

"I'll do it with you." He held out his hand for me to take.

But I stayed behind and crossed my arms over my chest. "I don't know. What if I break my neck?"

"You won't."

"What if—"

"What if you have a good fucking time?" He smiled at me, then walked back, and the other guys gave us some privacy by jumping into the water, their shouts fading once they were over the edge of the cliff. Then their bodies smacked the water loudly when they collided. "I would never put you in danger, all right?" He stopped before me, his body still glistening, breathtaking. "You don't have to do it. I'll help you climb back down. But I think you should."

"Why?" My eyes flicked back and forth between his, his height blocking out the sun and shielding me from the brightness. All the adrenaline and the fear left when I focused on him and nothing else.

"Because I think . . ." He made his hand into a fist and gently tapped my core. "You've forgotten just how fucking tough you are." He turned away from me and walked back to the edge of the rock, looked down into the water, and then turned back to look at me. "Now, let's do this." He took his own fist and beat it once against his chest, like a gladiator who'd clashed his sword against his shield.

I wasn't sure what it was about his words that made me snap out of my fear, but all my worries faded away. I'd spent the last few months hating and blaming myself, turning into a pathetic version of myself that I despised. I forgot who I used to be, how carefree I was, how self-assured.

I took a breath and moved toward him at the edge.

And the way he smiled at me, like he was proud . . .

He offered his hand to me.

The guys below had swum back to give us space to jump. "You got this!"

"Come on, Aurelia!" Francesco shouted.

"On the count of three," Constantine said, looking at me. "One . . . two . . ."

"Three."

Together, we jumped, became airborne over the rock and the water, and then came crashing down into the cerulean water of the Mediterranean. When I opened my eyes underwater, a cloud of bubbles was around me. His hand released mine so I could swim, and I pulled myself to the surface before I breached the water.

The guys all cheered and clapped.

Constantine shook his head to get the water out of his face and eyes. He threw a fist in the air before he swam toward me, slipped his hand into the water to squeeze my ass, and kissed me. "Attagirl."

"Let's do it again!"

For the first time since I met Constantine, he laughed. Laughed at something I'd said, the amusement entering his gaze. The other guys joined in too. "That's the spirit."

The restroom was a distant walk away, across the patio and the bar toward the stairs. I did my business, fixed my hair as much as I could, swiped the bleeding lines of mascara, and then headed back to the cabana.

"She's cute, Con."

The cabanas only had two solid walls. The back was the cliffside and there was a gap in between, so it was easy for voices to carry. I should walk away or continue into the cabana like I didn't notice anything, but I was curious to hear what Constantine might say.

"She is." He said it with a smile in his voice. One that I could hear.

"Really fine," one of the other guys said.

"She is," Constantine repeated. "But keep it clean. Otherwise, I'll have to punch you." Without seeing his face, I wasn't sure if he was joking . . . or if he was serious.

"Where'd you meet her?" I wasn't sure which one of the guys asked. I didn't know them well enough to recognize them based on their voices alone.

"The bar at the hotel," Constantine answered.

"Nice," one of the guys said. "I love tourists. They come for fun, and then they go back to their lives."

Constantine said nothing to that. Not that I expected him to. He never explicitly said it, but I assumed this was just for the week. Even though we both lived in Rome, just a couple miles apart, actually, I didn't expect to see him after this. I wasn't stupid. A man that handsome and that rich wasn't interested in monogamy. He'd probably had a ton of these summer flings with other women he met when he visited home.

I was just one of many.

But that was fine with me. His purpose in my life was to bring me back to myself. To give me confidence again. To rehabilitate me so I could go back out into the world. I'd just gotten out of a long-term relationship, and the idea of getting into another one so soon sounded like a bad idea anyway.

When the conversation headed in another direction, I came around the front and entered the cabana. My aim was for the corner of the couch, but when I passed Constantine, he grabbed me and pulled me into his lap before sliding my legs across his thighs. He slipped his fingers into my jean shorts under the hem. He didn't care about the PDA, not even in front of his friends. "They're about to close the bar. Want another drink?"

"No thanks. I've already had too much today."

One of the guys got the attention of the waiter, and Constantine closed out the tab. We all made the long walk up to the top of the cliff, said our goodbyes, and then Constantine and I got into the back of the black van and returned to Taormina.

We arrived at my hotel. Constantine got out of the van and stood with me on the sidewalk. "Pack your stuff and come stay with me."

I heard what he said, but I stared at him blankly as I waited for the second part of that sentence. Because there had to be more to it. When nothing else came from his mouth, I blurted, "Sorry?"

"You heard what I said."

"You want me in your hotel room until I leave?"

"Yes, that's what I said."

"Why?" I asked, surprised that he wanted more of my company and not less.

He stared for several heartbeats, thriving in that signature silence that would make anyone else uncomfortable. "Because I want you." It was a simple sentence, the same one he'd repeated several times, but each time he said it, it took on a new meeting. "So, go up there and grab your stuff, or I'll grab it for you."

The elation I felt was cosmic, but it was quickly swallowed by the protective shield in my mind, the reminder that this was temporary. I couldn't get too excited, not when our days were limited, that this was a very short-lived situationship. I'd already gotten so attached to this man, and it was hard to imagine not having him in my life, even if he was just a friend. To never see his smile, to never feel the warmth of his presence, to not have him in my corner when I felt alone.

But I was too weak to fight the warning. Too weak to protect myself. All I had left with this incredible man was a few days, and I'd rather cherish that time now and mourn it later than not have it at all.

"Give me ten minutes."

Chapter 9

Constantine

I woke up bright and early like I did every morning, and Aurelia was already on her side, the big shirt she wore scrunched around her hips, her panties gone because she'd never put them back on after last night.

I was a man in his prime, and sex was better than coffee, so I slid inside from behind, my arm hooked around her thigh to hold it up for her as I thrust. She slowly woke up, her breathing deepening, her moans raspy because she was still half asleep.

I finished within a minute, because this was just a means to an end, and then I left her there and slipped out to head to the gym. I did my workout, showered when I got back, and then headed into town to visit Rosticceria Da Cristina. We had two locations, one that was only a takeaway spot, and the other that was also a sit-down restaurant. I headed to that one, knowing the family would be there to prepare for the day.

I walked past the window and saw my mother and Aunt Chiara in the kitchen, preparing the rice that would be used for the arancini. Other members of the kitchen staff were there, preparing for the rush that would happen the second we opened.

The door was unlocked, so I let myself inside. "Need a hand?" I hadn't spent as much time with them as I should have, but I had a distraction in my bed that very moment . . . and she was quite the distraction.

Mom looked up from her work on the table, and her eyes lit up at the sight of me like they always did when she saw me. "That's my boy."

I washed my hands in the sink, then gloved up before I joined them at the table, giving each of them a kiss on the cheek. After working there as a kid, I knew exactly what to do to prepare the ingredients to be molded into a ball before it was fried, the rice, cheese, and vegetables warm on the inside, the surface crispy and strong enough to contain the contents.

"Haven't seen you much, Con." Aunt Chiara kept her eyes down on her work, and her tone was accusatory—like always. My mother and her sister were two peas in a pod, and after losing both of their husbands, they were even closer. The matriarchs of the family, the ones running the restaurants and hosting family dinners on the weekends.

I smirked as I rolled the balls of rice mixed with pistachio pesto and cheese together before piling them on the pan to be coated with the breadcrumbs. "Gotten sidetracked."

"By?" my mother pressed.

Shit, they knew.

I ignored the question as I worked across the enormous table, other staff members working on the dough for the pizzas in the other kitchen. "You know how it goes."

Aunt Chiara looked up from her work, giving that powerful stare that used to scare me as a boy. Like she could apply enough pressure to break a skull with just her eyes. All the while, she continued to work on the arancini . . . which made it all the more impressive. "Who's the girl, Con?"

My smile widened. "Nothing gets past you two, huh?"

"It's a small town," Mom said. "And according to everyone in it, you've taken her everywhere."

My eyes stayed down on my work, the smile still stretched across my mouth. "Well, like you just said, it's small." Now I felt both women staring at me, abandoning their work to give me that third degree.

I worked until the bowl was empty, and then I carried it to the sink so the dishwasher could take care of it later. I ripped off my gloves and tossed them in the trash.

They both stood there, demanding details in their lethal silence.

I chuckled. "If the restaurant goes under, the two of you can easily make a career of getting people to pay their debts with looks like that."

"What's her name?"

"Is she from Taormina?"

"She comes from a good family?"

"Does she go to church?"

They fired off a series of questions so fast I couldn't answer them all even if I wanted to. "Her name is Aurelia, and that's all I'm giving you."

My mom continued to stare me down. "Umberto says she's very beautiful."

"Oh, she is." I came back to the table and couldn't contain my smile, not even in front of these two meddlers.

"First time we've heard about you and a girl, Con," Aunt Chiara said.

I conducted my personal life in the privacy of Rome. Taormina was a tiny place and everyone knew everyone, so it was impossible to have a private life. So I was never seen with anyone in the village, and if I did meet someone at the bar, it was a onetime thing. I kept my life private because I didn't want my mother pestering me about settling down, and I also did it out of respect.

But with Aurelia . . . it all just happened.

"Son." My mom changed her tone slightly, deepening it, a clear warning that one of those *talks* was coming. "You're in your thirties now. Keep dragging your feet, and all the good women will be taken. Who will have your children then?"

I gave a slow nod to placate her. "Yes, Mother."

"It's time to settle down. Time to move back to Taormina. Be close to family. Have a son of your own." She continued on and on, reminding me of the importance of family and God, that I'd lost my way from everything that mattered.

I was tired of hearing this speech every couple of months, but I held my tongue like the good son I was. "I will consider it, Mother. Thank you."

"Invite her to dinner," Aunt Chiara asked. "We want to see just how beautiful she is."

"I'll think about it." Like I'd put Aurelia through that misery.

"So, this is serious?" Mom pressed, holding on to an invisible string of hope.

"That's not what I said."

"But you said you would think about it," Aunt Chiara said. "Which means that it's possible."

I chuckled. "You guys should be detectives." I stepped away and walked into the other room. My sister Beatrice was there with my cousin Antonio. She was talking about her kids, but she halted mid-sentence when I walked in the door.

"Con." Her mouth melted into a smile that reminded me of my mother's, just decades younger, cheeks fuller. She moved into me and gave me a hard hug. "What brings you here?"

"Wanted to help out." I kissed her on the cheek before I greeted Antonio. "I haven't seen you guys much this week."

"That tends to happen when you get a girlfriend . . ." Beatrice wore that knowing smirk as she returned to the large bowl on the counter and measured the salt, pepper, and basil before tossing it all inside.

So the entire town knew.

My eyes shifted to Antonio, and he shrugged as he continued to roll the pizza dough on the counter.

"So, tell us about her." Beatrice stirred the pot of hand-crushed tomatoes before she carried it to the stove and turned it on low so it could slowly come to a simmer.

I leaned against one of the counters, arms crossed over my chest. "I just got grilled by two hardcore detectives out there."

"And we're worse," she said. "So fess up."

"I never talk about the women in my life, so I'm not sure why you expect me to talk about one now."

"Oh, come on." My sister rolled her eyes. "You've never paraded anyone through Taormina where you know *everyone* will see you. So this is different, and you know it is."

My gaze shifted back to Antonio.

He gave another shrug, telling me I was on my own.

I looked at my sister again, knowing I shouldn't bother to fight it. I had been caught red handed, and they would all continue to dig until they uncovered every piece of information and there was nothing left. "I met Aurelia a couple days ago. I didn't expect anything to come from it . . . but I like her."

~

When I returned to the room, I found her on the back patio, lying in the lounger, reading on a device. She wore the bottom of a bright-blue bikini, but her top was missing, like she wanted to get sun directly on her tits.

I stared at her through the patio window, and that was all it took to make me hard.

The outdoor table held old dishes, like she'd ordered breakfast for herself in my absence.

I opened the door and stepped onto the patio, and she stirred at the sound of the door, sunglasses on the bridge of her nose. It was a beautiful day, not a cloud in the sky, perfect for the outdoor patio. "Hey." I sat on the lounger beside her.

"Hey." She hooked her sunglasses back over her head, and the bright playfulness in her eyes was magnetic. Flirtatious and affectionate, she moved her hand over my arms, and then she leaned in and kissed me nice and slow—like she wanted me to fuck her right on that patio. She slipped her hand underneath my shirt and up my chest before she brought it back down again, moving it over the front of my jeans to feel the outline of my rock-hard dick.

This woman.

She unzipped my jeans and popped them open so she could tug my boxers forward and let my dick come free. She dipped her head, her ass moving proudly into the air, and then she ate my dick like it was slathered in cream.

I dug my hand into her hair and reclined in the lounger, feeling the Sicilian sunshine and smelling the Mediterranean sea air. My dick was enveloped in her warm mouth and then sheathed in her throat.

I wanted her in my lap with her tits in my face, but getting my dick sucked on the patio was nice too. I lay back with my head propped on my arm and just enjoyed it, felt my breaths become shaky, felt every muscle in my core tighten because she gave the best head.

But then I wondered how wet she was, how tight.

I gripped her neck and I pulled her back, my dick slapping against my stomach when it left her pretty lips. I tugged her into me, telling her I wanted her in my lap, ass in my hands.

She climbed on top of me, pointed my length at her entrance, and then slid down . . . nice and slow.

I squeezed her cheeks in my hands before I guided her up and down, feeling her slickness coat me over and over, doing my best to be quiet because the walls that separated the patio from my neighbors' were made of tile and not stone.

With her beautiful tits in my face, I watched her bounce on my length, watched her work to stay quiet as she fucked me, as she enjoyed every inch of this dick that was rock hard at just the sight of her.

We ended up in bed, our fucking too loud outside, and I took her on the foot of the bed before we finished in a frenzy, clinging to each other and moaning and panting, utterly fucking desperate.

Then we lay on the bed together, a trail of clothes from the open patio door to the bed, the sunshine coming in and reaching the hallway across the bedroom.

She didn't ask me where I'd been. Her eyes looked heavy, like she was so relaxed she might fall asleep. Her makeup was already smeared from the workout we'd just done.

"Ready for lunch?"

She opened her eyes and looked at me, the sweat on her body already gone. Her nipples hardened like she was already cold in the air that came from the AC. "What did you have in mind?"

"Pizza."

"Ooh, I love pizza."

~

I took her to La Napoletana, a famous pizza spot far off the main path. The outdoor terrace was covered in white tables and chairs. Family friends ran the restaurant, so of course this would get back to my mother and aunt.

Like I gave a damn.

Humberto came to the table and greeted me warmly. "Your aunt told me you were back in town."

"Here for a couple more days," I said. "Humberto, this is—"

"Aurelia." He wore a full smile as he turned his attention on her, taking her hand as if in a handshake but just holding it instead, looking into her beautiful face so he could repeat all the details back to the detectives. "Lovely to meet you."

"You too," she said with a somewhat awkward smile.

Humberto turned back to me and winked at me—right in front of Aurelia.

Very sly.

We finished our small talk, and I ordered our pizzas. When Humberto left and it was just the two of us at the table, the heaviness settled over both of us.

She looked at me but didn't interrogate me. Didn't strike like a viper—like some people that I knew.

"I was with my family this morning." I decided to get ahead of it so she didn't have to wonder. "They've heard about you from people who have seen us together. So, naturally, they were curious." Curious wasn't even the right word. I'd thought my aunt Chiara was going to fight me for information in the middle of that kitchen.

"I know how that goes. If my mother were alive, she'd want all the details about this little fuck-cation."

I grinned. "Fuck-cation?"

"Yep." She said it unapologetically.

And I liked that. "Have you mentioned this to your friends?"

"No." Her good mood slowly deflated like a balloon with a minuscule hole poked in the exterior. "I haven't even told them about Enzo. I just didn't feel like getting into it yet. I'm not ready to hear the *I told you so*s or feel their pity or talk about where I'm going to live next and all that bullshit."

I felt like an ass for bringing it up. "Well, this is the best fuck-cation I've ever had." I said something to make the conversation lighthearted once again. To bring her back into the moment, not in the future or the past. I had never actually done this with anyone before. I had flings and short-term situationships, but nothing like this.

It worked, because light slowly returned to her eyes. "Me too. Well, it's the *only* fuck-cation I've ever had, but if I ever have another one, I'm sure it'll pale in comparison to this." She grabbed her can of soda and took a drink. "I hope I'm not taking too much of your time. I know you're here to see your family, and I don't want to get in the way of that."

"You aren't. To be honest, I'm not just here to see them."

"Then what else are you here for?" She took another drink of her soda.

When she'd asked me what I did for a living, I was intentionally vague. I didn't want to share something that sensitive with a stranger, with a woman I wouldn't ever see again. But that was days ago, and she was still here. "Work."

"Oh." When she got quiet, she showed her hand, that she suspected my occupation was serious. She'd probably connected some of the dots, my strength and my wealth, the fact that I said very little about it. She didn't pry, either because she didn't want to know more or she knew I didn't want to share.

"I have something to take care of tonight. Not sure when I'll be back." That was why I'd taken her out to lunch, because I'd be unavailable for the evening. I didn't want to invite her to my room just to be absent the entire day.

"It's no problem." She still didn't ask. "The room service menu looks pretty phenomenal, so I'll be just fine." She tried to force some playfulness into her words, but it fell flat. It was clear she was nervous, but it wasn't clear why.

Because she didn't want to make me feel guilty for leaving her?

Or because she was scared?

Chapter 10

Constantine

I arrived at the bustling city that hugged the coast, drove through the streets until I reached Villa de la Sirenuse, a sprawling estate secured behind magnificently tall iron gates.

The security remained out of sight for anyone on the street, relying on camera footage instead of a physical presence. When they scanned my face and the car, the gates swung open, and I was allowed entry.

The gardens were full of landscaped lawns and palm trees. The fountain in the center stood tall with water trickling down, reflecting the moonlight on this cloudless night. When I pulled into the roundabout, I saw the multitude of cars already there.

I arrived at the front door, was frisked by the guards, and the second I stepped into the house, I heard the sound of men cheering in some kind of commotion.

Gambling, probably.

I was escorted into the living room, a sea of tables across the expansive rug, smoke hovering just below the chandelier that hung from the ceiling. All the tables were occupied by men who smoked, drank, and gambled, cash piled into the center.

I approached Alfonso, standing there in a pin-striped suit with a cigar hanging out of the corner of his mouth. When his eyes made contact with mine, a smile entered his gaze, and he embraced me with a clasp of our hands. "Buy-in is twenty. You in?"

"You know cards aren't my game."

"Just Russian roulette . . ."

When I was young, I used to sit around with the guys and put a single bullet in the barrel. There'd be six of us, meaning one of us was destined to get hit and the others unscathed. We'd take turns, putting the tip of the barrel to our arm and pulling the trigger.

The longer you made it through the game without getting the bullet, the bigger hand you had in the prize. I always made it pretty far but never got the retribution of the bullet. "Tommaso around?"

"Just had a meeting." He nodded, and we moved through the hallway and different rooms, and then came to a stop in the drawing room. The fireplace was cold because it'd been a warm week, but it smelled of cigars, like Tommaso frequented this room for meetings. "I'll tell him you're here. I would offer you a drink, but the last time someone touched Tommaso's bar, they got shot." He grinned then disappeared into the other room.

I helped myself to the bar, made myself a stiff drink with a couple big ice cubes. I admired the paintings on the wall and surveyed the wealth of the room. Cosa Nostra had been in this part of Sicily since the mid-1800s, and they established their own collection of art and history.

Tommaso Sirenuse emerged from the other room, a decade and a half older than me, his T-shirt stressed in the stomach because he enjoyed Sicilian wine a little too much. His skin had a greasy texture, the aftermath of a diet heavy on Italian meats that seeped into his pores. He sauntered into the room as he slid his hands into his pockets. "Constantine, just the man I wanted to see." He came up to me, and I extended my hand.

"I'm sure." I took a seat on the couch across from his armchair.

He sat and then looked at one of the two henchmen who followed him around everywhere he went, his personal bodyguards who were present even at his home. "Make me a stiff drink."

They looked at each other, like they both agreed this wasn't in their job description, but one of them made a move and whipped up a drink.

Tommaso didn't reprimand me for helping myself.

When the drink was placed on a coaster in front of him, Tommaso dismissed them. "You can go."

They looked at each other again, knowing they weren't supposed to leave his presence.

"I said go."

Like scared cats, they scurried off.

Tommaso sat with his hands together, not touching his drink. "How's your family?"

"Good. Yours?"

"Elena says I need to lose weight." He grabbed the glass and took a drink. "So I picked up a mistress."

"Very diplomatic."

"Well, she doesn't seem to mind."

"Because she's getting paid not to mind. And I'm sure Elena just wants you to live as long as possible."

He gave an irritated look before he took another drink. "You always take her side."

"I do when she's right, which seems to be always."

He glared at me.

I smiled. "How's business?"

"The same. There's just been a lot of interference because it's a jubilee year. Harder to move product with the ferries. Not to mention the influx of tourists here getting in our fucking way. They usually stay in Taormina, but a lot of them have flocked over here."

"You'll manage."

"Easy for you to say when you have the whole country at your fingertips."

"Not that easy. Taking this week vacation will absolutely bite me in the ass."

"What's going on in Rome?"

"Organs hitting the black market, the truce agreement I have to comply with, according to Pope Zephyrinus, the graffiti problem, which annoys me more than all the other issues combined, by the way, and then everything else. President Barsetti has his agenda, and it doesn't always mesh with mine."

He gave a nod. "So you're going to uphold the truce?"

I grabbed my glass and took a long drink, needing the burn of the alcohol to wash away the bile. "It's complicated."

"I know."

"I felt coerced into it. Had to think about everyone but myself. But now . . . I don't know."

"But if you break it, you break your word."

"Exactly," I said. "But the older I get, the less I care."

He nodded like he understood, but to be frank, no one understood. "If the time ever comes, you know Cosa Nostra will have your back, Constantine. And not just because you're Emperor Constantine of the Roman Republic—but because you will always be one of us."

Chapter 11

Aurelia

I wasn't sure what time it was, but it was the dead of night when he returned to the room. He was quiet with the door, kept his footsteps light on the carpet and hardwood floor when he came inside. I heard the shower come on distantly from the bathroom in the other room. It was quiet, like the trickle of a fountain, and should soothe me enough to go back to sleep.

But now, I was wide awake.

I'd just left my hotel room and joined his, and the second I arrived, I knew him a little better. I reached for my phone on the nightstand, tapped the screen, and saw that it was almost five in the morning.

He'd been gone all night.

I returned the phone and lay there with sleep behind my eyes, feeling a twinge of fear because there were only two explanations for him being out all night. He was either with someone else, which I highly doubted with all the fucking we did. Or . . . he was doing that private security he mentioned before.

It was common knowledge that Cosa Nostra had been here as early as the mid-1800s. They were still active today on the west side of Sicily. They kept a low profile and stayed to themselves, so they didn't seem to be a problem among the general public—if you didn't cross them.

That was too much of a coincidence.

I'd wonder if Constantine was a member, but if he lived in Rome, that didn't make sense. It wasn't exactly a work-from-home type of gig. But he might be associated in some way, and that was terrifying . . . and a little thrilling.

Minutes later, Constantine left the bathroom and came to bed. A small amount of dull light came from the tiny crack where the two sides of the curtains met, and I wasn't sure if I'd be able to fall back asleep at this point.

He took a drink of water from the nightstand, then got between the sheets beside me. He didn't try to be quiet like he had when he'd first come in—like he somehow knew I was awake. He moved to the center of the bed, hooked his big arm around me, and pulled me close into his core, dropping his chin and pressing a kiss to my exposed shoulder.

I should be wary of this man, but the second he grabbed me like that, I was fucking spineless. I melted into him like he was heat and I was butter. I felt safer in his arms than I had in the embrace of my nine-to-five, aboveboard boyfriend. I was just as obsessed now as I'd been before he'd told me his plans for the evening.

He tugged up my shirt underneath the sheets to expose my ass in my little thong. His big hand squeezed one of my cheeks before he pressed his hips into me, shoving his big dick right between my ass cheeks.

He should have been exhausted from his long night, but his dick was so hard, it was as if he'd had the greatest night of sleep in his life. He turned and grabbed one of his pillows, then placed it in front of me before he gently rolled me on top of it, placing it beneath my hips and getting me onto my stomach.

My lower back arched, and when I looked at him over my shoulder, he was already tugging my thong down my thighs. He wetted the head of his dick, then mounted me, sliding inside my tight entrance that barely had any warning of his intentions. He gently pushed, eventually getting past my entrance, then sinking the rest of the way, releasing a quiet moan when he was fully sheathed.

His weight drove me into the pillow, my clit against the silky cotton, and when he started to thrust inside me, it hit just right, the pressure and friction against my sex enough to make me moan right away.

He took me at an even pace, not nailing me hard like he did at other times, but at a speed that was about enjoyment rather than a rush to the high. I'd never been taken this way in my life, so I could barely handle the fullness of his big dick, could barely handle the stimulation against my clit. It was one of those rare times when I didn't want to come, just wanted to hold on to this anticipation as long as I could before the explosion made my body jerk in odd and uncontrollable ways.

"Fuck," he said from above my ear. "This pussy hits better than coke." He started to thrust harder, giving me his full length even though he felt the dead end inside me, wanting me to take it all before he came.

It hurt, but fuck, it felt so good. "Yes . . ." It made me come, hard, and the tears that sprang to my eyes were instant. "Come inside me," I said breathlessly, wanting to hit an even greater high. "Please."

"*Fuck,*" he said in a rush, pounding into me as he finished, making the mattress bounce with his rhythm. Then he came to a stop, giving me his full length and ignoring the way I winced in pain when I took it all.

He breathed above me, his breaths deep and slow, his hands balled into fists as they propped his body above mine. When he started to soften, he pulled out of me and lay back on the pillow. He gripped my ass and gave it a smack before he closed his eyes, drifting off right away like he was spent.

I looked at the crack between the curtains and saw that the light had changed, growing brighter as the sun rose farther in the sky. I turned back to him, seeing him already asleep in just seconds, his normally hard expression a little softer when he was relaxed.

With the heft of his come inside me, I turned over and fell asleep quickly, somehow spent when I just lay there and he did the rest.

~

Tomorrow was my last day.

Then I had to go back to reality. I had to move everything out of my apartment so my replacement could move in—with her two kids in tow. I suspected she might already be there because her husband may have thrown her out on her ass. Now she needed Enzo to provide for her since he was knee deep in this with her.

Or balls deep, I should say.

I already had gigs lined up with clients who had booked six months in advance. Weddings on the weekends, private events, engagement photos, all sorts of things. I had enough clients and a strong enough brand, along with word-of-mouth marketing, that I could afford an apartment by myself, but not the one I'd shared with Enzo. That was a three-bedroom apartment with a full kitchen and a large living room, a mansion for a place like Rome. I'd have to move outside the city center, which meant I'd have to commute to every gig. I usually walked everywhere, but now I'd have to get a motorbike because a car was too expensive and too difficult to navigate on those kinds of roads.

I didn't want to think about all those things, but I had to. I should have done it sooner, because now when I picked up my stuff, I'd have to crash with a friend or get a room at a cheap motel until I could find a new place to live.

But fuck it, I'd rather enjoy my fuck-cation.

Constantine took me to an outdoor bar called Daiquiri, down the stairs off the main street, with a full menu of fruity drinks and cocktails that made it special. The outdoor terrace had a string of lights overhead, colorful chairs on the pebbled terrace.

They brought our drinks, bringing him a glass of wine and me a piña colada, because why the hell not? They also brought a bowl of potato chips, two plates of appetizers of potato coquettes with shredded beets on top, and then fresh bread slathered in fresh ragu. They gave you so much food that it could easily spoil your appetite for dinner if you went overboard.

So goddamn handsome and utterly fuckable, he sat there relaxed in the chair and just stared at me, in a dark-gray collared shirt, his sleeves rolled to his elbows and exposing the ink of his fore-arms. A damn tree that anyone would love to climb, he was a behemoth of a man.

He was so hot that I didn't care what he was doing last night. Killing people, selling drugs, whatever. He might be the most dangerous man in Sicily, and I still didn't give a damn. Because Jesus Christ . . . look at him.

His focused stare remained on mine, his confidence piercing my gaze with bullets. "What are you thinking?"

That you're fucking dangerous, and I don't care. "That you're so fucking hot," I said with a sigh because it was painful to look at him. It was the truth—at least half of the truth.

A hint of a smile moved into the corners of his mouth. He grabbed his wineglass and took a drink.

"And you're a great tour guide." I grabbed the frosted glass of the piña colada and took a drink out of the reusable metal straw before I returned it to the coaster. "What was supposed to be the worst week of my life has turned into the best. I'd just hit rock bottom when we crossed paths."

He gave me his complete focus like he always did when I spoke. Like every word out of my mouth mattered. Like he found me utterly fascinating.

"I completely lost myself . . . but I found her again." Found the woman who didn't tolerate bullshit. Who wouldn't put up with a man who didn't give me what I deserved—even if I still loved him. "It just makes it easier to get my stuff and move on with my life." To carry everything I'd learned into the next relationship . . . if and when I was ready to be in one again.

I imagined he broke a lot of hearts as he passed through life. I could easily be the type of woman who expected and hoped this would be something more, and he'd have the painful task of explaining that the situationship had a deadline. I'd be lying if I said it didn't bother me to imagine him replacing me with his next fling in just a couple days or a week—or if he already had a line of regulars back at home who were happy to settle for casual.

But I accepted it. "So, thanks for spending the week with me."

He said nothing, elbows propped on the armrests, his hands clasped together with his fingers stitched.

"How do you normally handle this? You know . . . when the time comes to go your separate ways."

He continued his hard stare, eyes flicking back and forth slightly, like I'd said something he didn't quite understand.

"I imagine they don't always take it so well." I knew there was no chance that I'd have something more with Constantine. Not because he'd made that clear, but come on, a man like him never settled down. You just had to be grateful for the dick and let him go give it to someone else. Just appreciate the moment rather than mourn the loss . . . or wonder what could have been if he'd felt differently. Maybe I wouldn't have taken this so well if I hadn't just gotten my heart crushed, if I hadn't just gotten out of a relationship and lost all desirability to be in another. I didn't think of him that way at all, but I supposed he was a rebound.

His strong silence continued for a while. "I make my intentions clear up front. Tell them exactly what will go down before anything happens. Never had a problem."

"Oh." My mind searched through the receipts I stored in my head, never recalling a time when he'd said anything to me of that nature. Never established what this was. Never confirmed that this would end when our vacations were over. "Well, you're lucky you haven't had any problems, because you aren't as clear as you think you are," I said with a laugh, wanting to sound playful rather than confrontational. "But don't worry, we're on the same page."

His eyes narrowed slightly at what I said, like he continued not to understand. The more time I spent with him, the more I witnessed his intelligence and his wit, and this was the first time it felt like we were actually on very different pages.

"You haven't said any of that to me," I explained.

His signature stare was visible, white hot and searing, branding my flesh like cattle. He almost looked angry, given the degree of intensity with which he stared at me, like I was his enemy rather than his lover. My words weren't meant to be offensive or perverse, but he appeared to have taken them that way. "I know I haven't."

I waited for more. Waited for him to realize his error, clarify what he meant, but as the silence continued, I realized nothing was coming. And then the understanding hit me like a bolt of lightning from the heavens. First, it was shock, and then the flames ignited from the collision and burned my flesh. I swallowed, and my own saliva felt like a bowling ball.

"I've never done this before. Never spent a week with a woman here in Taormina. Never invited a woman to pack up her things and share a hotel room with me. Back at home, my hookups are brief and transactional. I also don't go around fucking women bareback either."

I was so stunned I could barely feel my face. Barely feel my chest rise with the breath I needed to take. The shock hardened all my limbs and made it impossible to move. Temporary paralysis.

"I want you—and I've been very clear about that."

I swallowed, trapped in the power of his stare, losing all feeling in my body.

"I don't play games. And I don't want a woman who plays games." He didn't raise his voice, didn't deepen his tone either. But the way he spoke . . . it was unlike him. Unlike the man who was quick to flash a smile and bring sunshine to my clouds. "Do you play games, Aurelia?"

This wasn't the Constantine I knew. When we were at dinner at Osteria RossoDiVino, I saw a brief figment of this version, of the subtly lethal, subtly sinister man who existed beneath the surface. "No."

"Then tell me what you want from me."

I was backed into a corner by this man, the conversation turning from lighthearted to suffocating. Everyone else around us was having a good time at their tables with their drinks and apps, oblivious to the fire burning at our table.

I didn't know what answer I should give. I didn't know if I should be honest . . . or too honest . . . or right on the cusp. "How about you go first—"

"Don't play games."

"I'm not playing games—"

"Then tell me what you want from me. Is this really just a meaningless fuck-cation you're prepared to forget? Or is it something more?" He watched me with his unblinking stare, observing me, analyzing me like his eyes were fucking microscopes. "Because I'm tired of you saying this is temporary when you feel pretty fucking permanent."

Jesus.

He moved into the table, arms on the surface, bringing his lens even closer.

"I—I just assumed this was casual—"

"Answer the question."

"I would, but you keep interrupting me."

He remained serious, but a slow smirk moved over his lips.

"I assumed this was casual. I assumed something beyond tomorrow was off the table."

"Why?"

"Have you seen you?" I asked incredulously. "Men like you don't stick around."

"Men like me?" He cocked his head, furrowing his eyebrows. "What's that mean?"

"Ridiculously hot. Wealthy. Smart. You wait until the very last minute to settle down with a girl, usually in your forties, and then you'll marry a twenty-five-year-old. I assumed we wouldn't see each other after the holiday was over. Seems presumptuous to assume anything else."

That smirk deepened. "This is the part where you tell me what you want. Or do I have to ask again?"

"Of course I want you, Constantine." Of course I wanted this to continue, but this man could rip my heart out of my chest and kill me instantly—physically and emotionally. "But truth is, I just got out of a relationship, and I should probably heal first. What I've been doing this week is just . . . pretending the pain isn't there."

He watched me with those hard eyes.

"But yes, I still want to keep seeing you."

That seemed to be the answer he wanted, because he sat back in his chair. "You can stay with me when we return to Rome."

"What do you mean, stay with you?"

"You have to move out of your old apartment, right?"

"Yeah."

"Stay with me until you find your new place."

This man was too good to be true. I had to be missing something. Something that was right in front of my fucking face. "What aren't you telling me?"

His eyes narrowed at the question. "What do you mean, sweetheart?"

"They say if something is too good to be true, then it probably is. Knowing this was going to end made it easy not to think about anything too hard, but now I have to question everything. Because you can't be this perfect. It can't be this easy." It just can't. "So, what am I missing?"

He considered the question for a long time before he found an answer. "You're a smart woman. I can tell you've pieced things together."

I knew he was talking about his job.

"I'm in a dangerous and violent line of business. The most dangerous business you could possibly be in. I would never let anything happen to you, but I won't lie to you. Being associated with me puts you at risk. That's the catch."

It was my opportunity to ask the questions that sat heavily in my mind, but my tongue wouldn't move. I suspected his criminal affairs, but I wasn't sure how to confront them.

"I understand if I'm not worth that risk." He grabbed his glass and took a drink, like he didn't just dump a mountain of stress on my shoulders.

"Are—are you in Cosa Nostra?"

"No. But I'm well acquainted." He said it unapologetically, not sheathing parts of the truth or mincing words. "Take your time. Think it over."

"Have you had other relationships while . . . in this line of business?"

"No."

"Because they were too afraid?"

His eyes flicked back and forth between mine. "Because I've never wanted anyone more than a night. The last nine years of my life have been filled with one-night stands, hookups, casual situationships, and prostitutes."

"Prostitutes." I repeated the word because I couldn't believe he'd said it.

"Yes," he said like he was answering a question.

"What does a man like you need a prostitute for?"

He gave a shrug. "Sometimes it's just easier. Just say what you want. Get off the way you want. Transaction complete."

I couldn't believe he'd said that to me—point blank.

"You look disappointed."

"I—I just wasn't expecting that."

"I don't like to sugarcoat things. I'd rather get straight to the point. If you have a problem with it, then it's better I tell you now before we go any further down this road. Walk away if you want. I'll never lie to make a woman stay."

I was taken aback by his honesty. So much so that I didn't know what to say. "You just didn't *need* to tell me that. I didn't ask if you slept with prostitutes. So you wouldn't have lied."

"Not directly, but by omission," he said. "I don't do that either."

I was still a bit flustered by all this.

"Would you rather be with a man who gives it to you straight? Or be with a man who lies, drags out the truth, wastes your time? I thought I knew the answer to that, but maybe I don't."

"I'm sorry, you just caught me off guard. Offered to let me stay with you and then told me you were a criminal who fucks prostitutes. It's a lot to absorb in the span of a few minutes."

He smirked. "I wouldn't call myself a criminal."

"You kill people, don't you?" We probably shouldn't be having this conversation on the outdoor terrace of a small bar, but once it started, it just rolled.

"I kill men who hurt people like you."

"People like me?"

"Innocent people. There are men out there who don't discriminate between good and bad when they're chasing their bottom line. Who will shoot a woman in the head for being in the wrong place at the wrong time. Who will put a kid to work for cheap labor. Who will put drugs in the hands of the most vulnerable just to turn them into lifelong customers. Who will put guns in the hands of terrorists who just want to burn our world to the ground. That's what I do."

Now, I was speechless, realizing I had no idea who I was sleeping with.

"So yeah, a lot of people want me dead." He smiled the way he did at the beach, the way he did over breakfast, like we were talking about something far more agreeable than this. Like this was some kind of joke. "I'm clean, by the way. Got checked before I came home."

"I hope I can say the same." Enzo had been sleeping with someone else for months, but if her husband had been faithful to her, then I doubted anything had spread among the four of us.

"I'm not worried about it." He took another drink of his wine, finishing off the glass.

In the back of my mind, I suspected Constantine was associated with nefarious people, though I didn't realize how deeply invested he was. But when he said he wasn't a threat to people like me, I believed him. Because he'd been nothing but a gentleman—except when he fucked me. "You said for the last nine years you've been floating around. What about before that?" I wasn't sure why he'd specified the time period. Like something significant had happened before that.

"I was in a relationship."

"Oh." I couldn't contain my surprise because he seemed too elusive for anyone to keep. Too prized for anyone to afford.

"But men like me don't do that, right?" he said with a smirk.

"How old were you at the time?"

"Twenty-four."

He was a bit older than me. About five years. No wonder I found his company so refreshing. They said your thirties were the best decade of your life. You just stopped giving a damn what anyone thought of you—and Constantine was the epitome of *I don't give a fuck*.

I wanted to say he was young at the time, but that was just five years ago for me, so it wasn't that young. He didn't look old by any means, but his experience and wisdom were obvious in every word he spoke. "Can I ask what happened? You haven't been in a relationship in nine years, so something happened."

He was quiet for a while, sitting on the question as he decided what to do with it.

"You don't have to tell me—"

"There's a lot to it. It's complicated. But I've known her forever. I always knew we would get together, but I didn't want to pursue that until I was ready to commit. So when I was ready, I went for it. We were together for about a year before she fucked up." He said all of it in the same tone, like he didn't harbor any negative feelings about it. But it had been almost ten years, so that was plenty of time to move on.

"How did she fuck up?"

"That's where it gets complicated. She kissed my brother, thinking it was me . . . but chose not to disclose that. Then it got messy and soapy, and they kinda had this thing between them while I was oblivious to all of it. My brother is the one who came clean about it—not her. Then we were done."

She'd had Constantine wrapped around her finger, and she . . . threw him away? I would never understand people who did stupid shit like that. It selfishly made me feel better, because if Constantine could get cheated on, then it really could happen to anyone—including me. "That is complicated."

"That's not the reason I haven't been serious with anyone. I just haven't met anyone I want to commit my mind, body, and soul to." He'd just shared a really sad story, but he was starting to look at me with that intensity again, like I was the only thing that mattered.

It made me lose my breath—as always. "What happened with your brother?"

"I was fucking mad as hell for a while. He was an arrogant little shithead who instigated it. When she mistook him for me, he could have stepped out of her kiss, said who he was, but he'd always had a thing for her too, so he went for it. That was a separate issue that pissed me off even more because he took away her consent. She never would have kissed him if she'd known he wasn't me."

"How could she confuse you that easily? Unless you're—"

"Twins." He nodded. "Yes."

"There are two of you?" I asked in disbelief.

He smirked. "Don't get too excited. I don't do threesomes . . . at least not with men."

"I still feel somehow she should have known since she was intimate with you."

"Sometimes I wonder if it was intentional. If he wore my clothes to purposely confuse her."

"You can't ask him?"

His eyes flicked away for the first time during the conversation. "If she'd just told me what happened, I would have forgiven her and we could have moved on, but she didn't. And then they continued to have these moments together. Stares across the room that I noticed but didn't know what to make of. Private moments when I was nowhere around. I trusted her implicitly. If there was nothing to share, it's because there was nothing to share. She broke that, and trust can't be rebuilt—despite what some people believe." His eyes remained shifted away, like he was lost in the memory he continued to share. "I was gonna marry her. Had always wanted to see more of the world, live in Rome, Istanbul, and Paris, but she was enough of a reason for me to stay. We would have had a bunch of kids together and had a quiet life in Taormina with our families." He gave a shrug. "That event forever changed the trajectories of our lives."

I felt empathy for him because I knew how it felt to be betrayed by someone you loved. To watch them lie to you without an ounce of shame. To be reduced to ashes when they set your heart on fire. "I'm sorry."

"I know you are, sweetheart." His eyes came back to me, and then slowly, the smile stretched his lips. "But I think it worked out for the best." The warmth of his smile reached his eyes as he continued to stare at me in a way no one else ever had. Like I was all he could see, even when we weren't together.

Chapter 12

Aurelia

When I woke up that morning, I knew it was my final day in paradise. But while I was sad that the vacation was about to end, I didn't have to be sad that my time with Constantine was ending.

I wasn't sure where it would lead, but at least the door was open.

He fucked me quick and hard every morning like he needed it to start his day, went to the gym, and then showered. He took me out to breakfast, and then we had lunch together next door to my hotel at Trattoria da Nino, and he ordered the catch of the day for us to share.

When the waiter brought the white fish on the platter and placed it in front of Constantine, head and everything, I wasn't sure what we were supposed to do with it.

"Would you like me to clean it, sir?" the waiter asked.

Constantine brushed him off. "I've got this, man." With his utensils, he cleaned the fish like he'd done it a hundred times, working until just the meat was on the table. He handed the plate with all the pieces we didn't want to eat back to the waiter, and then he divided the fish between us.

"Where'd you learn that?" I asked.

"My father. When you grow up in a family of cooks, you learn the trade."

I took a bite of my fish, and I was a bit taken aback by the taste.

"It's all right?"

"Yeah, it's the best fish I've ever had."

He grinned. "The reason everyone comes here."

We finished lunch and then headed back to his room. The second we walked in the door, he came up behind me, lifted me into his arms, and then literally threw me on the bed. "I've wanted to fuck you in this little dress all day." He tugged me to the edge, lifted up my sundress, and ripped off my thong so he could sink inside me. "Jesus Christ." It was like he hadn't fucked me that morning, or the day before, or the day before that. Several times every twelve hours.

But it never seemed to be enough.

~

When I woke up from my nap, he was already getting ready.

But I continued to lie there because I never wanted to leave this big bed. Never wanted to leave this beautiful room and the man who occupied it.

He came out of the bathroom naked and pulled on a pair of boxers. "My family hosts a big dinner every Sunday. I want you to come."

"What?"

He ran his fingers through his slightly damp hair as he approached the bed. "Yes."

"Uh . . ." I sat up in bed, taking the sheets with me so my skin wouldn't be exposed to the cold air. "I—I don't know about that."

"It's not what you think. Everyone comes to these dinners—friends, family, neighbors. I wouldn't be surprised if there are thirty or fifty people there. It's casual."

"But your *family* will be there."

"Yes, I'm aware." That handsome, somewhat arrogant smirk moved on to his lips as he sat on the edge of the bed. "I've brought friends to these all my life. It's not a big deal."

"Friends . . . like me?"

He chuckled. "Well, no."

"And you don't think that will be a big deal?"

"They already know about you."

"They do?"

"It's a small town. Everyone knows each other. So yes, they already know I've spent the week with you. My mom has heard about it from about twenty different people."

I felt like I was under a microscope, under the careful surveillance of cameras and intelligence officers. "Now I understand why you've never done this with a woman in Taormina."

He gave a quiet laugh. "If my mother knew about all my extracurricular activities, she'd take me to an exorcist."

"Does she know what you do for a living?"

He raised his hand and twisted it left and right, indicating his knowledge was wishy washy. "Yes, but we don't talk about it. She chooses to pretend it's not happening. Helps her cope."

"You really think this is a good idea?"

"I've got to go. I haven't spent as much time with them on this trip as I should have—not that I have any regrets." Big and burly, he sat beside me on the bed, his weight making the mattress dip, all of his muscles hard and more like stone than human flesh. And he had this lightheartedness to his eyes, this contagious energy that drew me in. "And I don't want you to spend your last night in Taormina alone."

"I'll be fine—"

"Sweetheart, what are you afraid of? Because I thought you remembered how tough you are."

"Jumping off a rock is not the same as meeting an Italian mother. They're vicious."

He chuckled. "My mother is great, I promise you. There will be great food, wine, and people. It's the perfect Taormina send-off. One thing my family does well is hospitality. So, just come."

"You're sure?" I asked, not wanting to put him in a tough spot.

"Yes."

"I just don't want you to be bombarded with a million questions."

"They've already bombarded me. There's really nothing new they can ask me at this point. So you may as well come and have a good time."

"Well . . . if you're sure."

His hand slid into my hair at the back of my neck, and he tipped my head. "I'm absolutely sure." Then he kissed me, kissed me slow and tender, a tantalizing embrace with his soft, full lips. When he started to lean me back into the bed, I knew he wanted me again. Not a throw-me-on-the-bed kind of want, but a gentle want, the kind that would take time neither of us had before dinner. But we made time for it anyway.

We took a taxi farther up the mountain above Taormina because there wasn't a lot of parking in a city like this. We were dropped off outside, and I could see the terrace lit up with a stream of white lights, dozens of people already talking and drinking, music playing over the speakers.

It was a beautiful house, a grand two-story villa with unobstructed views of the sea. "Damn, the restaurant business does well," I said as I walked to the front door with him, wearing wedged heels with my sundress and jean jacket.

"Not *that* well," he said as he walked with me. "I bought this for her."

"Oh."

"After putting up with my bullshit all her life, she deserved it."

"What kind of bullshit?"

"Oh, pretty much anything you can think of." He opened the front door, that playful smirk on his lips, and he gave me a gentle smack on the ass when I stepped over the threshold.

It was a beautiful entryway with a round table in the center, an enormous vase of flowers atop it. Other people had already placed their purses and coats on the coat hangers and one of the couches. The smell of dinner hit us right when we walked in, and just when I thought I was too nervous to have an appetite, the hunger suddenly gnawed at my stomach.

"Beatrice, I told you to turn the arancini. Now they're going to burn."

"Ma, I told you I already turned it—*twice*."

"Then where is it?" I assumed it was his mother who did the yelling.

Constantine chuckled to himself like he was used to this. "Feels like home."

"Should we offer to help?" I asked.

"Antonio, where's the grated lemon?" she yelled. "I told you to leave it here. *Where is it?*"

Constantine shook his head and guided me to the outdoor terrace. "I think they've got it handled." He stepped through the open doors to the outdoor terrace. Quite a few people were excited to see him, or they were already drunk, because they all lifted their glasses and let out a unified cheer.

The exact same way everyone in town did whenever they saw him.

It was the first time I'd ever had social anxiety in my life.

Constantine was immediately overrun with people giving him hugs and embraces, sharing jokes and pleasantries. "Guys, this is Aurelia." He didn't explain further who I was, if I was a friend or something more. But how would he explain to people that I was basically a vacation fuck buddy?

They all seemed thrilled to see me, like I was automatically included in this club just by knowing Constantine.

A bunch of ice chests were scattered on the patio, so he walked over to one. "Sweetheart, what do you want to drink?"

"Water is fine."

"We don't have water."

"You don't have water?" I asked in mild surprise.

"We aren't really water-drinking people. How about wine?"

"Sure."

He grabbed an already uncorked bottle of white wine from a chilled bucket and poured two glasses. A group of guys came up to talk to Constantine, and I recognized one of them from the beach, Francesco.

He greeted me with a tight hug. "Aurelia is cool. She jumped off the rock with us at the beach the other day."

Constantine introduced me to the rest of the guys, and they all seemed to be first, second, and third cousins. They talked about tennis and football, and they joked they'd heard his mother screaming from the kitchen earlier.

It was definitely casual, and I didn't feel on display as I'd feared I would be. Looked at as an outsider. Judged for not being pretty enough for Constantine. Because, let's face it, the guy was way out of my league.

A woman I assumed to be his mother, because her voice sounded the same, stepped onto the terrace. "Dinner is ready."

Everyone raised their glasses and cheered.

It was definitely the most energetic and festive party I'd ever been to.

People filed into the house, and we joined the line.

His mother was in the hallway when we passed, and her eyes lit up at the sight of Constantine. It reminded me of the way my mother used to look at me, like I was the light of her life, the only thing that mattered.

"My boy." She hugged him tightly and kissed him on the cheek several times.

"You drunk, Ma?" he asked as she continued to hold on to him. He rubbed her back as she remained buried in his chest, a foot and a half shorter than him. She had to be five feet tall, and I didn't know how she'd pushed him *and* his brother out of her special place.

She pulled away without answering the question, and her eyes immediately landed on me, absorbing me with a slightly glossy stare. Analyzing me like every mother did to make sure I was good enough for her son, even though I was just fucking him at the moment. "Oh my god, Con. She's beautiful."

"I told you."

"Oh, you're so beautiful!" She hugged me hard and squeezed me tight.

The gesture was so unexpected I let out a laugh as I looked at Constantine over her shoulder.

He shrugged.

"That's sweet of you to say," I said. "Thank you. And thank you for having me."

"No, no, no." She pulled away and gripped both of my hands in hers. "You're welcome here, honey. I'm so happy you're here. Your hair is just beautiful. And you're nice and tall—"

"Ma." Constantine put his hand on his shoulder. "We're holding up the line. Can't let people go hungry, right?"

"Of course," she said. "You're right. We'll catch up later." She moved farther down the line, letting everyone else get their food first.

We walked a few steps forward, the people ahead of us slowly making their way to the kitchen, where the food was on display so people could load up their plates. All the dread I'd felt at meeting his family suddenly felt ridiculous because they'd all been so lovely. The matriarch was usually the least accepting, but she'd brought me into her arms like I was welcome before she even met me. "You have a really nice family."

"Yeah, they're pretty great." He moved into me, his arm curling around the small of my back, embracing me in the presence of his family the way he did when we were alone. "A little bit drunk and crazy, but still great."

"I'm excited to meet your dad."

There was a quick hesitation on his face, his eyes shifting away.

I knew him well enough to know that wasn't the right thing to say. "Oh, did he pass away?"

"Yeah, he's been gone awhile."

"Shit, I'm sorry."

"It's okay, sweetheart. You didn't know."

A man had never called me sweetheart and he probably called everyone in his bed by the endearment, but I still loved it when he called me that. It made me feel special, even if it was overused.

He quickly changed the subject. "So, if you *really* want my family to like you, I have some advice."

"I'm listening."

"Eat. *A lot.* It's the greatest compliment you can give my mother."

"I already eat a lot. You've seen me."

He chuckled. "That's not a lot. You'll see."

We were the next in the kitchen, every flat surface containing a platter of fish, a fresh salad, roasted potatoes, lemon-crusted asparagus, octopus, marinated red shrimp in olive oil, giant pots of pasta in homemade ragu, arancini, freshly baked bread . . . more things than I could even see. "How did they make all this?"

"Generations of experience." He handed me a clean plate. "Ladies first." He gave my ass a playful smack.

"Con!" A woman with dark hair moved over to him and gave him a hard hug.

"Hey, sis." He gave her a one-armed hug and kissed her temple. "Everything looks good."

"Well, I almost killed her to make it."

He chuckled. "Yeah, I heard when we walked in. Where are the boys?"

"With Aunt Chiara. Probably climbing on her like a tree."

"I'll help out after I eat. Beatrice, this is Aurelia."

I awkwardly held the plate as I extended my hand to shake hers. "It's lovely to meet you."

Beatrice clearly wasn't expecting me like her mom was, because she quickly glanced at Constantine before she looked at me again, a silent conversation passing between them. "You too. I've heard so many stories about the two of you in town, so I'm glad I can finally put a face to a name." She didn't hug me like his mother did, didn't even try to shake my hand. "Enjoy the food. I almost killed my mother when I made it."

I laughed, but I would have laughed a lot harder if it weren't obvious she was disappointed by me.

"Con, we'll catch up later." She left the line and headed toward the terrace.

I moved around the kitchen and made my plate, trying to take a bit of everything because a home-cooked meal was rare to come by. In Rome, I was usually too busy to cook, so I ate out most of the time, stopped by a little shop and got a slice of Roman pizza before I continued on my way.

Constantine and I found an empty table outside and took a seat. It was quickly filled by other people, and I was glad none of them was his sister. When I looked across the terrace, I saw her sitting with a woman her age, a young boy in her lap that I assumed was her son. The woman looked out of place with everyone there because of the way she sat, arms tight across her stomach, no food or drink in front of her, purposely staring straight ahead like she didn't want to see anything else.

Maybe his sister didn't dislike me. Maybe she was just occupied with this cousin or friend of hers. Maybe it had nothing to do with me.

"What do you think?" Constantine asked, arms on the table as he inhaled his food. When we went out to dinner, he executed better manners, but when he was at home, he let his guard down.

"Fucking delicious."

He patted my thigh under the table as he stabbed his fork into another piece of fish. "Attagirl."

When dinner was finished, I ventured into the house to use the restroom. I passed the kitchen on the way, and his mother's words made me stop in my tracks.

"Isn't she beautiful?" She didn't bother to keep her voice down. She must have assumed everyone was on the terrace while she prepared the cannoli. The smile in her voice was so obvious I could picture it on her face.

"Stunning," another woman said.

"And her hips. Did you see them?"

"Perfect for babies," the other said. "Beautiful and tall . . . she's a dream."

I couldn't believe they were talking about me. I was certain no one had ever said so many nice things about me—ever.

"I'm happy for you, Sofia," Aunt Chiara said. "It's unfortunate what happened with Isabella."

"Constantine is too smart for that," his mother said. "He knows a good woman when he sees one. I trust his judgment. I'll ask Pope Zephyrinus to pray for Constantine. He's thirty-three. It's time to slow down."

She knew the pope?

"You know how men are in this new generation," Aunt Chiara said. "Think they have all the time in the world . . ." They changed the subject, talking about people I didn't know, so I continued on to the bathroom.

I tidied up my hair and makeup and did my business. When I left the bathroom, I took the wrong hallway and ended up in the other wing of the house. It had its own terrace doors from a separate sitting area that no one occupied, so I didn't think it would matter if I used it. The windows on either side were open to let the sea breeze inside, and I could hear conversations from everyone having a good time and drinking.

And then I heard Constantine. "We really have to do this here?" He spoke in a way I'd never heard him before. He didn't raise his voice and yell, but his tone was fucking ice cold.

I stopped in my tracks and backed up a couple of steps, finding him talking with someone apart from the crowd. It was the woman I'd spotted with his sister at one of the other tables, and she looked as miserable now as she had then.

"I just think it's disrespectful, Con."

"Disrespectful?" he exclaimed. "This is my mother's house. This is my family. I can do whatever I damn well please. I can bring whomever I want."

"And you didn't think of my feelings at all?"

"No." The viciousness in his eyes was something he'd never shown to me. It reminded me of the way Enzo had looked at me toward the end of our relationship, like he wanted nothing to do with me. "Because your feelings aren't my responsibility, Isabella. They aren't my problem. The only feelings I care about are Aurelia's, and the last thing I want is

for her to feel uncomfortable. Unless that's what you're hoping for? That she comes back from the bathroom, asks me about this conversation, and then I tell her about all this nonsense because you know I won't lie to her, and then she walks away because she doesn't want the headache."

"So, this is serious?" She winced like he'd already given her the answer she didn't want.

"No."

"Then why would you bring her—"

"It's not serious *yet*. But it will be."

Her head made a distinct jerk as she looked away. It was as if he'd slapped her with an invisible hand. "You're an asshole."

"Oh, I'm an asshole?"

"You slept with me, dangled us in front of me like a fucking carrot—"

"Don't rewrite history. You'd just gotten divorced and said you wanted one night. I did not give you *any* indication that I wanted us again. I will never want us again. And don't act like I didn't make that crystal fucking clear before we hooked up. Now I would do anything to take it back because clearly that was a fucking mistake—"

He stopped talking when she started to cry, when her bottom lip trembled and she did everything she could to stop herself from crying.

Constantine bowed his head and squeezed his eyes shut, grimacing at the destruction he'd caused. Fortunately for them, everyone was too drunk and absorbed in the fun to notice the soap opera playing out in the corner.

She took a deep breath and brought herself to a state of semicalm. "We were practically kids at the time, Con. Why can't you just forgive me?"

Now, when he spoke, he was calm, like he really felt bad that he'd made her cry. "I have forgiven you, Issy."

"No, you haven't."

"Just because I forgive you doesn't mean I want to be with you."

"We were so young. It was a stupid mistake."

"We weren't *that* young. Girls were always throwing themselves at me, and I could have fucked all of them and you wouldn't have ever known. But I never did." He closed his fist to his chest. "Because I'm fucking loyal. Because I fucking loved you. This is so stupid to even talk about right now because it's been nine goddamn years."

"And we're still meant to be together, Con."

"Why?" he challenged. "Because our families are close? What kind of fucking reason is that? The only people meant to be together are the ones who work their asses off to be together. You didn't do that. You kissed my brother and lied to me."

"He kissed me—"

"I never cared about the kiss. I cared about the lie. Trust is broken, and in my book, that can never be fixed. You break a bone and you mend it, but it's never what it was. It aches in the cold, it hurts when you twist it a certain way. It's not the same."

Her bottom lip started to tremble again. She fought the tears from reaching the surface.

I wasn't mad about this at all. I actually felt for her, because if I'd had Constantine the way she did and lost him, I'd be devastated. Not devasted for a year or two. But my whole fucking life. Desperate to get him back, even after a decade.

He looked over his shoulder at the back door, clearly searching for me. "I never thought I'd say this, but I hope my mom ambushed her. The last thing I want is to scare her off and have her think I'm still hung up on my ex or some bullshit."

I knew I should leave and walk back to the main house in case he did look for me. He didn't want to explain his conversation with Isabella, and I didn't want to explain that I overheard the entire thing. Both of us wanted to keep those cards in our pockets.

If they said anything else, I didn't hear it because I headed across the house, back to where I came from. I walked into the kitchen and saw his mother and aunt finish preparing the cannoli and place them on multiple serving platters. "Need a hand?"

His mother looked up first, having the same kind of luminance in her gaze that her son had when he was excited. I recognized it well, saw the sincerity on the surface. "Yes, yes, yes. Come on over."

When I came to her side, she rubbed my back like I was one of her kids. "Put one of these on every table." She handed me two different plates of cannoli, an assortment of flavors of pistachio, vanilla, and chocolate.

I carried them out of the kitchen and into the hallway—and almost walked right into Constantine.

"What have we got here?" He looked at the two plates in my hand before he smiled, but it wasn't the same smile I'd seen from him through the night. It was strained, the weight of his confrontation with Isabella still heavy on his mind.

"Your mom asked me to help. It's nice to know she trusts me not to take these into the bathroom and eat them by myself."

This time, the smile was genuine. This time, it reached his eyes. This time, it lit up his entire face. "Here, let me help you." He took both the plates out of my hand. "And make sure you don't eat one of these in front of me."

"Why?"

He moved into me, coming closer like he might kiss me where everyone on the terrace could see if they looked. But he didn't seem to care about that, about Issy or his family or anyone. "Because the last cannoli you ate was on my dick."

~

Most of the guests had already left when we said goodbye in the entryway. His mother held him for a long time and struggled to let go, knowing he was leaving Sicily for Rome tomorrow.

"I don't see you enough," she said. "And you know how busy the restaurant is. I'd come see you if I could."

"I know, Ma. I'll try to come back soon."

"The last time you came was six months ago."

"I know, I know," he said. "I had a lot of stuff going on at work at the time."

The second he mentioned work, she physically and emotionally withdrew. "I love you, baby."

"Love you too, Ma." He kissed her on the cheek. "Thank you for dinner."

He was so good to his mom, and he was polite. God, he was a dream come true. It was hard to believe this was the same man that . . . I still didn't quite understand what he did. He sounded like a police officer for the worst criminals in the country. What was the name for an occupation like that?

She turned to me next. "It was so wonderful to meet you." She hugged me and kissed me, smothered me like I was already accepted. Like she didn't hope Constantine and Isabella would find their way back to each other. She wanted him to have whomever he wanted, and that was such a relief.

"You too. I had so much fun."

"I can't wait for both of you to come back. We'll need to spend more time together."

My heart squeezed because I already loved his mom. She reminded me of mine. "I look forward to it."

Constantine and I walked outside, and we went through the gate of the property, where he pulled out his phone to order a ride. "Couple minutes away." He stared down at the cliffs and the lights from the buildings, a quick rush of breeze moving through his hair. He seemed to feel my look before he turned to look at me.

"Thanks for bringing me. I had a good time."

"Yeah?" He grinned in his special way, the smolder entering his gaze.

"Yeah, it's nice to be around family, if that makes sense." They weren't my family, but it was like a memory of what a family used to feel like.

His smile slowly faded as his eyes filled with endless depth.

"But I noticed your brother wasn't there. Does he live in another part of Italy?" I'd noticed no one mentioned him either.

His stare didn't change, still locked in my gaze. "He's dead."

His words were so final and abrupt that it took me a second to understand what he'd just relayed to me. "I—I'm sorry. What happened?" I assumed his father passed from a health problem, but even if his brother died yesterday, he would have been in the prime of his life.

"I'm not ready to tell that story." He looked down the cliff again, crossing his arms over his chest.

"Of course. I understand." I continued to watch him stare, carrying a weight of hurt entirely on his own. I reached for his arm, and I rested my head against his shoulder, the only affection I could give him when he was closed off like this. "I'm always here, whenever you're ready."

He moved his arm away from my grasp and slid it around my waist. He pulled me effortlessly, resting his chin on my head. "I know, sweetheart."

Chapter 13

Aurelia

He quickly threw his stuff into his suitcase as if he had someone at home who would sort through it when he returned. He didn't care about keeping his shirts straight because someone would press them and hang them up in his closet. I noticed subtle indicators in his behavior that showed his wealth, and that was one of them.

But he didn't wear it on his sleeve like some of the billionaires I'd rubbed shoulders with. He seemed too secure to need everyone in the room to know he was the richest one there. He'd told me he bought that beautiful villa for his mother, but it hadn't felt like he was trying to show off.

I zipped up my suitcase and sat at the edge of the bed. "I don't want to go."

He wore jeans and a simple T-shirt, his muscular body filling it out well. He clasped the watch on his wrist as he smirked. "I know, sweetheart. We'll be back."

I loved Rome, the Eternal City, but it was a lot of hustle and bustle, motorbikes flying down the roads at full speed. Crowds all year round except for the month of January. I'd return to work and so would Constantine, so our easygoing, carefree fuck-cation was over. Now, it was time for reality.

"Staying with me?"

I tore my eyes away from the terrace and the sparkle on the surface of the water of the pool and looked at him again, not understanding the exact meaning of the question.

"At my villa," he added.

I got to my feet, dressed in jeans and a tank top, something comfortable for the short flight. I felt his stare with every move I made. "Actually, I told my friend what happened, and she said I could crash with her."

He finished fastening his watch, then relaxed both arms at his sides, staring me down without a specific expression.

"I just don't want this to go too fast."

"You aren't over him?"

"No, no, no." It wasn't that at all. All the warmth I'd ever felt for Enzo had died. Now I just kinda . . . hated him. "It's not that at all."

"Then why?"

"Like I said before, I need time to heal." It was hard to deny this beautiful man who inexplicably wanted me. It was hard to turn down another form of the fuck-cation. I was certain his place was a lot better than my friend's little apartment. "I don't want to ruin this by rushing." Now, we were back to reality, and having me at his home too long might actually suffocate him. I might overstay my welcome when I didn't mean to. What if it took longer to find an apartment than I realized and I annoyed him? I didn't want to leave one relationship bruised and battered and immediately jump into another one. There was only one Constantine. Only one shot with this man.

"I didn't ask you to move in. Just wanted to help you get back on your feet."

"I know, but you've done enough for me."

"What have I done for you exactly?"

"Well, you've given me the best week of my life."

"And you fucked my brains out. We're even." He smiled, then turned to the phone on the dresser. He hit the speaker button and called the bellhop to come grab our things and take them to the car. He didn't address the subject again, so he seemed to have accepted my answer.

A driver picked us up at the airport in Rome, but it wasn't a private chauffeur company. The two guys who got out of the car had guns stuffed into the back of their jeans, not caring about the public seeing the weapons, and they didn't say a word to Constantine as they grabbed the luggage and stowed it in the back of the SUV.

Constantine must have spotted my unease, because he moved his hand to my waist and gave me a gentle squeeze before he opened the back door for me. We sat together, his hand on my thigh, the radio on.

When we were on the freeway, I noticed the two black cars directly behind us. They seemed to be following us. It was as if Constantine was the president and he had a private motorcade to escort him wherever he went.

An hour later, we entered the city center of Rome and arrived at my friend's apartment. She was still at work and had left her spare key under the mat. I got the door unlocked, revealing a one-bedroom apartment.

The guys had carried all of my stuff up the three flights of stairs, probably because it was quicker than taking the elevator, and placed everything in a pile against one of the walls. They left without saying a word.

Constantine lingered. A man too big for this little apartment, so handsome dressed in all black. I should want no association with him after seeing the armored crew that picked him up, but all I felt was sadness at our separation. I didn't want to confront the reality of my life, that I had to get all of my stuff out of my old apartment, that I had to acknowledge the truth of what had happened . . . and feel it. I could already feel it squeezing me now, Constantine's presence not enough to erase the ugly truth.

He didn't ask me to change my mind. He just stared at me like he wanted to give me the opportunity to speak first.

I didn't have anything to say. And I certainly didn't want to say goodbye.

He moved into me and circled his big arms around me, bringing me in for a hard hug, his chin resting on my head. It was the first time he'd hugged me like this, face-to-face, affection that was friendly and loving at the same time. "You know where to find me." He pulled back and dipped his head to kiss me. One of those short, slow kisses. He felt my mouth with his for a couple of seconds, felt the heat burn between our lips, and then he pulled away.

And he left.

Chapter 14

Constantine

Rocco and I sat together in the stands of the small stadium at the Temple, the place where we conducted our affairs in the heart of Rome, a private building gifted to us by the Republic. We'd made a couple of changes and built our own Colosseum inside of it, a fraction of the size of the real one.

A large statue of Mars, the Roman god of war, was mounted over the prisoner's gate. The walls were carved with Roman numerals and Latin, the coffers on the walls gilded. The top of the ceiling was a dome, decorated in a similar fashion to the one in Saint Peter's.

I relaxed in the chair and waited for the games to begin. "Should have brought some popcorn."

"How's your ma?" Rocco asked.

"She's good. Health is good. Busy with the restaurant."

"She's one hell of a cook."

"Damn right she is," I said proudly.

"Didn't hear from you much."

"Because I was on vacation, and the last thing I wanted to do was listen to your bullshit." I didn't get much time off, so I treasured it whenever it was possible. As the First Roman Emperor of the Roman

Republic, not only was all of Rome my responsibility, but the rest of the country too.

He gave a slight smirk. “Figured you were buried in pussy.”

I was definitely buried balls deep in one pussy in particular.

When I didn’t confirm it or deny it, he turned to me. “Don’t tell me you fucked around with Isabella again.”

“God no,” I blurted, regretting that idiotic decision even more now. The god of fortuna had been on my side that evening, keeping Aurelia inside the house so she wouldn’t have to witness the very complicated drama with my ex. An ex I hadn’t been involved with for almost a decade. And I had been stupid enough to think we could just fuck and that would be the end of it.

“She give you any shit?”

“Yes, unfortunately.”

He slowly shook his head. “I fucking told you.”

“I know you did.” I fully admitted it. It was a mistake, and I should have listened to Rocco when he’d warned me not to give her any form of hope whatsoever.

“You could have any woman you want, but you decide to start shit.”

“She’d been married and divorced at that point. I thought it would be fine.”

“Still could have fucked literally *anyone* else, Con.”

“She’s crazy good in the sack, all right?”

“Not good enough to justify the bullshit.”

“Whatever,” I said. “It’s done.” I stared down at the bottom of the coliseum, the sand pit that was illuminated by the golden glow that came from the lights overhead. “We got into it at my mother’s house. I brought someone to dinner, and she lost it.”

He slowly turned his head to look at me. “You brought a woman to your ma’s house?”

“Yeah.”

“To meet your family?”

“That wasn’t why I brought her, but yeah.”

He looked ahead at the pit again before he turned back to me. "Why are you acting like this isn't a big deal?"

"I'm not acting like it's not a big deal."

"Whoa, whoa, then let's back up here." Rocco straightened in his chair and pivoted so he could face me better. "Who is she?"

Brick stepped out of the prisoner's door, a smaller door that was away from the gate. "We're ready."

"Ten minutes!" Rocco shouted across the coliseum.

"What the fuck? Why?"

"Fuck off!" Rocco yelled back.

Brick flipped him off before he walked back through the door.

"Who is she?" Rocco asked. "She lives in Taormina?"

"She lives in Rome, but we met there." I told him the whole story. How we met, that she'd just ended her long-term relationship with that little punk-ass bitch, and we spent the whole week together. "She insisted on staying with her friend and says she needs time to heal. So I'll give her some space."

"Or maybe she's just not that into you and is trying to let you down easy."

The smirk that stretched over my face was instantaneous. "No, she's into me."

"Then why would she sleep on someone's couch instead of in your bed?"

"She's got to figure her shit out. I get it, it's fine. She's gonna go through dick withdrawal at some point, so I'll hear from her then." I continued to smile, remembering all the faces she made when she came. She was so pretty when she cried, her tears like diamonds. Or when her face was pressed into the sheets and her makeup stained everything. "I'm not worried about it."

"What's her name?"

"Aurelia."

"Nice."

"Yeah, I like it too."

"So her last relationship ended a week ago?"

"About."

"And you want to get involved in that?"

"Doesn't bother me."

"Then you must really like her."

I hadn't stopped thinking about her. Every time I checked my phone, I hoped her name would be there. The second I got back in town, my regulars had started to hit me up because their dick withdrawal had kicked in before I'd returned to Rome, but my dick didn't even twitch. There was only one woman I wanted.

But she'd asked for space, and I wouldn't violate that request. I wouldn't be the first to make a move when she'd asked me to hit the brakes. I wanted her, but I had too much pride to chase a woman who didn't want to be chased. If I didn't hear from her after a couple weeks or a month, then that would be the end of it.

But I was certain it wasn't the end of it.

The iron gate started to lift. The beaters with bats took their positions around the edges of the coliseum so there was no escape for the prisoners, but of course, they ran out like they always did . . . as if there was anywhere else to go.

The music came through the speakers, music that would play over an action-adventure film.

In rags for clothes and covered in dirt from the cells they slept in, they ran forward across the sand, some losing their balance because they tried too hard, too fast. These were the criminals who had been gathered in the last week, those found guilty of rape, murder, and direct violations of the Roman Republic. Not every violation was punished with the same severity, but these men were the worst of the worst, those who chose to hurt innocent people for their own bottom line.

Now, they would be put to death.

"It's showtime." I got to my feet and walked down the stairs to the platform over the pit. "For your crimes against the Roman Republic, I give you the opportunity to fight for your freedom—or die." For every prisoner, there was a guard with a bat—but not just any bat, a bat studded with metal shards and nails. A single hit was a death blow. "Let the games begin."

~

Graffiti was a big problem in Rome. Assholes decided they had the right to stain our Roman history, and one of our agendas was to erase those marks from our beautiful city. President Barsetti couldn't do much other than enforce the law, which threw those assholes in jail for a couple of months before they were out on the streets again, doing the same shit.

Because Roman history was my history, I took that pretty fucking personally.

So, we stationed our men at all the main monuments, and whenever they caught someone, they smashed their faces into the cobblestones and forced them to eat the paint from the bottles. Most of them ended up in the hospital, and word had spread that the Roman Republic would come for anyone who tried that shit again.

Graffiti in the city had dropped exponentially. President Barsetti was happy, the locals appreciated it, and I defended the work of my ancestors. We paid for a cleanup team out of our own pockets to scrub all the paint off the walls and to carefully restore the stone.

Rocco and I approached the square of the Pantheon, one of the oldest and fully intact monuments that had survived all the ages. The Roman Forum contained pieces of our history, but that's all they were—pieces.

But the Pantheon remained.

We stopped and examined the side wall, the area that had been riddled with different-colored paint and gang symbols, marking this beautiful piece of history. Now, all of that was gone.

The stone had been restored.

Rocco held a piece of Roman pizza in his hand by the waxed paper. He took a bite as he examined it in silence. "How it should have been."

"Yeah. She cleans up good."

"Took a year to clean all this shit up, but it was worth it."

Anyone who was caught trying to graffiti the walls again would get a worse punishment—and lose a hand. That way, if anyone thought we'd relaxed our security, they would be sadly mistaken. And then they would fear what we would do next if they tried again . . . and they might lose more than a hand.

President Barsetti wouldn't agree with that measure, but we'd cross that bridge when we came to it.

Rocco stared at the monument in silence, just eating and appreciating the beauty before him. Other locals got used to the Roman landmarks and forgot their power, but for people like Rocco and me, we never did. We treated this city like it was our own home. Appreciated it every day.

"Heard from Aurelia?" he suddenly asked.

It'd been over a week since I'd dropped her off at her friend's house. I hadn't heard a peep from her. "No."

He took another bite of his pizza, chewing quietly.

I'd hoped I would have heard from her by now. I'd rejected all the offers that had fallen into my lap in the hope she'd call. In the hope she'd return to my bed where she belonged.

He moved his hand to my shoulder and gave it a squeeze. "Sorry, man."

"I haven't given up."

"A week is a long time."

The longest week of my fucking life. "She'll reach out."

He gave me another pat on the shoulder then finished his pizza. "We've got a long night. Let's get moving."

Chapter 15

Aurelia

It'd been a rough week.

The shit hit the fan, everyone knew what had happened, and all my friends told me I was better off without him. They took me out for dinner and drinks a lot, let me air my grievances in a way only girlfriends could. I lived out of my suitcase because I couldn't muster up the courage to go back and get the rest of my things. I wasn't sure what I would see when I got there. Evidence that she had moved in the second Enzo returned from Taormina, probably. Evidence that I'd never really mattered at all.

I also had a lot to do at work. I'd already booked the photo sessions long before we'd left on our planned vacation, and since my clients were relying on me for their special events and their weddings and their headshots and whatever else, I couldn't cancel.

And in the moments between all that chaos, I missed Constantine.

Missed him like crazy.

Our lives in Taormina were so easy. It was all sex and food and fun. We didn't have a care in the world. He was a man I'd known for a week, but by the end of that trip, I felt like I'd known him all my life.

I really fucking missed him.

But until I got my stuff back from Enzo and moved in to my new apartment, I felt like I wouldn't have closure. I wasn't in the right headspace to start something new with someone that I already cared so much about.

I was at my friend's apartment and she was at work when Enzo texted me. When are you coming to get your stuff?

It was the first time we'd spoken since he'd left me in Taormina. Since he'd walked out of our hotel room while I sat alone on the bed and watched him leave. He spoke to me like he was one of those coworkers I'd never gotten along with. Like we'd never been friends, let alone two people in love. I can come today. It was time to get this over with. Just face it and be done with it.

Alright. Let me know when you're on your way.

Why? Was it because he was going to be there?

All I had to do was ask, but I didn't want to give him the satisfaction that I cared. That his presence would make me uncomfortable. That I was worried Luna might be there, that cunt who smiled at me at the Christmas party while she was fucking my boyfriend behind my back.

I needed to man up and just do it, but I didn't want to.

I could bring some of my friends, but that felt like an ambush. Like it made me look weak. But could I realistically move all that stuff with just my motorbike? Probably not. That meant I'd have to rent a car and then store all that stuff here, in an apartment that was already small enough.

I should have searched for my own apartment sooner.

I grabbed my phone and stared at Constantine's name for a while before I typed the message. I need to pick up my stuff at Enzo's today. I know it's really lame, but I don't want to go alone . . . I didn't outright ask him, but the plea for help was easy to read between the lines. I sent the message and set my phone aside, unsure when he would text me back.

But the second I put my phone down, it vibrated.

I'll be right there, sweetheart.

My heart melted into a puddle when I heard his voice in my head as I read his words. I felt like he was there with me, jumping out of the screen and holding me tight. I'd missed hearing him call me sweetheart. Missed the way he made me feel . . . like I mattered.

~

I opened the door when he knocked.

It was the beginning of June, so the weather was getting warm outside. He arrived in a black T-shirt and black jeans, like he didn't care about the heat. With a clean-shaven jaw and a warmth in his deep, rich eyes, he was exactly what I remembered . . . but so much more.

How could I possibly forget how hot he was?

A wave of need passed over me, a desperation for his affection and warmth, a longing I couldn't describe in words. How had I come to care for someone so deeply and so quickly? My friends had been there for me ever since I'd come home, had been my surrogate family, but it wasn't the same.

The silence continued between us, both of us processing our emotions at the sight of each other. He eventually stepped into the apartment and came over to me, his eyes flicking back and forth between mine as he analyzed all my features. "Rough week?"

"Something like that."

His eyes dropped in a hint of sadness before he hooked his arms around me and pulled me close. He held me in my friend's apartment, chased away all my sadness and anxiety with his touch. He slid his hand into the back of my hair as he rested his chin on my head, holding me in a way no one else ever had.

Even when Enzo and I were at our best, I never felt *this*. This kind of depth. "I missed you." I probably shouldn't have said that, shouldn't put stress on a relationship that I was actively trying to avoid for the time being, but there was something about him that made me do stupid shit and say reckless things.

He pulled away from me, that devilish smile on his lips. "Come on. Let's get your stuff."

~

He drove us in a blacked-out Range Rover. He didn't have his team of guys with him this time. It was just the two of us. He drove with one hand on the wheel, the other propped on the armrest, the music turned down so low I couldn't really hear it. The vehicle smelled brand new, like he'd just bought it or hardly ever drove it.

My heart rate was irregular with him next to me, my peace interrupted by his momentous presence. When my longing had become too much, I'd looked at the few pictures of him I'd taken on our trip, just to see his face. Now, he was there with me, at my beck and call like I was an important person in his life—if not the most.

A guy had never treated me like that before. Let alone a guy who was six foot five with a hundred pounds of solid muscle and was so good looking it was painful to look directly at him sometimes.

"Find a place yet?" he asked with his eyes on the road, the SUV coming to a stop in traffic.

"I think so. Applied for it."

"Where?"

"Trionfale. By the university." It was much farther outside the city center than I wanted, but it was all I could afford on a single income. The neighborhood was decent, and I cared more about that than anything else.

He gave a nod but didn't offer his input. When he arrived at Enzo's apartment building, he pulled up right in front of it, up against the sidewalk where you weren't supposed to park.

"I don't think we can park here."

He gave that arrogant smirk before he hopped out. "I can park anywhere." He shut the door behind him, and the sound of the door closing concluded the discussion. He came to my side and opened my door for me before we stepped into the entryway of the building, where all the mailboxes were.

It was a nice building, with couches and rugs and flowerpots on a tiled floor. It also had an elevator. We took it to the third floor, then walked down the hallway and approached the front door of the apartment I'd called home for the last year and a half.

I stopped before it, suddenly losing all the courage that had gotten me this far.

He didn't rush me inside, didn't tell me to buck up. He leaned up against the wall and crossed his arms as he waited. "What are you afraid of?"

"Of seeing how easily I was replaced . . ." How my entire existence had been erased from Enzo's heart seemingly overnight. "I wish he regretted it, not because I'd take him back, but because it would mean he still cared. To watch the person who said *I love you* first, asked you to move in, said you were the love of his life . . . just become indifferent to you. I'd rather he hate me for something because at least hate *means* something." I took a heavy breath. "I know it's stupid. I should be over this by now—"

"This isn't the first time you've been abandoned. That's why it bothers you."

I turned to him slowly and felt the pain bubble in my stomach as I stared.

"Your father walked out on you, and now, someone you trusted did the exact same thing. The fact that he doesn't realize that or care shows his character."

I was surprised he even remembered that.

"It's okay that it bothers you." He pushed off the wall and came toward me, this man beautiful in more than his looks. He was intelligent and deep and aware. "It hurts like hell right now, and it'll hurt for a while, but it'll get better." He nodded to the door. "But first, you've got to do this. And it doesn't hurt to show him *his* replacement." He gave me a gentle nudge in the side, wearing that charismatic smile as he knocked on the door.

I went from the lowest of my lows to the highest high in the span of a couple seconds—thanks to him.

Enzo opened the door, made eye contact with me with a slight look of shame, but then he turned his attention on Constantine and kept it there. With wide-open eyes and a stillness to his entire body, Enzo clearly didn't know what to make of the big, muscular, sexy man who accompanied me.

"Con." He didn't extend his hand to shake Enzo's. He stared him down in a way he'd never once looked at me, and I was grateful for it. "Here to get my woman's things."

My woman. He'd never called me that before and I knew it was just for show, but it sounded so nice.

Constantine gave my ass a gentle smack. "Come on, sweetheart."

Enzo awkwardly stepped aside. "Uh . . . yeah."

When I walked inside, I could easily see how much it had changed. There were children's toys on the couch, a toy chest against the wall, a pink indoor bike visible from the kitchen. I noticed other changes too, blankets I'd never seen before, women's shoes by the door that weren't mine.

She'd already moved in—with her two kids.

I did my best to keep a straight face, to pretend I didn't care because Enzo clearly didn't even try to hide all the evidence. He obviously didn't address the last text I'd sent him with all the fuck-off emojis either.

Enzo moved to one side of the living room, where all my boxes were grouped. He'd packed everything for me, so who knew what he'd actually grabbed or how he'd organized it. My entire life was compartmentalized and stacked in the corner, a discreet reminder that I'd ever existed. It was how I felt to him now, just a thought in the corner of his mind.

Constantine walked to the boxes and got to work, putting the lightest ones aside for me to carry. He went for the boxes at the bottom of the pile, the ones that contained my books, shoes, and clothes.

It was an awkward situation, Constantine and me coming back and forth and grabbing boxes and putting them in the back of his Range Rover before returning to the apartment to grab more.

Enzo sat on the couch and waited. He didn't offer to help.

At the end, it was only the heavy stuff that Constantine didn't want me to carry, so I stood there awkwardly and waited for him to finish. Enzo stayed in the living room, and I stayed in the kitchen. We'd been close for years, but now we couldn't even be in the same room together.

When Constantine grabbed the last box, we headed to the front door together.

"Aurelia."

I stopped at the sound of Enzo's voice.

Constantine continued into the hallway. "I'll meet you downstairs, sweetheart."

I kept my back to Enzo, feeling weak without Constantine present to give me strength. But I slowly turned around and looked at the man I'd thought I would marry at some point. "What's up?" I folded my arms over my chest, did my best to pretend I didn't give a damn, that my heart wasn't racing like mad.

He held my gaze for a long time before he answered. "I'm sorry . . . about everything."

It was the first apology I'd gotten. The first admission of wrongdoing. I'd been waiting for that for months. I'd waited for it on the trip. I'd waited for it when he packed up his things and left. And now that I'd gotten it, I realized it didn't make a difference. It didn't make me feel better. It just . . . didn't matter. "Take care, Enzo."

Constantine pulled up in the cobblestone alley next to the apartment building. He parked his vehicle in a place where he wasn't supposed to park, but he did it anyway, like he could do whatever he damn well pleased.

He turned off the engine but didn't move to unfasten his safety belt. "Doing all right?"

I hadn't said a word after we left Enzo's. Our final parting was just so . . . anticlimactic. "If you'd told me this was how it would end a year ago, I wouldn't have believed it. It's hard to picture, but we were happy. Really happy."

"He'll come to regret it. I promise you that." He looked straight out the windshield, one arm propped on the armrest.

"I don't care if he ever does." He'd apologized to me, and I felt absolutely nothing.

"I wouldn't be surprised if he already does," he said with a slight smirk.

"What makes you say that?"

"Well, it's a lot more fun sneaking around and screwing in the back seat or in a dark alleyway than playing house," he said with a chuckle. "Now, he's got a live-in girlfriend and two kids that aren't even his. Must be a shock."

"Yeah, maybe." Enzo's shock couldn't have been worse than mine when I'd walked in there and seen my presence completely erased by his new family.

"What'd he say to you?"

"Apologized."

He gave a slow nod. "Yep, he knows he fucked up. Got caught up in the secrecy and lost sight of what mattered. He must be out of his mind to trade you for any woman."

"That's nice of you to say."

He turned to look at me directly. "I mean it."

And Enzo had said a lot of the same things when we'd started seeing each other . . . and look where we'd ended up.

"I've been thinking about you like crazy."

How in the world did I land this guy? He was insanely hot, but his looks paled in comparison to his other features, like his warmth and his smile and how quick and smart he was. The way he cared for his family. His only vice was how he earned a living. "I've missed you too."

He extended his hand over the center console, his arm long enough to reach my thigh, touching me like we were back in Taormina. The touch of his flesh was muffled by the denim I wore, but the pressure and weight of his hand both excited and calmed me.

"Thank you for helping me today."

"I've always got your back." He squeezed my thigh gently. "I don't think there's room for all this stuff in that apartment. Let me hold on to it for you until you move in."

"Oh, you don't have to do that."

"I've got a lot of space. It's fine."

"That's nice of you, but it's not your problem—"

"Think I'm going to go through your panties or something?" he teased, his smile forming. "I mean, I can't promise that *won't* happen . . ."

I chuckled quietly, the first time I'd somewhat laughed all day. "Well, thank you."

He stared at me for several heartbeats, his eyes, dark like the underworld, so comforting. "Let me take you to dinner tonight."

"I would, but . . ." I felt bad for rejecting him when he'd just done something nice for me. "I'm just not in that place right now."

If he was disappointed, he hid it well. "Then how about lunch? I know a good spot nearby."

"Now?"

"You aren't hungry after moving all those boxes?"

"Well, you're the one who carried all the heavy ones."

He gave my thigh a pat, the way he had with my ass. "Like I'd let my woman do a damn thing." He clicked the button to free his safety belt and started to hop out of the car. "Come on."

"I really don't think you can leave your car here."

He grinned as he came around the car and opened my door. "Oh sweetheart, you're cute."

~

We went to Cambio, a restaurant that had great Roman pasta. I'd been there a couple times. Of course Constantine knew the guys here too, just like in Taormina. He made small talk near the bar before we were given a table in the back, away from everyone else.

Also just like in Taormina, he ordered a bottle of wine for the table and barely glanced at the menu, as if he already knew what he would order. "What are you thinking, sweetheart?"

I'd had no appetite at all when he'd asked me to lunch, but now that we'd changed our surroundings, the desire for food started to come back. "The cacio e pepe."

"Excellent choice."

"What about you?"

"I like their steak."

The waiter came to the table, and the guys had a small conversation about tennis before Constantine ordered our lunch for both of us.

"So, you really know everyone, huh?" I teased.

"Yep," he said with a nod. "Got eyes and ears everywhere."

Whenever his profession was mentioned, I became more curious . . . and more wary. "How was your week?"

"Busy."

"What did you do?"

"Work."

"The entire time?"

"Yeah, that's how it works." He grabbed his glass and took a drink. "The job and I are the same entity."

A job I still didn't understand. "Could you . . . tell me more about it?"

"I'll tell you anything you want to know," he said. "So, I'm sure you already know that President Barsetti is the head of state of Italy and oversees the laws that govern this country. And I'm sure you also know that Pope Zephyrinus is the leader of the Catholic Church, the head of the Vatican. So you have the president." He raised one finger. "And then you have the pope." He raised a second finger. "But there's another ruler in Rome—and that's the emperor."

I felt a shiver down my spine, straight from my neck to my ass. It was ice cold and terrifying.

"And that's me." He raised a third finger. "Emperor Constantine. Leader of the Roman Republic, ruler of Italy. We all have very different roles in this country and abide by our own rules."

It was the first time in my life I'd been stunned into complete silence.

"Like it was for the emperors after Christ and the death of Julius Caesar, it's my job to protect this country, not just from enemies outside our lands, but from those within. To protect the civilians who call this place home. Some have called my tactics ruthless and savage, but I take that as a compliment."

I did not expect to get into this at lunch. But I did ask . . .

"I police the criminals operating within this country, make them adhere to humanitarian practices that keep people like you out of harm's way. I make sure that whatever drugs hit the streets are not laced with fentanyl. I won't judge anyone who wants to take a hit, but I'll make sure people aren't dying needlessly because the dealer wanted to maximize his profits. Trafficking has been outlawed under my rulership. I won't put up with that shit. Anyone working in a gang has to be at least twenty-one. No kids. I do that sort of thing." As if he'd said something insignificant, he took another drink of his wine.

I was still stunned. "How—how do you enforce all that?"

"With the men I employ under my rule. I have four barons who work with me, ones that I trust the most to enforce my laws. It's a large network of people. I also leverage resources from President Barsetti. My job is to focus on the crime aspect of the city, to protect the country from terrorism, and President Barsetti is more concerned with nonviolent legal matters. Like tax fraud and tax evasion, city and building codes, petty crimes, arson, stuff like that. The really violent assholes are my responsibility. And the pope . . . he brings me back to God when I stray too far."

"You know Pope Zephyrinus?"

He nodded. "I know him well."

This was the part where I should stand up and get the hell out of there. But I stayed. The part where I assumed he was a pathological liar. But I believed him. "How did you get into that?"

"It's a long story. But I basically worked my way up to the position and was elected based on my pedigree."

"Your pedigree?"

"I'm a descendant of the first emperor, Augustus." He said it with a straight face—like this was all true.

Now, my appetite was long gone. I realized I didn't know the man I'd been sleeping with. I had been too blinded by his handsome smile and eyes that were so confident they were borderline arrogant.

He studied me for a while.

I felt the heat flush my face. It was a warm day, but I felt unnecessary sweat start to collect at the back of my neck.

"You're scared." He didn't say it triumphantly, but with defeat.

"I—I'm not sure what I am."

"You're scared," he repeated. "But I'm the last man in the world you should be scared of."

Every breath didn't feel like enough. I felt the scream in my lungs.

"And I believe you." And that's what elevated me from scared to utterly terrified. I'd suspected he was in the Mafia or some other organized crime, but this was much, much worse. I felt like I'd stepped two thousand years into the past of ancient Rome, and now I sat beside Emperor Augustus himself.

He was quiet for a long time, just staring at me.

I wasn't sure if he was waiting for me to say something or was just giving me time to process it all.

The waiter brought our dishes, then departed.

Neither of us touched our food.

Constantine's attention remained laser focused on me. "Nothing has changed, sweetheart. I'm still the man you met in Taormina. But I'm not going to sugarcoat what I am and what I do. As I told you before, I'll never lie to keep a woman, no matter how much I want her."

"Has this been a problem for other women?"

"No. But like I said, I haven't been in a relationship in nine years. Most of the women I've slept with knew exactly what I was, and it only turned them on more."

I could absolutely see that. The ultimate bad boy. The draw of his power. The magnetism of his strength.

When the silence continued, he grabbed his glass and took another drink before he rested his fingertips on the edge and swirled it.

I wanted to know if Isabella knew this and still wanted him, but there was no way I could ask.

When he realized my discomfort wouldn't evaporate and follow-up questions weren't forthcoming, he changed the subject. "What did you do this week?"

It took me a moment to recover, to shift gears and head in another direction. "I spent a lot of time with my friends, had a lot of sessions. I already had these events booked months ago, and I couldn't cancel them, even though work was the last thing I wanted to do."

"What were they?"

"A wedding, a private shoot, a client's website, images for a realty company."

"That is a busy week," he said. "How's it been, staying with this friend of yours?"

"Her name is Cindy. And it's . . . fine."

He'd grabbed his utensils and started to eat, brushing off the intensity of our previous conversation.

I felt like I was sitting next to a mob boss who could get shot in a drive-by shooting any second—and I was right next to him. "The apartment is small, she's got a boyfriend . . . it's not ideal. But once my application gets approved, I'm sure I'll be able to move right away."

He didn't offer to let me stay with him again. He just listened. "You don't like her boyfriend."

"I wouldn't say that."

"Come on, you don't need to be diplomatic with me." Unlike how he was around his family, he ate with polite manners when it was just the two of us. Elbows off the table, taking his time, refined.

"I just get a weird vibe from him."

"Like he-wishes-he-were-fucking-you-instead-of-her kind of vibe?"

"No," I said with a scoff. "I can't really explain it. He doesn't talk about himself much, doesn't seem to have a job, like he's secretive. Like he's hiding something. He's a good-looking guy, so I think my friend has just fallen under that spell."

He took a bite and then rested his elbows on the table, taking his time chewing the food he'd placed in his mouth. He surveyed the restaurant as he sat in quiet contemplation. "What's his name?"

"Timothée. I think he's French."

"The offer to stay with me is still on the table."

"It's okay, Constantine—"

"You've got to be the most stubborn woman I've ever met. And that's including my ma."

"Your mother is lovely, not stubborn."

"Because you met her on a good day. Cut the bullshit and just stay with me."

"I'll probably be out in a week, and it's a hassle to move all my stuff."

"Your two suitcases?" he asked with a chuckle. "Could carry that in a single trip."

"Constantine, I appreciate the offer, but I'd rather stay put." I focused on my pasta instead of him, afraid to see how pissed off he was.

He stayed quiet for a while, but his rage was palpable. "You're that afraid of me?"

"It's not that."

"You're a bad liar, Aurelia."

"I'm not afraid of you in *that* way."

"Then be specific."

I looked across the empty restaurant and felt his heavy stare burn a hole in my cheek. "I already told you I need time to heal. I don't know how many times I can say it. I don't want to leave one relationship and then jump into another one. That always ends in disaster."

"I just want to make sure you're safe, sweetheart. This is not some ploy to get you into bed."

"I'll be fine. If I ever need help or feel unsafe, you will be the first one I call, okay?" I raised my chin and looked at him again, seeing his arms on the table as he leaned toward me, his dark eyes lethal. "I don't know how much time I need—weeks, months, I don't know. But you shouldn't wait around for me."

He held my gaze for a long time before he withdrew his arms and sat back. He released a quiet chuckle before he abandoned his approach and focused on the last bit of his steak. "All right." He grabbed the bottle of wine and refilled his glass, eating and drinking in silence.

"What?" I asked, picking up on the laugh he issued under his breath.

He continued to look relaxed, his eyes elsewhere, his behavior not matching the words that left his mouth. "I'll wait as long as it takes, sweetheart."

Chapter 16

Constantine

I arrived at Quirinal Palace, the residence of President Barsetti in the heart of Rome. I bypassed all the security checkpoints because I didn't have to waste my time with that. I was the only person in the world who could meet with the president armed.

I walked down the long hallway comprising Roman arches, sculptures, and artwork from the palace's private collection, and then I was let inside the double doors to his private office.

He was seated behind his desk, one arm propped on the armrest of his chair, talking to someone through the earbuds in both of his ears. Wearing a look of distinct indifference, he stared at me and then tried to wrap up the call. "I'll look into it. I've got another meeting, so let's circle back to this." His phone was on his desk, so he tapped the red button to end the call, then pulled the earbuds out of his ears and tossed them aside.

"Another day at the office, huh?" I dropped into one of the two comfortable armchairs that faced his desk.

He ignored what I said and straightened in his chair.

"One of the perks of my job—no meetings."

"What do you call this?"

I shrugged. "If you break open a bottle of scotch, I'd call it lunch."

His lips didn't smirk, but his eyes filled with mirth at the suggestion. He left his chair, grabbed one of the bottles from his private bar, and then poured two glasses.

"Here we go."

He came to me and handed me a glass before he dropped into the other chair, wearing a dark-blue suit and a black tie, a black Patek watch on his wrist. He crossed his leg on the opposite knee, his pant leg rising up to reveal the black sock underneath. The youngest Italian president to ever hold office, he was somewhere around my age. The previous legislation required the candidate to be at least fifty years old, but after enough money and lobbying were thrown at the problem, that rule was amended.

I clinked my glass against his before we both took a drink. "How's the family?"

"Pissed that I don't come home enough."

"Tuscany is just a short flight away, especially in a private plane."

"Unlike everyone else in this world, I don't have the luxury of working from home." He took another drink before he looked at me. "Not when my citizens are disappearing off the streets and their body parts are being harvested from operating tables."

"I knew this was coming."

"You said this would be handled by now."

"I'm working on it."

"Are you? Were you working on it during your trip to Taormina?"

No, I was busy getting hooked on the best pussy I'd ever had. "Rocco had it covered."

"Did he? Because I've seen no progress."

"Crow, I'll handle it, okay? Vladimir knows I'm onto him, so he's changed his tactics. He laid low when I was right on top of him because he's smart. But he's started up again, which means he's probably changed his mode of operations. I have Rocco tapping into health networks and evaluating names on the transplant lists to see if we can get information that way."

Crow looked away and took a drink.

"Have I ever failed you before?"

Too stubborn to concede, he ignored me. "I spoke with Prime Minister Foster this morning. He provided some intel from MI6. There are whispers of a terrorist act here, Paris, or London. Don't know when or where or how."

"Well, that's helpful."

"You keep your arms guys on a tight leash."

"A leash so short it chokes them a little."

He took another drink of his scotch before he set it on the table between us. Tall, slender, and ripped like a soccer player, he was the most popular president Italy had ever had. Not just because he was young and intelligent, but because women described him as a beautiful man. He was well spoken and articulate, but he also didn't settle for less than the best. He was passionate about the security and well-being of his country. I liked him a hell of a lot more than his predecessor. He accepted my position without reproach, understood the criminal underworld like he was already well acquainted with it. "I've dispatched our military to our most congested posts throughout the city. In case something happens, we need some kind of backup."

"And you need to send a message that you know what's coming."

"Exactly."

Roberto dropped me off outside, and I entered the bar, American alternative rock music playing overhead, every chair and table occupied. I found Rocco seated at a table for four, his back turned and propped against the brick wall as he watched the TV in the corner that showed a replay of the football game that had happened earlier that afternoon.

I dropped into the chair across from him, and he ignored me.

But the waitress didn't, and she came over in a flash. "Hey, Con. What are you in the mood for?"

"Whiskey and Coke."

"I was hoping you had something sweeter in mind." She winked, then headed back to the bar. She ignored the other patrons and delivered my drink right away. We'd hooked up a couple of times, super casual. She was a cute girl with blond hair and big tits, good in the sack. Nearly ten years younger than me, she was getting her degree in art history from the university, so she'd never had commitment on her mind—which was perfect for me. "Free tonight?"

Rocco's eyes were glued to the TV like he didn't even hear the conversation.

I could just tell her I was busy and that'd be the end of it, but I was incapable of lying, whether it was outright or by omission. "I'm seeing someone."

"Oh," she said, clearly surprised my dick was spoken for. "Well, maybe some other time." The second she knew she wouldn't get laid, she paid me no further attention. She focused on the other people at the bar because at least she might get a tip.

Rocco shook the ice in his glass before he took a drink. "So Aurelia is still in the game."

"Yeah. She reached out a couple days ago."

"That's good news."

"I helped her move her stuff out of that asshole's apartment."

"Did you see him?"

"Yeah." I took a drink. "She's totally out of his league."

"Then he's either gay or stupid."

"The *other* woman moved in with her two kids, so it's gotta be the latter. Guy's a fucking idiot. Mark my words—in a couple weeks, he'll reach out to her. When the last tendrils of the dream clouds start to fade away."

"You think she'll take him back?"

"Not a chance. She can't go from a stallion to a pony."

"Are you the stallion or the pony?"

I fought the smirk from hitting my mouth. "Fuck you."

He laughed then took a drink. He also had dark hair, but he was a lot burlier than I was, choosing mass and muscle over cut. He watched the game on the TV for a while before he addressed me again. "Glad things worked out. I know you're into her."

"Well . . ." That wasn't really the situation, and I could just stay quiet about it and keep it to myself, but I didn't have a filter with Rocco. If I were to have a best friend, it would be him, but I wouldn't say that pussy shit to him or anyone else. "It's complicated."

He turned back to me, his arm resting on the table as he waited for an explanation.

"She knew I was involved in organized crime before, but I painted a crisper picture for her." She'd been a bit skittish when I'd mentioned it in Taormina, but she was able to quickly move on because we were in paradise. "I can tell it freaked her out."

"This is the life we've known for so long that it's easy to forget how normal people live."

"Yeah."

"What are you going to do?"

"She says she needs to heal and all that, so I'll just take it slow. I know she needs time to adjust to the emperor thing, so taking it easy is really my only option at this point."

"What's the rush, Con?" He turned back to the TV, his head resting against the brick wall.

"Not a rush per se." I shook the ice in my glass before I took another drink. "I just miss what we had. Ever since we got back, she's been focused on her shit with Enzo and work and her friends."

"You mean, like a normal person."

"Why are you always a dick when there's a game on?"

"Because I'm about to lose a mill on Manchester."

I gave a slight shake of my head. "Could have bought a nice woman for that."

"What's Aurelia's rate?"

I gave a cold chuckle. "Keep it up, and a chunk of my glass is going to be impaled in your skull, asshole."

He turned his attention to the TV for a while, and when enough silence passed, I assumed we'd moved on from the subject of Aurelia, but then he broached it again. "Are you guys exclusive?"

"Haven't had that conversation, but yes."

"So, you're just going to assume? Is she even sleeping with you?"

"Well, no." It wasn't a dealbreaker for me, but fuck, I missed it. Wherever I was, pussy wasn't far away. I never liked to jerk off because I preferred to share the passion with someone. After touching Aurelia's flames, they were the only heat I wanted to feel on my skin. When I'd asked her to dinner, getting her on her back hadn't been my agenda, but I'd be lying if I said it wasn't on my mind . . . *a lot*. She told me she needed time to move on from her last relationship, that it could be months, so I was free to do whatever I wanted in the interim.

But she was all I wanted.

Rocco gave a quiet chuckle but kept his eyes on the TV.

"What?"

"You aren't gonna want to hear it."

"No, but say it anyway."

"I just think it's fucking hilarious that the one woman you want is the one you can't have."

Chapter 17

Aurelia

I finally got the keys to my new place.

What a fucking relief, because I needed to get out of Cindy's apartment. I'd gone from having a three-bedroom apartment with two and a half bathrooms to the two of us sharing a tiny bathroom. It was even more challenging when her boyfriend was around, and he stared at me *way* too much.

I paid for a taxi to get my suitcases to the new apartment. I would retrieve my motorbike some other time. I paid for a furnished spot because I didn't have a single piece of furniture to my name. Technically, Enzo and I had split the cost of everything at our old place, but I wanted him out of my life so much that I didn't even want to bother with that conversation. He could keep it all. Fuck her on every piece of it, for all I cared.

I texted Constantine my new address, and the second I saw his name at the top of the message box, I felt a thrill of excitement and hesitation. Excitement because he made me feel alive when I thought I'd never feel that way again. And hesitation because . . . well, he was the most dangerous man in the world I could have in my life. Just got the keys to my place. Excited to finally have my own space . . . and not share a bathroom. I wasn't sure when to expect a response because I didn't have a clue what his hours were. He said he worked all the time, but he had to sleep, right?

But the dots popped up instantly. Congrats, sweetheart. Now you can walk around in nothing but those cute little thongs you wear.

That same rush I felt anytime I interacted with him was immediate. The same fire-breathing dragons I'd felt when I'd seen him across the bar hit me right in the feels. Outside of our conversations, I felt like a walking zombie, but the second he was there, I felt good again. I hadn't talked to him in almost a week. I'd focused on editing all of my photos from the shoots I'd done last week. Now, I had to hustle a little harder than before because I needed to cover rent by myself, not to mention all the other expenses that came from just being alive. Did you go through my stuff?

No comment.

I knew I shouldn't have entrusted you with my belongings.

Yep, that's on you.

And just like that, I missed him like mad. Missed him like a best friend. Missed him like . . . something a lot hotter than a best friend.

I can come by in 15.

Okay, I'll be here.

See you soon, sweetheart.

When he knocked on the door half an hour later, he'd already placed all my belongings into the hallway, carrying them up from the Range Rover entirely on his own. He hadn't worked up a sweat either, as if moving my entire life had been a warm-up.

"Wow, that was fast."

He looked at me across the threshold, taking a pause to take in my appearance, wearing a black T-shirt that hugged his thick arms, the shade bringing out the color of his tattoos, ink that I'd never really looked at because I'd been so distracted by everything else.

The heat immediately burned between us, a wildfire that started with a single blade of grass before it engulfed an entire clearing. I could feel him pull me in with just his stare, like his soul was so intense it had its own magnetism.

He crossed the threshold and came toward me, eyes locked on mine the way they'd been across the patio at his family's restaurant. The hunter had found its prey, and there was no escape.

His arm circled my lower back, and he gently tugged me into him, my soft stomach feeling his rock-hard core. I was barefoot, so he was over half a foot taller than me, his head dipping and his neck bending as he moved in to kiss me.

There was a moment when I could have pulled away, but I was swept up in the way he looked at me, in a way no other man had ever done before. Even on my best day with Enzo, he'd never had this kind of obsessed intensity.

Constantine kissed me, slow and purposeful, a gentle collision of soft lips and easy breaths. He slid his free hand into my hair, and he cradled my head as he continued to kiss me, kiss me like I had a place in his heart, not just his bed. The arm that hugged my back lowered, and he moved his big hand over my ass and squeezed a cheek through my jeans.

I loved it when he grabbed my ass like that. Like I was a piece of meat. Like I was *his* piece of meat.

He pulled away, his strong hands leaving my body and taking all the heat he brought with him. He stepped into the hallway and then wordlessly started to pick up boxes and bring them inside, placing them in the corner of the living room where there was space against the wall.

I walked into the hallway to help.

"I got it, sweetheart."

"I want to help. You don't have to do all this—"

"You're my woman. I *want* to do this."

He called me that again. *His woman.* I'd told him several times I needed time to gain perspective and closure on myself as well as my failed relationship, but I didn't have the courage to tell him to stop. Because what if he never called me that again?

It was a hard line to walk. I didn't want anything serious right now, but I didn't want to lose him either. And I was utterly terrified by the information he'd shared—that he was basically the private security for the entire country.

"If you want to help, then get undressed and wait for me in bed."

Bumps formed on my arms when I heard his order, the way he just told me what to do. I hated it and loved it.

When I didn't move, he stopped his work and stared at me. "You heard what I said."

His footsteps grew louder as he came down the hallway, and my heartbeat thumped stronger with every step he took. When he rounded the corner, he was already in the process of taking off his shirt. He ripped it off and tossed it aside, his chiseled hardness on display, the different cuts of muscle, the beautiful ink on his tanned skin.

He approached the bed as he worked his jeans in a hurry, his eyes staring right at the little black G-string thong I wore. He clenched his jaw and released an anxious breath as he got out of his boots and dropped his bottoms in one quick swoop. His fat dick was plump with blood. His knees hit the bed, and then he was on me, tugging off my thong and slipping two fingers inside me without giving me a chance to prepare for it. He thrust into me hard with those big fingers before he pulled out and coated my slickness all over the head of his dick. And there was so much of it, like my body turned into a honey factory the second he walked in the door.

He tugged on my hips, then hooked his arms behind my knees to force my hips back and my legs open. The head of his dick found my entrance like it had a mind of its own, and it pushed past the tightness of my entrance before it sank inside.

I moaned when I felt him invade me with his girth, fill me with more cock than he'd given me before, even though that literally wasn't possible. The last time we'd been together had been in Taormina, and the harshness of my cold reality had made me lose all my desire. But now it was back, seeing his hard muscles flex every time he thrust, seeing the way he stared me down like I was his, feeling the way he kissed me in the doorway.

He brought himself to a stop, closing his eyes and releasing the deepest and sexiest moan he'd ever uttered. It was the first time I'd watched him edge himself, stop himself from filling me with all the come he wanted to give. "Jesus fucking Christ." He adjusted himself, bringing his body a little closer to mine, making me draw a deep breath because it was just a little too much dick.

Then he fucked me hard, right into the bed, grunting and moaning like he was buried deep in velvet heaven. He'd never been a verbal lover in the past, but the sound of his pleasure escaped his lips every few seconds as if he simply couldn't control it.

Witnessing and feeling how much he wanted me alone was enough to make me come. I palmed his chest as he kept my legs pinned back as far as my body could go, and the climax I released was like spewing lava from Mount Etna. "Yes . . ." When I felt the tears prick my eyes, I was swept away in the waters of the Ionian Sea, brought back to blue coves and beautifully colored tile.

He could only hold off long enough for me to start my climax. He started to thrust harder, releasing a loud, monstrous moan before he started to fill me, dumping a mound of desire deep inside me, as far in as I could handle him.

"Fuck, sweetheart." He dipped his head and kissed me, kissed me the way he had in the doorway, a slow embrace packed with sheathed passion, his dick still hard inside me like that single shot from his cannon wasn't enough to empty the barrel.

I cupped his cheek as I dug my fingers into his hair. "I missed you." Our mouths worked together in perfect sync, falling right back into our old ways, our bodies knowing the rhythm of music only we could hear. "I fucking missed you."

~

We lay in bed together until the light started to fade from the windows, the sunshine giving way to a dull blue. I'd only been in the apartment for a couple hours, but now it felt like home once it'd been christened by Constantine.

He didn't say much, just looked at me, his fingers trailing over my hip and down my thigh, lightly feeling the curves of my body as if he'd forgotten the details in the two weeks we'd been emotionally apart.

I hadn't forgotten how unbelievably good looking he was, but it'd been a while since I'd seen him in the flesh, and damn, he was perfect. His arms were thick as trees, his stomach was firm as a wall, and the ink on his flesh was both a warning and a depiction of artwork.

My hand moved up the hills and mountains of muscle on his arm as I studied the details of his tattoos, a sword that was used by gladiators, words written in Latin I didn't understand, and when my eyes moved to his chest, I saw the outline of Sicily . . . right over his heart. "That's cute." I traced the outline of the island like I could feel the mountains and the sea beneath my fingertips. "It must have taken a long time for you to do all of this."

"I started when I was young, to my mother's horror." A little smirk moved over his lips. "It's a miracle she's still alive, raising two boys identical in every way you can imagine."

"Well, your sister seems nice."

"Because she's an angel," he said. "Did well in school. Helped out at home. All about the family."

She'd been nice enough to me, but I could tell she preferred Isabella. She wanted only her as her sister-in-law, not anyone else. Now that I knew they'd hooked up some time recently, I understood why his sister still hoped they'd find their way back to each other. And that was probably why his mother didn't show preference, because she had no idea.

If she did know, would that have changed anything?

His hand left my hip and moved to my flat stomach, cupping it like a husband touched his pregnant wife's belly. "Hungry?"

"Why? Can you feel it rumble?"

He smirked. "A little." His hand continued to rub over my skin, and while I should feel self-conscious with him touching me like that, it made me feel somewhat petite. "Want to go out?"

"I dunno. Kinda tired." Now that I was in this warm bed with this gorgeous man, I didn't want to leave.

"What are you in the mood for?"

"Anything."

He left the bed to fish his phone out of his pocket, his rock-hard, tight ass on display.

I wanted to bite a chunk out of it.

He came back to bed with the phone and fired off a quick message before he set the device on the nightstand. "Be here in about an hour."

"What?"

"Dinner."

"You ordered from one of those food delivery apps?"

"No. Told my assistant to do it."

"You have an assistant?" I asked in slight surprise.

"Yes."

"Like . . . a female assistant?" He seemed so self-sufficient that he wouldn't need an assistant. But I forgot he had a demanding job, so he probably did have help. Help with his home, groceries, laundry, all kinds of stuff.

Amusement moved into his gaze. "You need time to heal, and now you're jealous?"

"I'm not jealous. Just curious."

"You're in luck, because I don't employ women."

"You don't? Seems a little sexist."

"Maybe. But my intentions are good."

"How so?" I asked.

"It's a dangerous business. I wouldn't want anything bad to happen to them. I like women a hell of a lot more than men, so . . ."

"Because you can't help yourself?"

He looked like he might smile, but that smirk never came to the surface. "Because they're better in every way. Morally. Emotionally. Physically. My father was a good man, and I loved him dearly. He taught me how to punch, but my mother taught me how to fight. He taught me how to fish, but my mother taught me how to cook. Whenever he'd catch a cold, he'd be sick in bed for days, but when my mother had the flu, she'd still get us ready in the morning, cook breakfast, and take us to school. My mother carried and birthed three children while running the house and taking care of everyone else. I'm the man I am today because my mother raised me that way."

And just like that, he pulled me in deeper. He trapped me in his magnetism like a moth to a flame.

"Emperor Augustus had a daughter. Her name was Julia. She had six children, and my line comes from one of those six." He propped himself up on his arm, looking down at me slightly. "But when his reign ended, he chose to adopt his nephews and make one of them the next emperor." He gave a slight shake of his head as if he was personally offended by something that had happened two thousand years ago. "Took away her birthright simply because she was a woman rather than a man. It's fucking bullshit, because this world would be a much better place if more women were in charge. The world we inherited would be better. Fewer lives would be lost because fewer wars would have been fought. Because women think before they punch. They can fight an entire battle and eviscerate you with just words, while most men can barely put a few words together and form a sentence." He looked away like he was reflecting on a memory. "My job is to protect women, so no, I don't employ them. But if I ever have a daughter and she ever wanted a job, it'd be hers."

"You wouldn't worry about her?"

"Of course I would. Every moment of every fucking day. But any daughter of mine would be fucking tough, and she could handle herself."

~

We sat at the round dining table together, me wearing his black T-shirt while he wore only his boxers. Thankfully, the apartment came with plates, eating utensils, and drinking glasses, so we were able to take everything out of the containers and eat a meal like I'd cooked it from scratch.

He'd ordered a steak with a side salad, and he'd ordered me cacio e pepe with a side salad. The perfect meal to hit the spot. We ate together in comfortable silence. His elbows were on the table, and he ate like he'd skipped breakfast and lunch.

"How was your week?" I asked.

"Same. Busy."

"What do you do when you aren't working?"

"Work out. Eat. Sleep. That's about it."

"You don't get burned out?"

"No," he said before he took a bite of his steak and chewed it. "It's not the kind of job that comes with burnout."

"But you must be tired."

He laughed uproariously. "Oh, I didn't say I wasn't tired. I'm always fucking tired."

"What have you been working on?"

He finished his bite before he sank back into the wooden armchair. "You really want to know?"

"Yes."

"Because every time I talk about it, you pull away—and I fucking hate that."

I pulled away because I was scared of what I was getting myself into. Scared what this relationship might cost me—an arm or a leg, or maybe my life. "Well, I can't keep my head buried in the sand."

He set his plate aside, only the juice from the meat left behind. I'd found a bottle of wine in the cabinet and we shared that, but it was practically vinegar compared to the stuff he usually ordered. But he was nice enough not to complain. "President Barsetti has received intel from MI6 that a terrorist attack is on the horizon. But that's all we know. No further details. We've forged an agreement with the European countries to make sure arms aren't being sold to enemies of Western civilization, but I fear some are slipping through the cracks. I usually confer with the First Emperor of the Fifth Republic on this matter, but that power recently changed hands. I'm waiting for the dust to settle. I fear a violation may be happening there. I'll know more soon. Within our borders, we've had issues with black market dealings. Young people have been disappearing in pockets throughout Italy, mainly Rome, and we know someone is harvesting their organs for a secret transplant list. I caught on to their scheme and tracked them down, but the head of the operation was killed by his own men, and they moved their operations. Now, I have to start over. But make no mistake, I will find them and kill them all."

He was a different man when he spoke about these things. No hint of a smile or bemusement. No jokes. His tone dropped, and a lethal stare burned in his eyes. Even his composure and body language changed, his muscles stiff and flexed, his jawline tight.

"We also implemented a new hotline, for lack of a better description. Do you know what the number one cause of death is for women under thirty-five?"

Frozen by his tone, I didn't speak.

"Murder. They're fucking murdered by their partners. If women ask for help at the wrong time and it comes back to them, they're murdered.

If their abuser goes to jail, he gets out eighteen months later and kills her. There's never been a good solution to it, because even if a woman is lucky enough to get away from him, he just finds another woman . . . and does the same to her."

"Then what is the hotline?"

"It's a service we started about six months ago. You call the number and hit one if it's an emergency. As in, she's gonna die in the next couple minutes if help doesn't get there. That location is broadcast to the entire force, and whoever is closest to that location heads over there. Because the police take forever and will just take him to jail, so the cycle continues. We kill him and make him disappear."

I was terrified and also deeply impressed.

"They hit two if it's not an emergency. As in, they're in an abusive relationship and need help getting out of it. We interview them and review their case, just to make sure their account is true before we ruin someone's life. And depending on the severity of the situation, we either kill him or we implement our own rehabilitation service."

"What's the rehabilitation service?"

He stared me down before he answered. "We treat them exactly the way they treated their victim. Stalk them. Blow up their phone with threatening messages. Show up at their apartment and beat the shit out of them whenever we feel like it. We keep an eye on the victim, and if he goes within a mile of her, we break his nose and his collarbone. And so far, it's worked pretty damn well. Once their rehabilitation ends, they've learned their lesson. In jail, they just sit there and fester in their rage. But in our rehabilitation program, they actually learn." He grabbed his glass and took a drink before he crossed his arms over his chest. "That's just this week."

I had no words for what I'd just heard. Speechless yet again, like all the other times. "I had no idea."

"There's a lot of other stuff happening too. Monitoring the dealers, making sure their product is meeting standards for consumption. Then there's the truce . . . or war . . . with the Skull King in Florence."

War? Skull King?

"Never ends."

"I'm surprised you have any time for me," I said with a slight chuckle, trying to break up the tension that poured out of him like smoke. "With how busy you are."

He stared at me across the table, arms crossed over his chest in a relaxed way, his eyes focused on my face like I'd said something serious rather than humorous. "I always prioritize the things that matter. I prioritize my family and everyone who's as good as family—like you."

Chapter 18

Aurelia

I parked my motorbike outside, carried my bag that held my camera and lenses on one shoulder, and then grabbed the grocery bag. I did my best to carry it all upstairs in one go. I'd been pickpocketed before, so if I didn't get everything, then it might not be there when I came back downstairs.

I made it into my apartment and set everything on the counter as my phone vibrated with a text message.

I'll pick you up for dinner at seven. It was Constantine.

We had no plans tonight, so I wasn't entirely sure that was intended for me. Maybe he meant to send that to someone else? I texted him back. Think you sent that to the wrong person.

I didn't, sweetheart.

We didn't have plans, so that meant he'd just decided this on his own. How do you know I don't have plans?

Do you have plans?

Well . . . no.

Then dinner it is.

I was a bit annoyed that he just told me what was happening, but I also kinda liked it. I liked the fact that I didn't have to think or wonder when I'd see him again. And if he did reach out, we didn't have to play that long game of deciding what to do or where to go. He picked the time, the place, and he picked me.

Truthfully, I had so many edits to get through tonight, and I should be a responsible adult and work on that.

But he was sooooo hot. Like gotta-jump-his-bones-at-the-sight-of-him hot. So, I put my groceries in the fridge and sat down to work to get as much as possible done now, before seven came around.

He picked me up in a collared shirt with his sleeves pushed to the elbows. He wore black jeans and boots, and his head nearly touched the top of the doorframe. His shoulders almost touched both of the walls too. His eyes dropped down at the sight of me as he obviously checked me out—from head to toe. "Hey, sweetheart." He hooked his hand around the small of my back and pulled me close to kiss me.

To kiss me so good that I didn't even want dinner. I just wanted this man spread on a cracker.

He moved his hand underneath my dress and squeezed my ass like routine before he took me by the hand. He walked with me down the stairs, and when we approached the SUV outside, he opened the back door for me and seated me inside before he joined me on the other side.

His hand went to my thigh, and the drive was spent in silence. The two guys in the front didn't say a word. They didn't even have the radio on, just dead silence from three enormous men all carrying guns.

I'd never been around guns, so seeing one sticking out of the driver's side made my heart race a little faster. When I looked in the rearview mirror, I could see the shotguns propped up in the row behind me like this was a SWAT vehicle.

Constantine's huge hand took up most of my thigh, so when he turned to look at me, I assumed it was because he could feel my quickened pulse. His eyes roamed over my face, checking for the signs of distress I tried so hard to hide. "Pull over. We'll walk the rest of the way."

I couldn't hide my surprise.

The guys didn't say a word, just pulled over like he asked.

Constantine helped me out of the car and took my hand, and we walked together down the sidewalk before we crossed the street and headed down a small side road.

I was in my heels, so I wouldn't be able to make it far, but it was still better than being in a fully armored vehicle like someone was about to launch a nuke at us.

"Let me know if your heels bother you. I'll carry you."

"I'm okay."

"It's not much farther." He didn't give me a hard time about the quiet scene I'd made in the car. He walked slowly to match my pace, every one of his steps two and a half of mine.

A couple minutes later, we made it to Il Gabriello, a restaurant that was constructed underneath the street. After a steep walk down the stairs into the cavern, we were taken to a table right next to the curved rock that reached overhead. Constantine had to be mindful of the walls because he was not built to be underground.

The second we took a seat, he ordered a bottle of wine and still water for the table. He didn't even look at the menu, like he already knew exactly what he wanted because he'd been there before.

I was still flustered by the ride here. "I'm sorry about—"

"Don't be sorry. It's fine."

I knew he wasn't just saying that to dismiss the conversation, because he'd always been truthful with me. "I don't know why it makes me uncomfortable."

"Because you aren't used to it," he said. "I won't put you in that situation again."

I didn't want to ruin the night before it even started, but he seemed to be okay with it. "You already know what you're getting?"

"The steak with pepper sauce."

"You really love your steak, don't you?" I teased.

"This place makes the best steak I've ever had."

"Ever?"

He nodded once. *"Ever."*

"Wow, you're really selling it."

"Go for it. I would love to buy a woman a steak."

"You never have?"

"Maybe my mom one time . . ."

The waiter came back with the wine and the water, and Constantine ordered for the two of us, getting each of us a steak and a side of greens and potatoes for us to share. He always took the lead so I didn't have to say a word.

When the waiter was gone, he turned his complete focus back to me, staring at me intently like we'd never met before. Like he needed to get to know me all over, commit my features to memory, study me like he didn't know my body underneath the black dress.

"Your mom must really hate that you live here, especially after your brother passed away."

He didn't flinch at the mention of his twin. "She was really upset about it, initially. She's gotten better about it. Or at least she's gotten better about keeping it to herself."

"So, she does know . . . what you do?"

He nodded. "The main points, yes. But she's asked me to spare her whatever details I can—otherwise, she'll never sleep again."

"She must be proud of you, though. I would be if you were my son."

His body remained rigid, but there was a change in his gaze, a hardening of his stare. A hint of a smile crept on to his lips, just a ghost of it, and then it was gone. "I'm glad you feel that way. That's what I've always wanted in a woman."

I realized I'd shoved my foot into my mouth, made a step toward him that I hadn't meant to make, a commitment that still seemed out of reach.

"A woman who will always stand by me. A woman who believes in what I do just as much as I do."

I wasn't sure if that was me, judging by the way my heart pounded. "You said you would never hire a woman because it's not a safe environment. So, how does that work with a partner?"

"Because everyone in the Roman Republic is there to serve the Republic—including me. We understand and accept the risks. But my partner is not under the same obligation. She's not a part of it whatsoever."

"But based on association—"

"She is my Roman Republic. My Roman Empire. And my first job, before everything else, is to serve and protect her." We hadn't even gotten our food yet, and we were already in the thick of it. "I would let Rome burn to the ground before I let anything happen to you, Aurelia."

Everything was perfect between us, but the more we discussed it, the more I was uncertain what I wanted. Constantine was the ideal man, and I should be the one begging him to be with me. But I wasn't stupid. I knew a life with Constantine would be different from one with someone else. Full of guns and danger and instability. And while my heart went wild for this man, my mind continued to question it all.

When he spoke again, his tone was quiet. "Tell me what you're thinking."

"That I'm crazy about you but not crazy about this." I blurted it out because I couldn't contain it in my chest for another second. I should be more calculated in my responses, but all of this made me so uneasy that I couldn't.

"I promise nothing would happen to you."

"You can't make a promise like that, Constantine."

He suddenly looked provoked, as if I'd said the wrong thing. "Yes, I can."

"You said you don't like to lie, and if that's true, then there's no way you can say that—"

"Yes, I fucking can."

One step forward. Twenty-five steps back. Over and over. Our relationship worked in Taormina because it was just a summer fling. Maybe we needed to go back to that. Accept that was the only thing that would work between us.

"A lot of people don't like me. A lot of people want me dead. Me—not you."

"And I'm the perfect target to hit you where it hurts."

"You know how pirates have a code among thieves? We also have a code among criminals. We don't fuck with people's families. Period."

"And you trust that every asshole out there is going to stick to the code?" I asked incredulously.

"I believe most would, yes. But I would never let you be in danger, regardless. Would never let you be accessible to the wrong people. If you were mine the way I want you to be, you'd be guarded better than the fucking pope."

I didn't want to be guarded like the fucking pope. "Has anything ever happened to your family? Your brother . . . is that why he died—"

"*No.* And I don't want to talk about him."

"I'm not asking you to." I had no idea what could make him so distant like this. He was never evasive or closed off. An open book. So whatever happened with his brother, whose name I didn't even know, was serious. "But has anyone ever come for your family—"

"No. My dad died because he drank too much wine and ate too many cold cuts."

"How long have you been doing this?"

He started to calm down as we steered away from the topic of his brother. "I've been the emperor for five years. The four years before that were spent with Cosa Nostra and their partners in Florence."

So in the five years he'd been doing this, no one had ever tried to hurt his family. "You don't have anyone there to protect them in case?"

"Cosa Nostra look after them on my behalf."

"So that's where you were that night you left." I'd stayed in the room while he'd left late in the night, not coming back until an hour before morning.

"Yes."

"Do you pay them?"

"No. We built a close relationship through my years of service. And I've also pardoned them from the jurisdiction of the Roman Republic—and as a thank-you, they protect my family."

"You pardon them?"

"All the criminals throughout the country pay tariffs to the Roman Republic. That's the price they pay for the operations to continue without impediment by the police. Sicily was part of the great unification of Italy in 1860, but because they're technically an island, I was able to get them an exemption."

"So, do they traffic and—"

"No. They adhere to my laws. They just don't pay tariffs."

His job really was complicated and complex and . . . just a lot.

"I would do the same for you. And if it came down to it, I would fall on the sword, jump on the grenade, take the bullet, whatever it fucking took to keep you safe. My life is dedicated to my country and the people in it, but they all become second to my family—and you."

This had become heavy so quick. "Let's talk about something else."

"No. This problem isn't going away."

"Well, I'm not sure if this is a problem I want to have."

He winced like my words really hurt him.

"I'm not sure if I *want* to be guarded every hour of every day. I'm not sure if I *want* every car I get into to be filled with guns. I'm not sure if I *want* to have a husband who could literally die any day. To have children with a man who could leave them without a father. It's just . . ."

"That's the price you pay to be with me—and I promise I'm worth it."

A wave of guilt washed over me. "I know you are."

"You don't need to decide right now. Let's just see where it goes."

"The longer I wait, the harder it's going to be."

"Sweetheart," he said calmly. "Let's just put a pin in it for now."

The calmer he was, the more panicked I felt. He didn't understand the stakes, didn't understand the depth of implication. "I'm already falling in love with you, and if I let this go on much longer, I'm never going to be able to leave." I said it all in a single breath, needing to get it out but also regretting the fact that I let it out at all. "So, I do need to decide . . . while I still can." My eyes shifted away the second I finished speaking, not wanting to see his reaction to what I'd just vomited across the table.

The waiter crossed the room at that moment and placed our dishes in front of us. Hopefully, that would be enough of an interference that we could both forget what I'd just said. I watched him leave out of the corner of my eye. I glanced down at my steak before I found the courage to look at Constantine.

He just sat there . . . and fucking smiled. Smiled wider than I'd ever seen him. Like this wasn't the most difficult conversation I'd ever had in my life. Like my pain was his pleasure. Anyone who watched us across the room would assume I'd said something to make him laugh, judging by that goddamn smirk.

Then as if nothing had happened, he grabbed his fork and knife and cut into his steak. "Good, I'm starving."

Chapter 19

Constantine

"Would you stop doing that?"

"What?" I asked, sitting in the seat beside Rocco and looking out the window.

"You've been grinning like a goddamn dog for the last fifteen minutes."

"I like dogs, so no offense there."

"You look ridiculous."

I turned to look at Rocco in the back seat next to me. "I've been told I have a nice smile."

"By your mother, maybe."

I smirked, then punched him in the arm. "That was a good one."

"Seriously, tell me why."

"I locked it down with Aurelia." Now, I grinned wider, remembering what she'd said to me over and over . . . and over and over. It was definitely a favorite memory of mine.

"That was a one-eighty."

"Well, I can be very convincing."

"Am I gonna meet her?"

"Not sure you want to. Because I'll look like this the entire time." I leaned toward him, smirking widely once again.

Now he was the one to punch me. "Come on, let's set something up. I gotta make sure I humiliate you in front of her."

"I don't think you can. I've got nothing to hide."

"What about that time we had to share a shower at the gym because all the others were broken?"

I laughed at the memory. "Honestly, she'd probably think it's hot."

"Jesus . . ."

"What?" I asked with a smirk. "We're both good-looking guys. Could have recorded that and put it on OnlyFans."

"I'm gonna punch you for real this time."

"Now it looks like I'll be the one embarrassing you at this dinner."

He made good on his word and really did punch me hard in the arm.

I grimaced as I leaned forward. "Still worth it."

The car came to a stop in front of the pavilion.

"Need a minute?"

"Nope." I shook my arm to get the cramps out of the muscle. "Let's do this."

The iron gates opened, and we were let onto my private property, a three-story villa that wasn't connected to any other building—a very rare find in Rome. The security guys were outside, some stationed on the roof incognito, and I had a few positioned in certain corners of the house.

The only place they weren't was in my wing on the top floor. The only two allowed there were my butler, Elio, and Medusa. It was a long walk to the very top, over the thick carpets, passing the Egyptian statues that belonged to my family by birthright, and past the sculptures and other collectibles that made my home a personal museum—and reminded anyone who walked in there exactly who the fuck I was.

I had an elevator, but I always took the stairs to keep my ass tight. I was almost there when my mom decided to call me.

I pulled the phone out of my pocket and answered. "Hey, Ma."

"My boy," she said with so much pride that only a mother could produce. "How are you?"

"Good. Just had a meeting with—"

"How's Aurelia? She still around?"

"Ah, that's the reason you're calling," I said with a chuckle. "You don't give a damn about me."

"Of course I do, son. I haven't heard from you in two weeks, so I wanted to check in."

"Check in on my personal life, you mean."

She became a lot sterner, the authoritative disciplinarian, because my dad hadn't had the balls to fill the role. "Answer the question, Con."

"All right, all right," I said. "I think you're going to be seeing her around. That's all I'll say."

She was quiet over the line, probably hiding her tears or muffling the phone as she jumped up and down with Aunt Chiara, who pretended not to be there. I was pretty sure that's exactly what happened, because when she spoke again, she was so deadly calm. "Oh, that's great."

"*Oh, that's great*?" I teased. "All you've got to say?"

"I just don't want to pry."

"This whole phone call is a pry," I said with a laugh. "But you know what, it's fine."

Her voice suddenly changed, and then it was Aunt Chiara on the phone. "Con, we love her. We love her hair—"

My mom was in the background now. "Give me back the phone. That's my son."

"She's so beautiful, Con. Like a mermaid."

I chuckled. "If you put the phone on speaker, I can talk to you both, you know."

"Speaker?" my mom asked in the background. "Ugh, I can't remember."

"Right on the screen." She refused to keep up with technology. She'd had a rotary phone for the longest time before I forced her to get a cell phone. No matter how many times I taught her how to use it, it always baffled her. "Just hit the button."

"Let me try it," Aunt Chiara said.

They fought back and forth.

I stopped outside my bedroom door.

"Give it back—"

Click.

"Well, so much for that." I put the phone in my pocket, then opened the enormous golden door that led to my bedroom, a door that cost fifty thousand euros, completely bulletproof and impenetrable—and stunning.

My wing of the house had a private bedchamber with its own dining room and living room, basically a luxury apartment within the villa. And the second I opened the door, I heard Medusa jump off the bed and sprint across the room toward me with the speed of a jet.

I took a knee right when she crashed into me. I let her knock me over as I laughed. "That's my girl." She licked my face as she moved over me, her paws on my chest, looking down at me with those brown eyes that always made me a sucker. I gave her a good rubdown behind the ears before I pulled her into a bear hug. She let me hold her for a second before she was anxious to break free.

I got back to my feet, grabbed a tennis ball from the floor, and chucked it across the large room, watching her sprint after it. She was quick like a racehorse, grabbing the ball and running straight back to me like she was in training.

I played with her for a while because I hadn't seen her all day. My butler took care of her walks and made all of her meals from scratch, so she was well taken care of. She hung out with the security guys during the day so she would feel like part of the team. But like everyone else at this time of day, she got a little tired and retreated to my room for some peace and quiet.

I sat on the couch, and she immediately jumped with me, cuddling into my side and resting her chin on my thigh, her eyes glancing up at me every few seconds. I gave her a pat before I rested my arm on her back.

My phone vibrated in my pocket, and I pulled it out, hoping it wasn't Rocco or more bullshit for me to handle for the day. I hoped it was one person, the person I always hoped to hear from, the one who made me smile in a way I hadn't since I was a boy.

Hey. It was her.

The woman who was falling in love with me.

Looks like I wasn't the only sucker in this relationship. Hey, sweetheart.

Can I take you to dinner?

Damn, she really was into me. No. But I'm happy to take you out.

So you're one of THOSE guys . . .

Yep. I'll be there in an hour. And let's stay at my place tonight.

Bit presumptuous.

Am I wrong, sweetheart?

The three dots were visible for a while before she finally responded. No comment.

Good. I want you to meet someone.

Who?

The woman I've been sleeping with for the last four years.

Sorry, what???

I chuckled to myself before I took a picture of Medusa as she lay across my thigh.

Oh my god, you have a dog??? Oh, she's so cute. I already love her.

Well, not gonna lie, you're going to be a tough sell for her.

Yeah, I can totally see why.

I picked her up in my Range Rover, which was stocked with guns, just out of sight so she didn't have a clue. If you lifted the floor panel in the back, five loaded shotguns were on racks beneath. A handgun was stashed both underneath my seat and hers. And if she checked the glove compartment, she wouldn't like what she found.

She wore this little dark-blue dress with a ton of boobage . . . *and damn.*

I parked my car wherever the fuck I wanted, then I took her hand, and we walked inside together. I didn't have reservations, but that wasn't an issue when I was friends with the owner. They whipped up a table for me, and the two of us were seated where there'd been open space just a moment ago.

"So what's her name?"

"Medusa."

"Whoa, that's quite the name. Is she a sea monster?"

"She's definitely a monster," I said with a grin. "She's a police dog. Met her at work one day, but you know, it was love at first sight, so I took her home."

"Aww, that's cute. How old is she?"

"Four."

"Good, she's still young. Why didn't you mention her before?"

I shrugged. "Didn't come up."

"I can't believe you went a week without her in Taormina."

"I mean, I missed her, but she's well taken care of. She still has a family at the house when I'm not around. She sleeps with my butler, Elio, when I'm out. Everyone loves her. She's a great estate dog."

She didn't react to the words *butler* or *estate*, as if she'd already assumed I was wealthy. But she probably didn't understand exactly *how* wealthy I was. "How have you been?" It'd been a couple days since we talked. I gave her some space after the whole *I'm falling in love with you* thing.

"Kinda overbooked myself with shoots," she said with a quiet chuckle. "So I'm working a lot, which is good."

"Why is that good?"

"I feel better when I'm busy. My mind doesn't linger in places it shouldn't."

Was she referring to Enzo? Did that loser really still have space in her beautiful head? I almost asked, but I didn't want to ruin the night by being combative.

"I hope one day I'll have a studio and an assistant . . . and work will be less chaotic."

"Why do you want a studio?"

"It's a lot easier for the fine art photography I want to do. I can manipulate the shot and the lighting and all that. I can bring a model in and control the environment. And for all the shoots I do to pay the bills, I can book them back-to-back in my studio to make my life more efficient. Most of the photography I do now is on location, which is great, but it eats up a lot of time hustling from one place to the next. And then there's traffic . . ."

I shouldn't be so enthralled by her work, but there was something about it that interested me. Or maybe it was just her enthusiasm for the job. She had a lot of passion for it. I could see it in her face every time she talked about it.

She pulled out her phone, then looked through her photos. “Here are some I took in Taormina. I took most of them before we met.” She slid through the images, a close-up of the sign outside of Bam Bar, a few photos that were taken in the caverns of Isola Bella. And then there was one of me standing on the rock from the day we went to the beach. With my arms by my sides, I stared down at one of my buddies in the water, grinning from ear to ear at something someone said. “I love this one.”

“Can you send it to me?”

“Of course.” She took the phone back and texted it.

“I don’t know shit about photography, but I know you’re good at it.”

“Yeah?” she asked.

“I feel something when I look at it, so yes.”

Her eyes found mine again, and I swore they melted like butter over warm bread. I’d told her she was beautiful, told her she was tough, but she never reacted this way when I did. Her photography was her heart.

“Have you ever done boudoir photos? You know, get nearly naked and take a bunch of sexy pictures.”

She smirked at the suggestion. “Not really my thing. And even if it was, I would never show you their photos without consent.”

“No. Have *you* done a boudoir session? As in, been the subject.”

Realization came into her eyes, followed by a blush to her cheeks. “No . . .”

“Something you’d consider?”

She shook her head slightly, like she couldn’t believe I asked. “I prefer to be behind the lens rather than in front of it.”

“What a shame. Might learn something.”

“About photography?”

“Why not?”

“Well, Maximillian Cattaneo has dominated that space. It pays his bills so he can pursue his art. He’s really, *really* good.”

"Better than you?" I asked incredulously.

"Uh, yeah," she said with a laugh. "He's won the Elite Photographer Award four out of the last five years. He's always doing something different, sometimes capturing a shot in the studio and other times spontaneously in the field. My favorite photograph of his is the one he captured of Princess McKenzie. She was being surrounded by photographers while she signed an autograph, and he just perfectly captured how overwhelmed she was. I have no idea how he got the shot. Someone must have tipped him off where she'd be so he could be in the perfect spot."

I had no idea the world of photography could be so competitive. "Is he gay?"

"Excuse me?" Her eyebrows rose.

"Are these women getting naked for a straight man or a gay one?"

"Oh . . . yes."

"Good to know," I said with a nod.

She smirked when she caught on to my thinking. "Not gonna happen. And even if I did consider it, he is very particular about who he photographs. I wouldn't make the cut."

I released a chuckle I couldn't suppress.

"I'm serious."

"Whatever you say, sweetheart."

The waiter came over and took our order, and after we made our selections, it was just the two of us again and a bottle of wine. "I talked to my mom today."

"How is she?"

"Other than being a little fake, she's good."

"Fake?"

"She called to catch up, but all she wanted to talk about was you."

The smile that was in her eyes slowly started to fade, like I'd said the wrong thing.

"She asked if you were going to be around for a while. I said yes."

Now she looked visibly uncomfortable, eyes dropping down to her wineglass like she was having a conversation with it instead of me. "I've been thinking . . . and maybe we should just keep this casual." Her eyes remained down like she didn't want to see my reaction.

My blood turned cold, but I didn't let my face change. "What's casual?"

"You know . . ." She ran her finger around the rim of her glass. "We just hook up whenever, no strings attached."

I would be more upset about this if she hadn't already shown her hand. Now, she was trying to redraw the deck, but I wouldn't let that fly. "And what does that solve?"

Her eyes finally lifted to mine.

"No."

"No?"

"You aren't the kind of woman you wear a condom with."

"What's that mean?"

"It means I don't want to fuck other people, and you don't want me to either."

"But it could—"

"How about we just give this relationship a chance instead of finding ways to end it?" I asked. "You already said you're falling for me, so you're stuck. Don't pretend you want to take a step back when you don't. Don't pretend you're fine with me fucking other people when you aren't."

Her fingers rested under her chin, and her eyes searched the faces of other people in the restaurant. When she opened her heart to me, it was fucking beautiful. And then when she withdrew, all I felt was darkness. "When I said that, you were supposed to freak out."

The smirk that moved on to my lips was uncontrollable. "You thought that would scare me off?"

"I didn't say it *to* scare you off. But afterward, I thought it might."

"You can't scare me off, sweetheart." But any little thing I did spooked her. "Look, this is already a serious relationship, whether you like it or not. You know why? Because all we do is talk about how it's going to work. If this were just two people fucking for a couple of weeks, there would be no talking. I understand you're scared of everything my life entails, but you've forgotten just how tough you are."

I knew I struck a chord when her eyes flicked away for just a nanosecond, like my words cut her deep, reminded her of the mess she'd been in Taormina. She'd been afraid to jump off that rock, but once she felt the high, she wanted to chase it forever.

My hand tightened into a fist and moved over my chest, just the way it had on top of that rock. "Tougher than my fist. Tougher than my mother. Tougher than the Roman Empire."

She shifted her eyes away again as her fingers remained under her chin, looking like a Roman queen without even trying, her hair dark like winter soil, her eyes bright like the emeralds that should hang from her neck. "Doesn't it bother you that I just got out of a relationship?"

"No."

"Even though it's been three weeks?"

"Could have ended yesterday, wouldn't make a difference."

"When you got out of your relationship, could you picture being serious with someone this quickly?"

She asked me the tough questions. Put me on the spot. Made me consider a situation that had never crossed my mind. She was smart, really thought things through, and while that held her back sometimes, considering the gravity of her decisions was a good way to be. It made me respect her. And it made me realize what I meant to her, because she had every reason to leave, but she continued to stay.

"Now I think you understand."

I'd planned on marrying Isabella. Was about to buy a ring, about to tell my mom about it, but then it all came burning down. To jump into another relationship within a few weeks of that, even if she was in the wrong, was impossible to imagine. She'd really broken my heart. "Yeah, I get what you're saying." It took me a while to sleep with someone new. At least a couple months. I broke things off between us with no intention of ever going back, but a part of me still felt like I was in that relationship. Until one day, I wasn't. "But there's a difference between us. You said your relationship had fallen apart a long time ago and you were still holding on. Mine was great until the moment it wasn't—and then it was just done. I needed time to recover from that, while you'd been preparing for the end for months. You jumped into bed with me right away because you were ready."

"Jumped into bed . . . thanks."

"Trust me, I don't say that judgmentally. He stuffed your heart in a garbage bag when it should have been in a safe. When you were free, you were ready to be free. You were ready for me. So, no, it doesn't bother me at all. This feels right." It'd been nine long years since someone had made me look twice. Since someone made me feel anything at all. After a while, I wondered if Isabella had destroyed my ability to ever love again.

And then I met Aurelia.

"Can I ask you something?"

"Anything." There was only one subject off limits.

"You could have literally anyone you want. I mean, Jesus Christ, look at you . . ."

I didn't smile. I was too focused on the upcoming question.

"Smart, sexy, funny, easygoing . . . protective. Why me?"

"Why you?" I asked, almost not understanding the question.

"Yes. I'm not saying I'm unattractive. But I'm not, you know, bombshell-on-the-runway, front-cover-of-*Vogue* type of attractive. And I'm not successful, I don't come from a nice family, I don't come from wealth. It's just me and my camera. I put up with some asshole's bullshit for far too long and lost all self-respect. I hate myself for not just getting up and leaving. I judge myself every day for being so . . . pathetic."

I fought the urge to smile. Everything she said was ridiculous, but I reminded myself that it felt very real to her. That she actually believed all this nonsense. "Let me tell you what I thought when I first saw you, all right? *God fucking damn.* That's what I thought. I've seen and been with a lot of beautiful women, but none of them have ever captured my attention the way you have. If you wanted that fine ass on the cover of *Vogue*, we could absolutely make that happen. Why do you think I want some boudoir photos of you? I want to put them on the walls of my office. Add them to the collection. And the fact that you're on your own, standing entirely on your own merits and talent, is exactly *why* I like you. Everyone has someone to lean on, but all you've ever had is yourself. I like that—*a lot*. And in regard to what's-his-fucking-face, you would have made very different decisions if he'd had the balls to be honest with you. But he deceived you, gaslighted you, and then you didn't know what was true and what was false. You didn't know what was wrong, so you naturally assumed that you were the problem. So you stayed because you continued to search for the problem in the hope you could fix it. And the last thing I want to say is, Jesus fucking Christ, you're *way* too hard on yourself."

There was a blast of emotion in her eyes before she quickly looked away, like she didn't want me to know how deeply my words hit her.

"Would you ever say those things to a friend? To any other human being?"

Her eyes stayed elsewhere.

"It's one thing to take responsibility for your actions. Learn and grow. But you treat yourself like a punching bag, sweetheart." I pointed my finger and pressed it into the surface of the table. "Starting today, you don't do that anymore."

Her eyes lifted to mine.

"All right?" I hated seeing a man rip apart a woman. I hated seeing a woman forget that she was infinitely more powerful than he was. But for centuries, women were oppressed by misogyny and sexism and just plain bullshit.

She let the words sink in for a while before she finally gave a nod. "All right."

Now, I smiled. "Attagirl."

"I think I'm going to head home . . . if that's okay with you." She sat beside me in the passenger seat, her dress up to the very top of her thighs because she didn't adjust herself when it was just the two of us. "I want to meet Medusa. I just . . . it feels a little heavy right now."

I was a bit disappointed, but in my book, no meant no. Simple as that. "Of course, sweetheart." My hand moved to her thigh, pushing her dress up even higher, touching the silky material of her thong. She looked so sexy in the material that it got me every time, even just a glimpse.

I drove back to her apartment, left my Range Rover on the street, and walked her to her front door. I didn't want the night to end there. If she came by my place and fell in love with it and didn't want to leave, it wouldn't even bother me. "Good night, sweetheart." My hand moved to her ass under the dress and gripped it right there in the middle of the hallway. I kissed her with her back pressed to the door, feeling her hand squeezing my arm through the sleeve of my collared shirt. I could easily change her mind about the end of this night, get her to beg me to come inside, but that wasn't my style. Not just with her, but any woman.

I ended the kiss before it could burn into an inferno.

"Good night," she said, a look of longing in her gaze that she couldn't hide. It took her a moment to let me go, to fish her keys out of the tiny little purse that hung over her shoulder.

Chapter 20

Aurelia

I worked on my edits at the dining table throughout the day, working through a wedding I shot last weekend and a couple other events. It was one thing to get the shot, but it was another to make the photo as aesthetically appealing as possible. To smooth out the complexions and blemishes of the subjects. To change the tint of the photo, remove the red-eye that popped up. I didn't dramatically alter anything, but I did manipulate it quite a bit. At the end of the day, people wanted to see the best version of themselves—not the real version.

After lunch, I made another cup of coffee and continued to work. There were still lots of boxes around the apartment because I hadn't fully unpacked. Between work and Constantine, I hadn't had that much time to finish the job. And I'd much rather spend my time getting nailed by the sexiest man who ever lived than moving shit around my apartment.

A knock sounded on my door, and my first hope was that Constantine had come by for a visit. But he'd never done that before, stopped by unannounced, so I assumed it was a neighbor or maybe a delivery for something that I'd ordered.

I checked the peephole before I opened it—and spotted Enzo on the other side.

What in the actual fuck?

I opened the door and blinked a couple times, staring at a man who that now felt like a stranger. "Uh . . . what do you want?" I blurted, not thinking before speaking. I felt a little guilty for my rudeness, but it wasn't like we were friends . . . or even ended on good terms.

"You got a minute? I wanted to talk to you."

"If you can say everything in a minute, you should've just texted."

"Okay, well, maybe it'll take a couple minutes." He slid his hands into the front pockets of his jeans as he shifted his weight to one leg. The shadow on his jawline was thick, like he hadn't shaved in a while. I used to find him really attractive, but now I felt nothing. If I had a dick, nothing about him could get me hard.

"Um, okay . . ." I stepped aside and let him into the apartment.

The second the door was closed, I felt guilty. Guilty for being alone with my ex when I was seeing someone, I guess. I wasn't sure if Constantine was my boyfriend or what, but we were definitely together. "Everything okay?"

Enzo took a long time to start the conversation, scanning my apartment as his hands remained in his pockets. "Nice place."

I ignored what he said. "Everything okay?" I repeated.

"Yeah," he said with a sigh as he reached into the back of his jeans, pulling out an envelope. "Found these under the bed the other day. I knew you'd want them, so . . ." He handed them over before he returned his hands to his pockets.

I opened the envelope and found old pictures of my mom. Pictures from when she was young. One of her on a motorbike, one of her outside her secondary school. Pictures of her before I was born. There was one of my father too, the two of them together. "Thanks." I returned them to the envelope and tossed it on the dining table next to my computer. When I looked at him again, I expected him to be headed for the door already.

But he continued to stand there.

"Something else?" I asked, just wanting him out of my apartment. I wasn't sure how Constantine would react to this because I didn't know if he was a jealous guy or not, but the last thing I wanted was to risk what we had over this doofus.

"Yeah, um . . ." He rubbed the back of his head as he gave a sigh. "I just want to apologize for everything—"

"You already did, Enzo." I didn't need to hear it again. I could hear it a million times and would still feel nothing. "We've both moved on. It's fine. I'm happy. You're happy. It's all good." I'd say anything to ease his conscience if it just got him to leave.

"Are you happy?" he asked, dropping his hand to his side.

"What's that supposed to mean?"

"Are you seeing that guy who came by the apartment?"

It took me a second to realize what was happening. "Are you serious right now?" My eyebrows furrowed before I issued a laugh. "You've got a lot of balls to ask me that, especially since I asked you what was wrong, what, fifty times? And you lied each and every time. But yet, you think you deserve the 411 on my life?"

"Look, I didn't mean to upset you—"

"Yes, I'm seeing him. He didn't just move all my stuff because we're friends." Oh, we were definitely not friends.

He dropped his gaze before he gave a slow nod. "I wanted to explain what happened with Luna—"

"Why? I don't care."

"Well, I think it might have been a mistake. I mean, I don't think, I know." He looked at me, self-loathing in his gaze. "It started as a kiss at work, and then it just got carried away and—"

The front door flew open.

Constantine walked inside—a fucking menace.

His maniacal gaze was reserved for Enzo as he approached, leaving the front door wide open. He didn't say a word, but his presence was utterly terrifying. The way he carried himself, the stiffness in his shoulders, the palpable anger that radiated off his body like hot rays from the summer sun.

Enzo took a step back . . . and then another.

I was so utterly shocked by all of it that I couldn't move.

I couldn't really describe the phenomenon, but when Constantine spoke, he didn't yell . . . though his voice was loud. It carried, shook the walls, reached all of my neighbors down the hallway. *"Who the fuck do you think you are?"*

Oh Jesus.

I was tall, so every man I dated was also tall. Enzo was a little over six feet in height, but he looked tiny in front of Constantine. Not just in height, but in size and strength and masculinity. Completely dwarfed by Constantine's potent presence.

"You don't belong here, asshole. You forfeited the right to a minute of her time when you stuck your dick in someone else." He continued to move forward, crowding Enzo, moving him back until there was nowhere else for him to go.

I wasn't Constantine's target, but even I was fucking scared.

"She's mine now." He slammed his fist hard into his chest and made a loud thump—like the muscle that covered his sternum was unbreakable. "Come near my woman again, and I'll carve your eyes out of your fucking head and feed them to my dog." Then he yelled. *"You fucking understand me?"*

His voice was so loud, it made me flinch and step back, moving toward the kitchen counter.

"Yes—yes." Enzo raised both hands like he had a gun pointed at him. "Sorry . . . I'm sorry."

Constantine stepped aside so Enzo could pass. "Go."

Enzo made a step for the door but glanced at Constantine, like it was a trap.

I wasn't sure if it was a trap or not.

So Enzo moved around the kitchen table, walked past me, and went all the way around to get to the door.

Constantine turned his head and watched him the entire time, a hawk observing its prey slither through the grass. "Like a fucking table will save you, little punk-ass bitch." Then he barked, barked like a fucking dog, and Enzo took off at a run. He smacked his shoulder into the doorway and grimaced before he made his way around it and into the hallway.

The door was left wide open.

Constantine miraculously dropped his ire when he looked at me—as if he could just turn it on and off like nothing. "You all right?"

"Yeah. But I was fine before you burst in the door like that." Like a fucking guard dog.

He seemed to understand that I was upset, read it on my face or heard it in my words. "I'm not sorry."

"You acted like you were going to kill him."

"Your point?"

"You said you don't hurt innocent people."

"Did I hurt him?" he challenged, taking a step closer to me. "Why are you defending him?"

"I'm not. But when you scared the shit out of him, you also scared it out of me." I'd never witnessed Constantine act like that. He was all smiles and jokes and sexy, smoldering looks. He'd never . . . lost his mind.

"I would never hurt you."

"I know that, but you were still fucking terrifying."

"Well, I'm a terrifying guy." He remained completely unapologetic.

"I've just never seen you like that. I'm a little shaken up." I always believed him when he told me he was the Roman Emperor of the Roman Republic. But now, I really saw it, witnessed it with my own two eyes. I could imagine how lethal he was when his intention was to kill.

"It's over now," he said. "But I promise I would never come at you like that."

"I'd probably start crying if you did."

He smiled slightly. "You wouldn't. But it doesn't matter, because I don't raise my voice to women. So, what did he want?"

"Um . . ." I crossed my arms over my chest, and I looked at the envelope he'd left. "He brought some pictures I'd left at the apartment. Some of my mom's old stuff. I was glad he brought them back, because they're important to me."

"And that was it?"

I wanted to keep it from him so this conversation would end, but he said he was an honest guy, and if he would always be honest with me, then I would always be honest with him. "He apologized for everything—not that I needed to hear it."

"And what else?" His tone hardened like he knew exactly what else.

"Said he made a mistake."

His stare was stone cold.

"That's when you came in. So he didn't say anything else."

"I didn't feel bad before, but I sure as fuck don't feel bad now. A fucking peasant coming to a queen like he deserves a moment of her time." He shook his head. "Better not show his fucking face around here again."

"Are—are you jealous?"

He laughed, but it was packed with sarcasm. "Sweetheart, I don't get jealous. But I'm protective, and if some asshole who broke your heart thinks he can kick up some dust, he's fucking mistaken. I was there to pick up the pieces that he broke—so he can fuck right off."

"How did you even know he was here?" Had he just happened to stop by at the right time?

He didn't say anything for a while, like he wanted to hold on to his words a little longer before he set them free. "Because my men told me he was here."

"Your men . . . ?" It took me a second to understand the implications of his words. "You're—you're watching me."

"I'm not watching you," he said. "I'm protecting you."

"From?"

"Just because this relationship has barely begun doesn't mean it's not obvious to anyone watching me that you mean something to me. I don't take risks, so yes, I've put some of my guys on your surveillance."

"And you didn't think you should tell me this?"

"You were already freaked out enough," he said. "And to be clear, they don't report your movements to me. I don't know where you go or how you spend your days. They keep you safe—that's all."

"Is there someone to keep me safe from?"

"No. Not that I know of. But as I said before, I don't take risks."

I felt violated, and I didn't know why. "I feel like this is something you should have told me."

"If that asshole hadn't swung by, you never would have known."

"And that makes it okay?"

"Sweetheart." He didn't say it affectionately like he normally did, but sternly. "Did you see how quickly I got here? He was here for, what? Three minutes? And my men would have been here instantly if it was necessary. You're afraid to pursue this with me because of the risks, but I've proven to you I don't take risks. I protect you—*always*."

"I still feel like I had the right to know."

"All right, that was an error on my part. I'm sorry I didn't tell you." He dropped his arms to his sides. "Can we move on now?"

My heart was pounding so hard in my chest that I wasn't sure if we could just move on. "I—I don't know."

"You don't know?" he challenged.

"In the last fifteen minutes, you've threatened to carve my ex's eyes out of his head and informed me that every move I make throughout the day is being watched by men I don't know. That they could be watching me through my fucking windows, following me on my motorbike when I go to the grocery store, watching me do my photoshoots by the Trevi Fountain. Jesus, it's *a lot*. Not to mention I just witnessed you go ballistic . . ."

"Sweetheart," he said calmly. "That was nothing."

"I just . . . need some space. And I don't want to be followed anymore."

He stared me down.

"Not without my consent. And right now, I'm not giving my consent." Every moment I thought I was alone, I was under the watchful eyes of a handful of men. When I hopped on my motorbike, they were probably right behind me—and I had no idea. I was a bit embarrassed that I hadn't figured it out.

Constantine said nothing, but in silence, his anger was like a scream. "What does space mean?"

"I don't know. Just some space." I felt impaled by the bullets from his eyes. "The last fifteen minutes have been chaos. You're the perfect guy, and I can't believe that you're real. I just wish you were . . . normal." I regretted what I said the moment it came out of my mouth. I knew I fucked up the second I took a breath after I completed the sentence.

He wore a hard stare, all the cords in his neck popped like taut rope. His eyes were still and locked on my face, but there was no discernible emotion underneath, like he was sequestering his rage so I wouldn't have to see it. "Normal . . ." He tested the word in his mouth like he'd just added it to his vocabulary.

"That didn't come out right."

"I've been really patient with you. More patient than the fucking pope." He spoke calmly, but something about that sheathed tone was just as scary as when he'd yelled at Enzo a couple minutes ago. "One step forward, fifty steps back, back and forth, back and forth. But it was fine because you were worth it. But let me tell you something right now." He took a step toward me and raised his hand to point at me. "I'm proud that I'm *not* normal. I'm proud of what I do for my people and my country. I need a woman who feels the same way, and that's clearly *not* you."

Shit.

"I thought you were tougher than this. I thought you just needed time to remember who you are, what you're capable of. But I see now that you're just a coward."

Fuck.

"I want the woman who jumped off that rock. I want the woman who carried herself when she had no one else to help her to her feet. I don't know what happened to her, but I think she's gone." He stepped back, his eyes filling with disappointment. Not the kind of disappointment he showed when he didn't get what he wanted. But disappointment in me . . . as a person. "This is over." He turned toward the door to leave.

"Wait, Constantine." I went after him.

He didn't stop. Ignored me.

"Please, wait. I'm sorry."

He moved into the hallway and walked off like he didn't hear me. Like I didn't exist.

I grabbed onto his arm. "I'm just overwhelmed right now, and I didn't mean it like that—"

He twisted out of my grasp. "I said I'm done." He looked at me with such resignation, like I already meant absolutely nothing to him. "Goodbye, Aurelia." He walked down the hallway again, turned the corner to take the stairs, and disappeared.

The tears were immediate—and they poured down my face. "No, no, no . . ." I knew I'd just ruined the greatest thing that had ever happened to me.

Chapter 21

Constantine

Rocco and I sat with Antoine Allard, a Frenchman who had moved to Rome once his kids were out of the house. His daughter had chosen to make a career in Milan and his son in finance, so he decided to move to where he wanted to live—in the Eternal City.

"I have it on good faith an attack is coming," I said, sitting in the parlor with the sunshine coming through the ten-foot-tall windows. The garden was visible outside, but the moment summer had hit, it was already too hot to enjoy it. "I want all your intel about shipments so I can make sure we're doing everything on our end—" My phone vibrated for the third time in a row—and it was Aurelia.

Rocco glanced at me like he was just as annoyed by it.

I couldn't turn off my phone with the kind of job I had. People could die—literally. "Excuse me." I pulled out my phone, ignored her call, and blocked her. I set the phone on the table and focused on Antoine again. "You know how those telemarketers are."

Rocco knew better, but he came to my defense anyway. "I've been made aware of all the parking tickets I haven't paid many, many times."

Antoine chuckled before he took a drag of his cigar. "My partners are my allies, the French, the Italians, and the British. All my contracts are exclusive to the EU, so I'm certain that the break in the line isn't coming from me. But could someone in the chain be breaking protocol and sending batches of arms to our enemies? It's possible. I run a tight ship, but it's a big operation and someone could go rogue."

"Can we conduct an investigation on your behalf?" I asked. "We could send a team to comb through all the inventory and all the numbers. They're good at what they do, so if there's a discrepancy, they'll find it." It was also a tactic to make sure he was truly innocent, because if he refused, that meant he had something to hide.

"Have at it, Constantine."

Rocco shared a quick look with me. He was the one who assumed Antoine was a traitor, and I was the one who insisted he was a patriot. We'd made a bet on it—and now I was a million richer.

"I'll get a team together. We'll make sure it's delicate so we don't tip anyone off."

"Sounds good to me."

~

We got into the back seat of the Range Rover and left through the iron gates that kept the public off his property. We were immediately back in the Eternal City, on the congested roads with motorbikes that drove like they were invincible.

"I've been waiting for you to bring it up on your own, but you clearly aren't going to." Rocco stared out the window for a while before he turned to look at me. "You used to grin like an idiot, and now, you look pissed off every moment of every day."

I knew he'd seen her name on the screen. Which meant he knew I'd blocked her number. "It's done."

"Yeah, that's obvious. But the reason isn't obvious."

I looked out the window and shut down the conversation with my silence.

"You weren't even in a relationship, so what could she have done—"

"Not in the mood to be interrogated."

"All right."

~

We sat together in the parlor, an elaborate room with twenty-foot sculptures of Roman emperors, Augustus and Constantine, and sculptures of the gods who once watched over ancient Rome. Bookshelves were spaced between the sculptures, rising from floor to ceiling, containing tomes that no one had touched in centuries. Priceless artwork was on the walls. The only thing modern was the furniture and the rug in the center of the room.

I read off my device. "Antoine is a work in progress. That scrawny little snitch wasn't a snitch at all, and now we've got to find another lead. President Barsetti wants an update, and I don't fucking have one. Not to mention it's jubilee this year, so we've got to add security to Pope Zephyrinus's detail—" I stopped in mid-sentence when I saw Aurelia's name appear on the screen, along with a text.

I would give anything in the world to talk to you. I read the sentence twice before I lowered the device and looked across from me at Rocco, who was lounging on the couch, arm over the back, a drink in his hand like this was a fucking hangout rather than a work meeting. "You unblocked her."

He gave a slight shrug, then took a drink.

"You crossed a line."

He shrugged again, like he didn't give a damn.

"Never thought I'd have to tell *you* not to go through my phone."

"Didn't go through it."

"Stay out of my fucking business."

"What happened, Con? You were fucking gaga over this woman."

I set the device aside, sunlight fading through the windows that faced the garden. "Doesn't matter."

"It does matter. You've got a good head on your shoulders and a moral compass that doesn't deviate, but sometimes you get carried away when you're emotionally charged."

"That's not true—"

"Carl Athenios."

I released an irritated sigh.

"You were so fucking mad that you pulled his tongue out of his fucking mouth and then crushed his windpipe. It took us twice as long to get the information we needed because you jumped the gun."

"That is not the same thing as what's happening now—"

"Then what's happening now?"

I felt like a bottle of shaken champagne. The second I was uncorked, it'd be a mess of bubbly rage. "We don't do this—"

"I just want to make sure you aren't fucking this up, Con."

"Me?" I gave a laugh because it was fucking ridiculous. "I've been going after this woman hard—"

"I think you were too hard on Isabella. I think you prematurely ended that relationship."

"Asshole, I didn't even know you at the time."

"All I've heard is your side of the story, and I still think you're in the wrong."

"Wow," I said as I shook my head. "Now it all comes out."

"She didn't know he was your brother and, of course, was so confused by the whole thing. She was fucking twenty-three—"

"I'm not going to rehash a decade-old relationship, Rocco." It was dead and buried, and I'd moved on long ago.

"Why won't you tell me?" he asked. "I thought we were closer than that."

"Not saying we aren't."

"Then why?" he pressed. "Because you might be wrong?"

"Fuck you. I know what you're doing."

He sat up from the couch, forearms on his knees, leaning toward me with the coffee table between us. "Just fucking tell me."

He wasn't going to let this slide, so I decided to save us both the time and just tell him. So I shared the details of that afternoon, storming into her apartment and chasing off that little cunt like the pussy he was. And then what she said to me at the end of all of it.

Rocco was quiet when I finished.

"I've bent over fucking backward for this woman since I met her. One minute, she's there with me, and then the next, she pulls away. I'm just fucking sick of it. So many women would be happy to take her place in my bed."

"But you don't give a shit about any of those women."

"Well . . ." I grabbed my glass and took a drink.

"You're being too hard on her."

"I didn't ask your opinion!" I yelled, my voice reverberating off the coffered ceilings.

"Was her ex abusive? Did he hit her? Did he do anything to give you any indication that he was there to physically cause her harm?"

All I did was stare, fighting the urge to get up and punch him in the face.

"You didn't storm in there because you were worried about her. You went because you were jealous."

"I was not fucking jealous."

"Jealous and fucking insane. You barked at him like a dog?"

I looked away. "You should have seen him run."

"So this poor woman, who's already nervous just getting into the car with a bunch of dudes and guns, has you storm into her apartment and verbally assault her ex who stopped by to deliver some *pictures* she'd left behind. And then you reveal that you've had a security team watching her for who knows how long? And you wonder why she was upset?"

I was gonna do it. I was gonna punch him in the goddamn face.

"Con." He raised both of his hands slightly. "I don't get you, man. You're a smart fucking dude, but sometimes you get tunnel vision and you can't see the whole picture. She said she wished you were normal in a moment when her way of life was under threat."

"Still crossed a line."

"You've never said something in the heat of the moment that you regretted?"

I looked away.

"Has she ever given you any indication that she doesn't respect what you do?"

She told me if I were her son, she'd be proud of me. I remembered it so well because it meant a lot to me. Maybe that was why I lost my temper when she contradicted it.

"I've never met the woman, so I don't have a dog in this fight. But I've never heard you talk about someone the way you talk about her. There's Con before Aurelia, and then there's Con after Aurelia. Her impact on your life has been that distinct. It's been nine years since you've felt this way for someone, so maybe you should think about granting her a little grace instead of waiting another nine years." Rocco studied my face for a reaction, waited for a response.

"I don't need your input."

"I think you do," he said. "Because you act like you don't have any fault in this situation. It's like chasing a dog into the corner with a baseball bat and then getting mad when the dog barks. Remember, she's not like you or me. She was scared and overwhelmed and reactive. Text her or don't text her. But just think about what I've said, Con."

"You're awfully insightful for a man who's never been in a relationship."

"And you're awfully stupid for a man who's been in two."

Chapter 22

Aurelia

A week came and went—and Constantine ignored me.

I fucking ruined it.

A man infinitely out of my league and a dream come true came into my life—and I lost him. My two-year relationship ended in a dumpster fire in Taormina, and the hurt was like an open wound right in the center of my chest. But this . . . this hurt so much worse.

Because of what it could have been.

When it was time to pass away, your life would flash before your eyes. When my relationship with Constantine flatlined, so many of our memories hit me. We'd known each other for less than a month, but there was so much substance and depth to what we had. I remembered our morning trips to Bam Bar in the little town, waking up next to him in the softest bed I'd ever known, spending the day at the beach with him and his friends, meeting his mom and aunt, two of the most beautiful women I'd ever seen.

And now all of that was just . . . gone.

He wouldn't text me back. Wouldn't take my calls. When my text messages stopped going through and my calls went straight to voicemail, I realized he'd blocked me.

He fucking blocked me.

I'd hit rock bottom after Enzo left me in Taormina, but Constantine took my hand and helped me climb the tallest mountain. Showed me the view from the sky, cleansed me in his warmth and praise. But then I tripped and fell . . . and rolled all the way to the bottom of the sea.

I'd never recover from this. I'd end up like Isabella, still wanting him a decade later. I'd move on eventually, but Constantine would always be in the back of my mind. I'd wonder what could have been. Wonder if he'd met someone else. If he'd gotten married, had children.

I finally stopped trying to get ahold of him, knowing my messages weren't getting to him anyway. When he said he was done, he really meant it. He'd probably replaced me with someone else by now.

The thought made me cry . . . once or twice.

~

Cindy and I went out for a drink, sat together at a table and shared a bottle of wine.

"I want to ask if you're okay," Cindy said. "But that's a stupid question because I can tell you aren't." In a navy blue dress and heels, she had her dark hair in curls, a bracelet with charms on her wrist. She was beautiful, and I didn't understand why she was with a guy who wasn't of her caliber.

But I guessed people thought the same thing about me and Constantine.

"Yeah." I swirled my glass by the base of the stem. "I feel like shit, every moment of every day."

"But you said he was mixed up with some bad people?"

I'd never told my friends what he actually did. I'd kept it vague. He never told me I couldn't tell anyone, but they might think I was crazy if I told them the truth. "Yeah. Something shady, not sure what it was."

"Then maybe it's for the best," she said. "Got some good dick out of it, so that's all that matters."

The best dick in the fucking world. Whenever I slept with someone new, it would be a massive disappointment. In size, performance, passion, everything. It was hard to imagine ever wanting to take my clothes off with someone else. "Yeah."

Her eyes moved past me, and a smile broke out on her face, like she recognized someone who entered the bar.

God, it better not be Timothée.

"Hey, babe." She stood up to greet him.

Ugh, no.

His arm circled her lower back, and he pulled her in for a kiss.

What the fuck happened to girls' night?

Timothée looked at me when he finished their kiss. And he stared and stared . . . right in front of her. "Hey, Aurelia."

"Hey, Timothée." He had these lidless eyes that never seemed to close. Like a lifeless doll that you had to shove in a toy box because it was too creepy to leave out.

"This is my friend, Pierre."

I turned to see the other guy who came to the table. He had dirty-blond hair, green eyes, and was slender in the arms. He extended his hand to shake mine. "Lovely to meet you," he said with a French accent.

"Uh, hi." Did that skank set me up on a double date? I looked at her across the table.

She mouthed, "Just go with it."

We all took a seat, and the guys ordered their drinks.

I glared at Cindy so fucking hard. "What the fucking hell?" I mouthed.

"Just trying to help," she mouthed back.

I stopped mouthing and just spoke aloud. "You're unbelievable."

Both men turned to look at me.

Like I gave a shit.

~

Pierre made conversation the entire night, and to his credit, he was really patient with my attitude. Frankly, I was fucking rude, but he didn't seem to be bothered by it, like he'd already been told that could happen.

I felt guilty as fuck. I felt like I'd betrayed Constantine, when I didn't consent to this. I felt like I'd betrayed him, when he'd blocked my number and said he wanted nothing to do with me. This was a taste of life without him, of mediocrity, and I cursed myself for ever wishing he'd been normal.

I loved that Constantine wasn't normal.

It was the worst pain ever, to wish more than anything in the world to go back in time and have a do-over. To swallow the words before they had the chance to leave my mouth and pierce our relationship like bullets.

Maybe if I'd had the opportunity to actually apologize, I would have been able to change his mind. But he wouldn't even give me that. I didn't know where he lived, didn't know how to track him down. When I searched his name online, he wasn't present anywhere, not on social media, no hits at all. Like he'd been completely wiped from the internet.

My only option was to call his family's restaurant in Taormina . . . and ask his mom to relay a message to him. He'd get so angry that I'd crossed the line that he'd probably confront me, and then I would have my chance.

But what would I accomplish when he was out-of-his-mind pissed off?

Nothing. I'd accomplish nothing.

"We're gonna take off," Cindy said. "Timothée has to stop by and feed his cat."

What kind of man had a cat?

They left cash for their drinks and left.

She fucking left me there—with him.

There was an awkward bout of silence before he pivoted farther in his chair to look at me. "Cindy said you do photography—"

"I don't want to be rude because you did nothing wrong, but I'm just not into this."

He shut up, and his eyes flicked away. "I'll ask for the tab, then . . ."

"I'm sorry. I just got out of a serious relationship." I'd said that to Constantine a few times, but now Constantine was the serious relationship I referred to.

He waved for the waiter to come by as I took a few sips from my fresh glass of wine.

"I'm gonna pee." I headed to the bathroom, did my business, and when I came back to the table, I was disappointed he was still there . . . waiting for me.

"Let me walk you home."

"I'm fine." I moved to the table and grabbed my purse. My nearly full glass of wine was still there, so I took a few big gulps so it wouldn't go to waste. "I have my motorbike."

"You don't look in any shape to drive."

"Excuse me?" I said as I turned. "I've barely had two glasses of wine."

"Well, you seem a little loopy to me. I don't mean to offend you." He got up and raised his hands like that would somehow soothe my ire.

I stood there in my heels and felt a slight wobble. I wasn't sure if he'd put the thought in my head or if I actually was a little drunk, but now, I didn't feel so sure of myself. I felt a hesitation and then a wave of heat from my stomach as if I'd just drunk a glass of acid.

He watched me for a second before he offered his arm. "Come on. I'll walk you to the taxi stand."

I ignored his offer and moved past him, my purse over my shoulder. Instead of wearing stiletto heels, I wore wedged heels, so when we hit the cobblestone street, I wouldn't have to walk like I was in a field of land mines.

But the second I felt the fresh air outside, I felt worse. I would have taken a taxi if there had been any on that street.

"Come on, this way." He guided me around the building and down a side street. There was a gelato place still open, and across from that were a couple of cafés that had been closed for hours.

I felt weak and nauseated . . . and then downright confused. "I do not feel well."

He continued to walk beside me. "Not much farther."

I wasn't even sure what taxi hub he was referring to. I came to a stop and pulled out my phone. "Just gonna order a ride." It usually took longer than flagging down a cab and it was more expensive, but my body was not cooperating.

Maybe I did have too much to drink. Maybe in my anger and nervousness, I'd lost count of my drinks.

"I'll wait with you."

I leaned against the wall and continued to work the app, trying to order the ride, but the more I went through the steps, the more confused I became.

Something was not right.

My heart suddenly started to race in a way it never had before—like there was something in my system that was making my heart work to get it out.

Pierre pulled out his phone and made a call. His voice was hard to hear from where he stood. "That alley around the corner."

It didn't sound like he'd just ordered a ride. It didn't sound like he'd talked to a friend either.

I was fucked, wasn't I?

My mind started to slip further, my heart raced like it was about to explode, and I should have called the police, but I literally couldn't think. So I did something that made no sense. I texted Constantine. 112.

He'd blocked my number, but I still texted him the number to indicate an emergency anyway. I tried to type in the actual number to call, but then I couldn't feel my thumbs. And then the phone was taken out of my hand.

"Yeah, she's just had too much to drink," Pierre said to a passerby. "Just waiting for a ride."

The people continued on, unaware that I was slowly losing all my motor functions. I was exhausted, but my body was also unresponsive.

What the fuck did this asshole give me?

Sometime later, a black van pulled up. The side panel slid open, and two guys got out and came toward me. "She looks healthy."

"Get her in the car and check her blood type," Pierre said.

What in the actual fuck?

Each guy hooked a hand underneath one of my arms and dragged me up.

In a burst of rage, I was able to shove one aside and scream. Scream bloody fucking murder.

The guy clamped a hand over my mouth and nose, so I was silenced and smothered.

Pierre joined in, grabbing me by the legs to help me into the van.

"Did you give her enough?" one guy asked.

"Yeah," Pierre said as he walked backward toward the van. "Maybe she weighs more than I thought."

When they got close to the van, I found another surge of strength and tried to free myself from their grasp, but all I did was tumble slightly and almost hit the ground. My dress was forced up to my waist, my thong was exposed, but my bare ass on the street was the least of my problems right now.

Headlights suddenly came toward us down the small alleyway.

"Fuck, hurry," Pierre said. "Just throw her in."

I tried to fight again, but whatever poison was in my body had reached critical levels, and I couldn't do a damn thing.

Another pair of headlights came from the opposite direction. They grew closer and closer, a beam of light from both directions.

Oh, thank god. Surely no one would see what was happening and just leave me there.

The guys tried to shove me into the van, but only half my body made it. My head hit the edge of the van, and then my knees smacked into the cobblestones. One of the guys stepped on my wrist, and all I could do was groan, not even scream.

Doors slammed. The headlights stopped moving.

"Oh, we're fucked," Pierre said. "Guns, quick."

I tried to crawl away from the van, but all I could do was drag myself an inch or two. Then I jerked when I heard gunshots, a machine gun firing a hundred rounds into the air in just a couple seconds.

I pulled myself away again, my broken body useless, and then I saw the silhouette of men coming near. I hoped they were friends instead of foes, because I couldn't do shit right now. Not even write my own name.

Then I heard a voice I'd recognize anywhere, in a crowded room or in my dreams.

"You picked the wrong woman, boys." The machine gun fired again, the noise so earsplitting I thought I went deaf. "Rocco, take Aurelia."

"Con—Constantine?" I said it so quietly that no one could have possibly heard me.

A man came near, dark hair and eyes like Constantine, but it definitely wasn't him. He pulled down my dress before he scooped me into his arms like I weighed less than the shirt on his back. He turned me away from the commotion and toward the headlights.

"Round them up," Constantine ordered.

I heard the sound of fighting and a gunshot or two. I heard a man scream so high pitched he sounded like a woman.

Rocco got me into the back seat of the Range Rover, and the guy who was already seated there put a blood pressure cuff on me and then put the cold metal bell of the stethoscope to my chest as he listened to my heart.

I looked out the front window and watched the horror unfold.

The four men in the van had all of their limbs zip-tied before they all dropped on the cobblestone. Constantine's men stood back, covered in bulletproof vests and carrying machine guns and shotguns.

I watched it all in the brightness of the headlights.

"Who did this to you?" Rocco asked.

I stared at him, unable to move my mouth.

"I know what they gave her." The other guy opened a container, pulled out a vial and a syringe, and then injected it into my arm. "Give her a couple minutes, and she should be responsive."

Rocco left my side, then walked to Constantine. He seemed to report what he'd just learned about me.

Constantine had a look on his face I'd never seen before. When he said his confrontation with Enzo was nothing, he meant it. Because it wasn't just the wideness of his eyes that struck me, but the bloodlust. His neck was stiff, the veins underneath his skin strained so much they looked like they might snap. He held his body differently too, his shoulders squared like he was in a boxing match. He was the only one who didn't carry a machine gun, so he must have handed that to someone else.

When Rocco finished the message, Constantine strolled over to one of the men on the ground, stared at him with a stone-cold expression for several seconds and, with lightning speed, raised his boot, then slammed down hard—snapping bone.

The guy on the ground shrieked more than he screamed.

Constantine continued his stroll to the next guy. "While we wait for the meds to kick in so she can tell me which one of you motherfuckers is responsible, we'll play a game. See how many bones I can break in five minutes."

My thoughts and reactions were still suppressed. Otherwise, I probably would have screamed in horror.

Constantine continued to walk and stopped near the next victim.

He trembled on the ground and waited for Constantine to strike.

Constantine remained still, watching the anxiety and fear cripple him without actually doing anything. Then he moved to the next guy and, without a moment's notice, slammed his foot down onto his knee and snapped the socket.

"Ahhhhhh!"

Constantine went back to the man he tortured a second ago but didn't draw it out. He just went for the ankle.

The guy screamed in horror when Constantine barreled down on him, screamed just as loud as the moment he'd snapped his ankle.

Then Constantine moved fast, going to each one and breaking another bone . . . and then another bone. Stomping his boot down with enough force to shake the ancient cobblestones beneath us. It was the most violent thing I'd ever seen, all of the men screaming and crying as Constantine continued to pace and find something else to break.

The police never came. No one intervened.

Rocco addressed me again. "Which one, Aurelia?"

"Um . . ." I couldn't believe I could talk. I started to feel myself return. "Dirty-blond hair . . . green eyes . . . skinny."

He left the Range Rover and walked over to the men who writhed on the ground.

Constantine took a break from the torture and let Rocco survey the sea of future corpses.

Rocco stopped at one and then motioned for the guys to lift him from the ground so I could see him clearly. "This the guy?"

"Yes," I shouted from the back seat.

The guys immediately dropped him, and he slammed back to the cobblestone.

Rocco stepped aside so Constantine could finish.

"Get the gas," Constantine ordered.

Gas?

Two of the men went to the other Range Rover behind the van and retrieved canisters. Then they started to douse all the prisoners on the stone, drenching them in gasoline so strong I could actually smell it through the open door.

Constantine pulled out a book of matches from his back pocket. He ripped one out and struck it across the edge, making it light up.

All the guys on the ground started to plead, whimpering when they knew what was coming.

He went to the first one and stood over him, holding the lit match before him. "You've violated the laws of the Roman Republic, and as Emperor Constantine of the Roman Empire, I hereby sentence you to death." He flicked the match on the body, and flames immediately ensued.

The screams . . . I would never forget them.

The guy desperately rolled as he tried to put them out, and he rolled into his comrade, who also caught fire. Another wave of screams erupted as they were both burned alive, screaming for a reprieve that hadn't come yet, not until the flames made it past all the layers of skin.

The screams abated, but they continued to burn.

Constantine went to the third man and did the same. Lit the match and read out his sentence before he tossed the fire onto the pile of gasoline. Another ball of flames exploded and illuminated the alleyway between the closed businesses.

That left Pierre.

I knew there was something wrong with Timothée. He knew this entire time. He didn't stare at me because he was attracted to me. He stared at me because he thought I was a perfect target. No family. No boyfriend. And I lived alone. He assumed no one would notice I was gone until it was far too late.

"Tell me who you work for, and I'll be merciful." Constantine pulled out the handgun from the back of his jeans and cocked it. "Or don't—and you'll burn."

The answer was clear to me.

"I'll tell you everything you want to know," Pierre said as he trembled from the ground. "If you let me go."

Constantine smiled down at him, but it was fucking eerie. Then he raised his gun and shot him in the leg. The gunshot reverberated off both the walls, amplifying it to reach across the entire city.

Pierre screamed like he'd been set on fire.

"I've laid out your options—now choose."

Pierre continued to writhe, blood pooling out of his broken leg, his body already a crumpled pile of messed-up bones. The flames beside him made him perspire. He already looked like he was on the precipice of death. "His name is Clement . . ."

"Where can I find him?"

"I've never met him."

"How do you get your orders?"

"He calls."

"Where were you supposed to take her?"

"To a warehouse. The address is . . ." He struggled to hold on to consciousness. "Via di Casal Boccone . . . 283."

Constantine raised the gun and shot him in the head. "Thank you for your cooperation, asshole." He turned to Rocco. "We take the warehouse now. Might already be tipped off."

Rocco nodded in agreement. "What about Aurelia?"

"I'll have the doctor look after her until we're done."

Rocco headed to the other car. "I'll send a cleanup crew and meet you there."

Constantine headed toward my Range Rover, and my heart gave a lurch when he neared. His enormous body came through the open doorway, and then he was there, his neck bent down to look at me. "Are you okay?"

"Yeah, I'm fine."

"My doctor is going to take care of you until I finish this. Meet you at the house."

"Oh, okay." I wasn't sure what I expected, but I hoped for something more. Like a passionate kiss, even though the situation didn't permit it at all. The bodies in the road were still on fire. Constantine had just shattered a dozen bones with just his boot minutes ago. And just because he saved me didn't mean he wanted to be with me. He'd slept with Isabella and that meant nothing, so maybe this meant nothing too.

Chapter 23

Aurelia

When Constantine said he would meet at the house, I wasn't sure which house he meant. His or mine.

But when the driver pulled behind a colossal gate and we arrived at a villa I could only describe as a palace, I knew he meant his residence. Security was stationed on the property, on either side of the enormous thirty-foot doorway, near the potted olive trees and along the solid wall that separated his private home from the rest of the bustling city.

The doctor came around the other side and helped me out of the car because I was still weak. I felt like ash was burning in my body. My muscles didn't respond to commands the same way, and I could never really catch my breath. My lungs' need for air was simply out of sync with what my body needed.

Security opened the double doors, and I stepped into a whole different world. An entryway guarded by two Egyptian statues of the god Anubis. They were enormous and flanked the short staircase that led to the next part of the house. The expansive room had a long table in the center, which held another sculpture of the Eye of Horus. And the walls were covered in paintings and artwork, and the floor-to-ceiling window on one side showed some kind of garden space.

I didn't have time to take it all in because the doctor continued forward up the stairs onto the next level, which was another greeting area that branched off to several different spaces, a grand dining room to the left and a sitting area that looked like it was used frequently, despite the fact that it was lavishly decorated.

A man in a black tuxedo appeared, in his early fifties, his dark hair combed back. "His Highness just informed me of the situation."

His Highness?

The man in the tuxedo approached me and gave a slight bow. "I'm Elio, butler to Constantine and the caretaker of this home. Let me guide you upstairs so you can rest. This way." He took the lead up a large staircase, and when I said large, I meant five people could walk side by side all the way up. He guided me to the third level of the villa, and every floor had incredibly high ceilings. Statues erected in hallways, artwork on the walls, vases of real flowers.

I felt like I was in the residence of royalty.

Elio escorted me to a private bedroom, one that had a king-size bed, a private living room, and its own bathroom.

Every room in this house probably had its own bathroom.

The doctor guided me to an armchair and then opened his bag to get to work. "How are you feeling?"

"Better . . . but still pretty fucking terrible."

"The drugs they gave you are supposed to make you brain dead."

"What?"

"Don't worry, I was able to prevent that from happening. But you're going to feel unwell for at least several days." He took my heart rate and other vitals. "I'm going to give you something to put you to sleep. You're going to need to rest so your body can fight the effects quicker."

I wanted to talk to Constantine, but I didn't know when he'd be back. "Okay."

He grabbed another vial and a needle and gave me a shot. "I can help you get into bed."

"No, it's okay. I've got it." I kicked off my shoes, then moved to the bed, fully prepared to take off my dress and sleep in just my underwear. I already felt the medication start to kick in. He helped me pull the covers back and tucked me inside. "Here's your phone." I'd lost track of it, but Con or Rocco must have taken it back from the would-be kidnappers. The doctor set it on the nightstand. "Feel better soon."

I was asleep before he left the room.

~

As I woke up, I was aware of the daylight piercing the closed curtains and my eyelids. It took me a moment to stir, to realize I felt well, that the sickly feeling of poison had dissolved from my bloodstream.

I was on my side, and when I cracked my eyes open, I came face-to-face with dark eyes. But not the dark eyes of Constantine. There was fur and a long snout . . . and the smell of dog. I blinked several times, watching the German shepherd study me like I was a little mouse they were about to pounce on.

Then I remembered who she was—Medusa.

"Hey, babe . . ." My voice was raspy and cracked, and my arm felt weak as I lifted it and petted the side of her cheek. "Nice to meet you."

She dipped her head and licked my cheek.

I chuckled as I felt the streak of saliva from the swipe of her tongue.

"Settle down, baby girl." Constantine's voice was quiet and commanding but with a hint of affection, and it came from somewhere behind me.

Medusa hopped off the bed, and I saw her tail over the edge of the duvet as she walked around and out of sight.

When I realized he was there with me, my entire body went still. I'd been so calm just seconds ago, but now, I was rigid and on high alert. I lay there for a second before I forced myself up, forced myself against the padded headboard.

He sat in an armchair a short distance away, in the same clothes as the last time I saw him, minus the tactical vest. He was wearing a black T-shirt and dark jeans, his knees wide apart, and his arms were sprawled across the armrests—like a king on his throne. "You all right?"

"Yeah. I feel a lot better than I did yesterday." I was in nothing but my bra and underwear, but he'd seen me in less, so I didn't care what was on display.

He stared me down through a veil of coldness. "Still wish I were normal?" It was a cutting jab, and I could tell he'd been sitting on that for as long as he'd sat there, maybe for hours. His eyes weren't full of relief that I'd come out of this mostly unscathed.

Just emotionally disturbed.

Whatever hope I'd had that this event could change things between us was gone. He didn't look at me the same. He was still mad as hell . . . *clearly*. So mad, I didn't bother to apologize again. As much as I wanted Constantine, would want him the rest of my life, I knew it was done.

I was devastated . . . and defeated. "Thank you . . . for saving me."

"It's what I do."

I gave a slow nod, realizing I wasn't special, that he would have done that for any woman who called. He was as invested in my well-being as a stranger off the street. I pulled the covers back and got out of bed. I retrieved the dress from the other chair and started to get dressed so I could leave.

"What are you doing?"

"I should get home." I wanted to beg for another chance, but I respected him too much to waste his time. His mind was clearly made up, there was a queue of women ready to replace me, and whatever we'd had was dead.

Because I'd killed it.

"What's the rush?" he asked as he watched me. "Take a second."

I pulled the dress over my head, then slipped on the heels. "I'm fine." I stopped looking directly at him. It was the last time I would ever see him, and I couldn't look at him. I didn't want the memory, didn't want to carry that sad image in my head for the rest of my life. "Thank you . . . again." I moved for the door, a little wobbly in my heels.

He blocked my path—like a broken tree that had fallen across the road in a storm.

I felt myself take a harsh breath, not out of fear, but out of some misguided hope.

"Sit." He nodded to the other armchair.

The room was more like a suite in a hotel room than an actual bedroom. Basically an apartment within a villa. With my exit barred by the humongous mountain, I was forced to take a step back and comply with the demand.

I sat and crossed my legs, painfully aware that I looked like I'd been hit by a car. My makeup must have been a complete mess. My knees were all scraped up from trying to get free of Pierre and his cronies. I looked at the rumpled bed where I'd slept all night and then at the floor, where Medusa lay with her chin resting on her paws.

I looked at anything but him.

He stared at the side of my face for minutes, like he expected me to be the one to speak. "I'm the one who's angry, but you can't get out of here fast enough."

"Yes, because you still hate me."

"I don't *hate* you."

"Whatever. You know what I mean. You want nothing to do with me, and I've blown up your phone for the last ten days and never got a reply. Your message is pretty clear, and I don't want to waste more of your time." I still wouldn't look at him, because it felt like a goodbye. A goodbye from my eyes to his. "I thought maybe there was a chance something had changed because . . . I could have died, but it's clear nothing has changed."

"I shouldn't have made that last jab," he said. "It just slipped out."

"Yeah, I get it."

"No, it was pretty fucked up, considering everything you've just been through."

I stared at a painting across the room, some kind of colored sketch of the Roman Forum.

"Sweetheart, look at me."

Sweetheart. I never thought he'd call me that again. Hope blossomed in my chest, and I turned to him.

All the anger and resentment left his eyes. "This time apart has given me some perspective on the whole thing. And I fucked up too. I broke down your door with my toxic masculinity and set the place on fire. If I'd never done that, I'm sure you and Enzo would have finished an unremarkable conversation, he would have left, and that would have been the end of it. But I went in there like a psychopath . . . and provoked you."

I did not expect to hear him take accountability for anything. "I still shouldn't have said that—"

"Yeah, it still bothers me. But you did say previously that you would be proud if I were your son, so I don't think you fully meant what you said. Just partially. But partially is still enough to wound me. Now that you've had firsthand experience with what I do, I'm sure you can figure out why I felt that way."

I gave a nod. "Yeah."

He sat there, arms relaxed on the armrests, knees wide apart. His eyes moved elsewhere for several heartbeats before he spoke again. "I've had a rough time since I walked away. When I'm angry like that, it's usually pretty easy for me to forget the person ever existed. But I spent a lot of time on the couch with Medusa, and she could tell I was hurt. She kept looking at me like I had an injury that she couldn't find."

My heart ached in pain but also ballooned in hope. Hope that I would get this man back.

"Something about me that you may have already figured out—I don't do second chances. If someone betrays you once, they'll betray you twice. But because I'm also at fault here, I don't think that applies to us."

My heart raced like I was at a full sprint rather than seated in a cushioned chair.

"And even if that weren't the case, my feelings for you haven't changed."

It was happening. Really happening.

"But I need some time to get to where we were before. Because I've been all in since the day we met, and I'm tired of the constant back-and-forth, tired of you being unsure if you can handle everything my life entails. So take some time to think about it—"

"I don't need to think about it, Constantine."

His entire body went still as he stared at me.

"I'm in."

"You are?"

"Yes. For better or worse. Whatever comes our way."

He studied me for a while longer. "Just so we're clear, this is it. I will die in the line of duty, or I'll be lucky enough to live long enough to retire. I will never step down from this position, regardless of the threat it brings to either of us. If I ever marry, it will be to a woman who understands that this is bigger than both of us. I will never walk away from this, not for her or any children we may have. So if you think that, in time, my priorities will change, they won't. If you think if we ever have kids I'll walk away, I won't. I've been delicate and patient with you these last few weeks, because goddamn, I've never wanted a woman more. But that leniency is over. You're either in this with me fully—or you walk away now."

That speech should have scared me off, but I knew a life without Constantine was far worse. "I'm ready to be tough."

His stare remained hard, but a hint of a smile moved onto his lips. "Attagirl."

I couldn't keep my distance for another moment. I launched out of the chair and into his lap, my arms circling his neck as I brought my mouth to his lips and kissed him. Kissed him like I only had in my dreams. I felt his hard chest against mine like a wall of bricks, and I was reminded that this was real. Not wishful thinking. Not a fantasy.

He slid one hand into the back of my hair while his other hand went to my ass. He tugged up the dress, then grabbed one of my cheeks and squeezed it hard before he gave it a hard smack and let the dress fall back into place. He was on his feet a moment later, carrying me with him to the bed.

Oh my god, I couldn't believe this was real.

He set me down on the edge, then yanked his shirt over his head.

"Oh yes . . ." It was like he was already inside me.

He smirked as he worked his jeans. "Missed me, sweetheart?"

"Uh-huh." I practically drooled at the sight of him.

When he was naked, he slipped off my heels, then yanked my dress to my waist before he grabbed my thong and pulled it free.

I hadn't shaved in over a week because I hadn't expected anyone to see me naked. My dark hair was everywhere, an unmanicured mess. The heat left my lungs as the embarrassment filled me like a balloon.

He grabbed the tops of my thighs, then tugged my ass to the edge of the bed. "Sweetheart, I'm not picky." He slid his hand underneath my back, and he lifted me to his hips, the height of the bed too short for his six and a half feet. He guided me onto his length instead of pushing himself inside me, and I sealed him nice and tight.

He moaned like the only thing around his dick in the last ten days was his hand. "Fuck, I missed this pussy." He sheathed himself, then yanked up my dress to reveal my tits. His enormous hand gripped my side, his thumb over my belly button with his fingers over my hip. He thrust his hips and pulled me into him, nailing me at the edge of the bed, giving me his whole length like he wasn't in the mood to be considerate.

Every time he thrust too far, it hurt, but it was the best pain I'd ever felt. "Constantine . . ."

"Missed this dick?" he asked, pushing into me and making me wince with every thrust.

"Yes."

"Show me how much you missed it." He pulled me a little closer, ramming me harder than he ever had.

I should have cried out in pain, but I started to come instead. "Constantine . . . god . . . yes."

Chapter 24

Aurelia

We left the guest bedroom and headed down the hallway until we reached the double doors to his bedchambers. The doors were fifteen feet high and appeared to be made of solid gold. The outside was engraved with an image of the Roman Forum as it was believed to have appeared at the time of the ancient Romans. The Arch of Titus next to Palatine Hill, the temples dedicated to the gods, Roman arches used in every building. A piece of the Colosseum was also visible in the background.

The door itself must have been worth a million euro.

He opened the door, and the movement was so slow that I could tell it was as heavy as it looked. I studied the series of hinges attached to the wall. Thirty of them to keep the door up.

When we stepped inside, I saw he had an entryway with a table holding a vase of flowers in the center. The table was brilliant blue and yellow, reminding me of the tables I'd seen all around Taormina, constructed from the stone of Mount Etna. The table was on top of a bright rug, and the wall behind the table had pictures and paintings from floor to ceiling, arranged in a way that made it appear to be a single piece of art.

I wasn't ashamed to admit I was intimidated.

I followed behind him and Medusa, moving past a large sitting room with several couches on an expensive rug, with an enormous TV on one wall. There were two statues in the room, one that appeared to be Venus, goddess of love and beauty, and then Minerva, goddess of wisdom. I'd noticed statues throughout his residence, pots and paintings, works of art that did *not* look like replicas.

I trailed behind him, seeing a full dining table that could seat ten people in one room, and then we made it to his actual bedroom, which had a bed that was definitely bigger than a king. Custom made so he had plenty of room for him and his dog . . . and his guests. Another smaller sitting area was off to the side of the room near a fireplace with a TV on the wall. The bed frame had Roman soldiers engraved directly into the wood, and the matching dressers had the same design.

When I peeked into the bathroom, I saw a room with a large shower, a bathtub that was more like a small pool, a private sauna, and two separate vanity counters on opposite sides of the space.

I occasionally rubbed shoulders with wealthy people through work. Saw them arrive at events in Bentleys and Ferraris. Saw their expensive watches, recognized the high-end brands they wore. But I knew I'd never encountered a single person as rich as Constantine. Rich wasn't even the right word.

I walked to the window and looked outside, seeing the extent of his property. He had expansive gardens that reached to the wall, and I could see more sections of the building we were in, but he had other, separate buildings too. One that looked identical to the Pantheon, just on a smaller scale, and then another that looked like the Temple of Saturn from the Roman Forum.

The property itself, in the heart of Rome like this, had to be worth . . . a billion euros.

And it belonged to one man.

"Let's take a shower and have lunch."

I turned away from the windows and looked at him. How was this billionaire so . . . so normal? So down to earth? How could someone so rich care enough about other people to put his life on the line? "Uh, sure."

"Got other plans?" When he moved past the bed, Medusa jumped on it like it was where she slept every night. Constantine absentmindedly petted her, then gave her a kiss on the head—like he did it so often he didn't think about it.

I'd never had a dog, but seeing the way he treated her made my heart gush. "No."

"Then why are you being weird?" he asked bluntly as he walked up to me.

"I'm being weird?"

He cocked his head slightly. "A little."

"Well, if I'm being honest—"

"Always be honest with me. Never mince your words."

"I guess I'm just a bit overwhelmed by all of this."

"All of what, exactly?"

"Uh, maybe you're used to this, but I'm not."

He cocked his eyebrow.

"You live in a palace. Like, a Roman palace . . ."

When he finally understood my meaning, recognition came into his eyes. "Don't be intimidated."

"Hard not to be. Your art collection alone . . ."

"It's not *my* collection. It's my inheritance. Everything you see belonged to my family before it came back into my hands."

"How did you get it back?"

He shrugged. "Asked for it. And since people want to stay on my good side, they complied." He smiled before he headed into the bathroom. "Come on, sweetheart." He pulled off his shirt along the way, revealing the hard muscles that hugged his spine. He had been so vicious and cold when I first woke up, but now, he was himself again.

I joined him in the shower and watched him rub the soap into my body. He felt me everywhere, like I'd been found in the mud instead of in his clean bed. Both of his hands squeezed my ass before he kissed me, and then he smiled at me as I stood under the falling water, looking at me the way he used to.

We dried off and got dressed, and since I had nothing to wear, he gave me some of his clothes, a pair of sweatpants that I had to roll so they'd stay on my hips and one of his T-shirts.

When we left his room, I felt ridiculous walking around in the hallway dressed like that because I didn't feel like we were home. It felt like we'd left our hotel room and ventured onto the rest of the property—and I looked homeless.

The rest of his villa was just as grand, every hallway jam-packed with art and sculptures, free of a single sprinkle of dust, even though almost the entire place was probably never touched. Every floor had very high ceilings, all coffered and outlined in gold and flowers. I felt completely and utterly out of place.

When we made it downstairs, we walked through the enormous glass doors shaped like a Roman arch, and stepped into the gardens. In the shade of the trees and under a large umbrella was a circular table and four chairs, along with a small vase of flowers.

We took a seat, and then someone immediately came to serve us. We were given a pitcher of ice water along with a chilled bottle of wine. A basket of fresh bread and a bowl of marinated green olives were placed on the table. But we barely had time to eat it before our salads were presented to us, leafy and green with tomatoes and mozzarella and a seared piece of salmon on top.

No one said a word to Constantine. It was like the guys in the car when he'd picked me up. To me, he was just a man I'd met in Taormina, but to everyone else, they either respected him . . . or feared him.

He dropped his linen across his lap and started to eat. "So, what happened last night?"

My morning with him had been so magical, I'd nearly forgotten about the nightmare of last night. I should be debilitated by the memory, but once again, Constantine brought me back to life. "I went out with my friend Cindy. Thought it was supposed to be the two of us until her boyfriend showed up—"

"The one you don't like."

"Yeah," I said. "And he brought his friend. Cindy and Timothée left, and I was stuck with the guy. And when I went to the bathroom, he clearly spiked my drink. I tried to leave, but he insisted on helping me find a cab. It was clearly a setup."

"Have you talked to Cindy?"

"No." I hadn't spoken to anyone.

"You know I have to talk to Timothée, right?"

"Yeah. I'm not sure if he was in on it or not."

"He might have gotten a kickback. Set up the meeting with the target, and he gets a cut."

"I really fucking hope not."

"You got a bad vibe from him for a reason."

My intuition had been firing off, and I hadn't listened to it.

"You could have stayed with me like I offered, and maybe none of this would have happened." His tone dropped like he was angry again.

"Yeah . . . hindsight." I wished I'd just stayed with Constantine. I wished I'd just accepted everything that came with the package from the beginning. There were a lot of things I didn't love about his line of work, like the fact that he could be killed at any moment, but losing him romantically had felt like a death anyway, so . . .

"I hoped you've learned from that hindsight."

"I have." I picked at my salad before I took a bite, and it was the best salad I'd ever had.

"Good," he said. "The entire time, we haven't been able to actually have a relationship because we've been so busy focusing on why it won't work. Well, *you've* been focused on why it won't work. I'm excited for us to just be. To see where it goes. To see what it becomes."

"Yeah, me too." All the dangers and concerns simply weren't important anymore. This relationship might get me killed, but I was ready to accept those consequences. I was in too deep now. Dead either way—in a lot of ways. "So, if Timothée was in on it . . . what will happen to him?"

"You know what will happen to him, sweetheart."

"Even though he didn't actually hurt or kill anyone, he's dead?"

"He's an accomplice to murder, so yeah."

"I just wasn't sure how you decided the punishment."

"I don't give much leeway for violent crimes," he said. "You rob a bank, don't pay your taxes, deal on the street, I don't care. We might even be friends," he said with a smile. "But if you're committing violent crimes against innocent people, you're done."

"Yeah . . ."

"And I won't go easy on Timothée, even if you ask me to."

I shook my head. "I wouldn't ask. I just . . . feel bad for Cindy."

"You don't think she knew?"

"God no," I said immediately. "She's a little ditzy sometimes, but she would never participate in that. If she knew he had a hand in this, she'd cut his dick off. No, there's no chance she knew. But she'll be heartbroken when she finds out."

"I could set it up to make it look like he took off, if you want."

"Yeah, maybe that will be best."

"All right, I can do that." He took a few more bites of his salad, then poured water into his glass. He filled my glass as well before he set down the pitcher. "I've been trying to find this employer for a while. Hopefully Timothée knows something decent."

"Can I ask you something?"

"Anything, sweetheart." He rested his elbows on the armrest and stared at me.

"You're obviously very wealthy . . ." So wealthy I felt like I'd crossed a line just acknowledging it. "So, why do this? Why risk your life for people you don't know? Why spend so much of your time working, when you could be on a yacht full of supermodels who would gladly take turns sucking sunscreen off your dick?"

He released a quick and harsh laugh, like he hadn't expected me to say that. "That is quite the picture." His hands came in, his fingers stitching together. "I believe we all have a personal destiny, and this is mine. President Barsetti rules over the civilians. The pope rules over the church. And I rule over the criminals. We make a tripod, and without one of the legs, we topple over. I'm proud of my history and the roots of my ancestors, and I'm proud of how I serve my country and my people. Like a painter or a poet, I'm passionate about my work. And quite frankly, no one can do it better than I can. Money is important to everyone, but family and purpose are more important."

I nodded in agreement.

"I'm lucky I have a job that I would do for free." He grabbed his wine and took a drink. "But I'm glad I make money hand over fist." He smiled before he set the glass down, then grabbed his fork again.

"Your residence . . . there's nothing else like this in Rome."

"There's Villa Aurora," he said. "But yes, this is the largest personal residence in Rome. I didn't buy it. It was handed down to me, gifted to me from the government in exchange for my service, but also because it was rightfully mine."

"Then doesn't that mean your sister and the rest of your family have a claim to it?"

"Yes, but they didn't want it. Their lives are in Taormina, and they aren't leaving for anything—which I respect."

I'd felt like I knew him before, but now, I really knew him. I knew a version of him that had gone incognito for a while. I finally saw behind the curtain and everything that was off the stage. I'd met this man in Taormina and expected one night together. But that one night had turned into a week . . . and then beyond.

"You're pulling away again."

My eyes flicked back to his. "I'm not."

"I can feel you growing distant." He had unparalleled intuition, reading me even at times when I had nothing on display.

"I'm just . . . intimidated by you."

"Intimidated?" he asked incredulously and with a smile. "Sweetheart, you've got nothing to be intimidated by."

"I feel like I'm sitting in the presence of a real emperor." I was in modern times, but I felt like I was in ancient Rome, somehow getting the attention of the Roman Emperor. Becoming ensnared as his obsession . . . inexplicably.

"You are in the presence of a real emperor," he said seriously. "Emperor Constantine II. But of all people in the world, you should be intimidated by me the least."

"Why?"

He stared at me for a long time, eyes focused and stern, seeing something on my face that I couldn't. "Because you know the guy who jumped off the rock in Taormina with his friends. You know the guy who helps his mom with dinner in the kitchen. You know the guy who's just like everyone else. Because you know me for me."

OTHER WORKS BY PENELOPE SKY

Golden Retriever in Another Republic

Fifth Republic Series

The Butcher

The Carver

The Saint

Golden Retriever in a Mafia Romance

The Betrayal Series

It Kills Me

It Breaks Me

It Ruins Me

It Hurts Me

It Pains Me

It Destroys Me

Morally Gray Hero in Organized Crime

The Buttons Series

Buttons and Lace

Buttons and Hate

Buttons and Pain

Buttons and Shame

Buttons and Blame

Buttons and Grace

Morally Gray Hero That Doesn't Care About Boundaries

Skull Series

The Skull King

The Skull Crusher

The Skull Ruler

Arranged Marriage with Alpha Protector

The Wolf Series

The Wolf and the Sheep

The Wolf and His Wife

The Lone Wolf

Alphahole That Falls First

Banker Series

The Banker

The Dictator

The Tyrant

Alpha Male That Wants Revenge Through Arranged Marriage

Betrothed Series

Wife

Husband

Lover

Committed

First

Second

Forever

Lie

Secret

Truth

Morally Gray Alphahole

Lesser Evil Series

Lesser Evil

Better Man

Harder Betrayal

Golden Retriever Mafia Romance

Empire Series

Bartholomew

Barbarian

Morally Gray Antihero in a Romantic Thriller

Chateau Series

The Chateau

The Camp

The Boss

The Palace

Alpha Male Protector in Romantic Thriller

Cult Series

The Cult

The Catacombs

Alphahole Captor Falls First

Queen Series

Protect Your Queen

Love Your Queen

Worship Your Queen

The Barsetti Clan from the Buttons Series Continues

Beyond Buttons Series

Buttons and Revenge

Buttons and Betrayal

Buttons and Devotion

Buttons and Power

Buttons and Despise

Buttons and Beauty

Buttons and Loyalty

Buttons and Blood

Buttons and Death

Buttons and Lies

Buttons and Deceit

Buttons and Hope

Buttons and Belief

Buttons and Desire

Buttons and Shadows

PENELOPE SKY WRITING AS PENELOPE BARSETTI

Morally Gray Alphahole Necromancer

Death Series

The Death King

Blood of Dragons

The Dragon King

The Dragon Queen

Princess of Death

Empire of Death

Alphahole Hell-Bent on Revenge

Forsaken Series

The Forsaken King

The Broken Queen

The Three Kings

Obsessed Golden Retriever Vampire

Dirty Blood Series

Bite The Woman That Feeds

Bite The Terror That Feeds

Bite The Power That Feeds

The Forsaken Vampire

The Broken Prince

Clash of Kingdoms

About the Author

Penelope Sky is an international phenomenon and multiple Amazon Charts, *New York Times*, *Wall Street Journal*, and *USA Today* bestselling author. She's best known for her dark romance, mafia romance, and romantic thrillers, and with books translated into dozens of languages around the world, she's sold more than five million copies worldwide. Sky also writes fantasy romance under the pen name Penelope Barsetti. Follow and connect with the author on Instagram or TikTok at @penelopeskyauthor.